HELICOPTER HELL

The chopper pilot cursed and fired his 50-caliber machine guns into the Iraqi position. In the confusion, Hawkins couldn't make out what they were up against, but it was some serious firepower for sure. He tried to hail the ground team, but they weren't answering—probably because they were dealing with the same Iraqis as the choppers.

Hawkins yelled and pointed to the spot where he wanted the chopper to land, and the pilot swung over toward the target area. A new line of green tracer bullets erupted on the right, and Hawkins felt the helo twist to get a better aim on this new threat. The line of green began to turn toward them as they did.

He shouted, "Get that son-of-a—" and then the front of the helicopter seemed to come apart with a roar. Hawkins looked at the pilot, who was bent over the control stick, and then felt the ground slam against the skis beneath his legs as his head smashed into something hard and very dark . . .

Berkley Books by James Ferro

HOGS

GOING DEEP

HOG DOWN

FORT APACHE

HOGS #3

FORT APACHE

JAMES FERRO

BERKLEY BOOKS, NEW YORK

HOGS: FORT APACHE

A Berkley Book / published by arrangement with the author

PRINTING HISTORY
Berkley edition / January 2000

The Penguin Putnam Inc. World Wide Web site address is
http://www.penguinputnam.com

ISBN: 0-425-17306-2

BERKLEY®
Berkley Books are published by The Berkley Publishing Group,
a division of Penguin Putnam Inc.,
375 Hudson Street, New York, New York 10014.
BERKLEY and the "B" logo
are trademarks belonging to Penguin Putnam Inc.

PRINTED IN THE UNITED STATES OF AMERICA

10 9 8 7 6 5 4 3 2 1

PROLOGUE

SOMEWHERE IN NORTHWESTERN SAUDI ARABIA, NEAR THE IRAQI BORDER
24 JANUARY 1991
1655 (ALL DATES AND TIMES LOCAL)

Private Smith and Private Jones had spent the whole day arguing about the Super Bowl. So when their duty shifts wound down, Private Smith found a football and tossed it to Jones.

"Go long," said Private Jones, dropping back to unleash one. "Here comes a bomb."

Smith had played tight end in high school. He'd done pretty damn well too—made all-county his junior and senior year. People used to say he ate defensive backs for breakfast, or at least lunch.

So when he put his head down and darted across the Saudi desert in a post pattern, he felt as if he were reliving a little of his old glory. He felt damn good, turning back with impeccable timing as Jones's bomb arced overhead.

One second, the pigskin fluttered in the evening sky, headed for his outstretched arms.

The next second it was swallowed whole by a dark angel of Hell.

The demon swallowed the ball and kept coming. Smith

threw himself head-first into the sand. He thought—he knew—he was dead. He said the only prayer he knew.

"Now I lay me down to sleep."

His words were drowned by the roar. The ground shook so hard that he thought the devil beast was chewing him whole.

Then he realized it had passed him by.

"Yo, what the hell are you doing?" asked Jones, nudging him in the back with his foot as the ground stopped shaking.

Smith turned over. "Didn't you see that? Shit. I've never seen anything like it. That—thing—came right for me."

"What? The Warthog? They always fly low around here."

"Warthog?"

"Yeah. It's an A-10. Motherfucker of an airplane. Ugly as hell. Kills Iraqis just by lookin' at 'em."

Smith pulled himself up. "That was an airplane?"

"Meanest stinking bomber in the whole damn Gulf," said Jones. "Say, how'd your pants get wet?"

PART ONE

INJUN COUNTRY

1

Over Iraq
24 January 1991
2200

This was what happened when you had a big mouth:

You ended up staring through the open door of a C-141B Starlifter, 35,000 feet over Iraq, sucking oxygen from a mask, waiting to kill yourself.

You also shivered your damn butt off. But at least the cold took your mind off what was going to happen when you jumped.

A little.

Air Force Lieutenant William "BJ" Dixon would have given anything—anything—not to be standing in the dim red light of the unpressurized cargo hold, wind whipping everywhere, weighed down by what the Special Ops paratroopers around him swore was only thirty-five pounds of equipment but which felt like at least five hundred.

But it was his fault. He had opened his big mouth.

Worse. He had committed the unpardonable sin.

He had volunteered.

Idiot.

Technically, Dixon hadn't been lying when he told the Delta

Force officer in charge of the operation that he had parachuted at night. He had—once, as part of a recreational skydiving program in college.

But that jump was a lot different than this. Much different. And while the Special Ops people had obviously thought he was a heavily experienced jumper, the truth was Dixon hadn't even made the hundred jumps necessary for a Class A skydiving license.

In fact, he hadn't made half that.

Or a quarter.

But five jumps did qualify in his mind as "a lot," which were his exact words when asked how often he'd parachuted.

It had been a seemingly innocent, offhand, and irrelevant question at the time, precisely the kind that demanded a vague and even baloney-squash answer.

You'd think.

Until tonight, the highest altitude Dixon had ever jumped from was twelve thousand feet. Or eight thousand. He couldn't quite remember now as the commando in charge of the team—a Delta trooper named Eli Winston—gave him a thumbs-up and nudged him toward the Starlifter's door.

All these guys were certified nutcases, but Winston was the worst. The rest of the commandos had M-16's or MP-5's, serious but lightweight submachine guns. Created by Heckler & Koch, the MP-5's could spit through their thirty-round clips in less than three seconds and were generally accurate to two hundred yards. Impressive, but not gaudy.

But Winston, a wiry black man who stood maybe five-seven, was carrying an M249 Squad Automatic Weapon or "SAW," a fierce machine gun more than twice the size of the MP-5. Winston had four plastic boxes of belted ammo strapped to his chest, augmenting the bulky clip of 5.56's in the SAW's gut. Dixon was convinced the sergeant was planning on using all five clips before he hit the ground.

Thing was, to a man the Special Forces troops he was jumping with thought Dixon was as crazy as they were. Crazier. He flew a Hog, after all. He'd shot down a helicopter, after all. And he'd accepted the surrender of an entire platoon of Iraqi soldiers while riding along with some friends of theirs on a rescue mission just a few days before.

But what cinched it was the fact that he'd volunteered.

So no wonder they figured Dixon would have no problem jumping out of a cargo plane going, oh, must be Mach 25 by now, more than a hundred miles into Iraq in the dead of night.

Hog driver? Shit, those guys are born crazy. Ever see the plane they fly? How low they go? All the bombs they carry?

Got to be nuts.

Jumping out of orbit in the middle of the night's like going to a drive-in movie for those guys.

Dixon's decision to volunteer had actually been part of his plan to get back to his squadron, the 535th Tactical Fighter Squadron, affectionately known to Saddam and anyone else who tried messing with them as Devil Squadron. Punished for an admittedly stupid screwup the first day of the air war, Dixon had been temporarily shunted into a do-nothing job in Riyadh. So naturally he'd salivated when one of his newfound Special Ops buddies suggested he tell a certain colonel he was available to help train ground FACs.

Ground FACs—also known as forward air controllers—worked with attack pilots to pick out targets on the front lines. In some cases, the job was actually handled by pilots, but that wasn't particularly necessary; mostly all you had to do was work a radio and have a good sense of direction and a rudimentary understanding of a plane's capabilities. Telling a Hog driver what he needed to know would take all of three seconds: Point to something big enough to blow up, then duck.

It was a time-honored profession, and Dixon figured he could make as worthy a contribution to it as the next guy. A few lectures, a bunch of donuts, and the job would be done.

And since the Special Ops units were headquartered at King Fahd—also his squadron's home drome—the assignment seemed a perfect chance to worm back into his squadron commander's good graces. The boss, Colonel Michael "Skull" Knowlington, would certainly have cooled off by now, and volunteering to help a brother service would surely count in his favor.

It was all going to be a piece of cake, especially since there was no real need for FACs until the ground war started—weeks if not months from now. Dixon had figured that with a little luck, string-pulling, and maybe some strategic whining, he'd be back dropping bombs with Devil Squadron inside a week.

Except something had gotten lost in the translation. Because there wasn't anyone to train.

And the Special Ops troops weren't waiting for the ground war to start. They needed somebody north right away.

Far north. As in: Iraq.

By the time Dixon realized what was involved—a night HAHO jump into central Iraq, for starters—it was too late to back out without looking like a complete coward.

There was also the fact that he had fibbed slightly about his colonel's permission regarding the assignment.

It wasn't a fib exactly. He had given an accurate and direct response, though the question had been posed unartfully and—like the parachuting one—in what seemed like idle conversation.

Or maybe it hadn't. Because who in their right mind would expect someone to actually give permission for something this nuts?

Or volunteer, for that matter?

Dixon and the six men around him in the C-141B who constituted Team Ruth were jumping into an area just south of the Euphrates River. They were part of a small but carefully coordinated covert operation to nail Scuds and otherwise wreak serious havoc in Saddam's kitchen. A larger group, code-named "Apache," had parachuted into the southwestern desert a few minutes before. Their mission was to establish a permanent base to support Dixon's team and others Scud hunting in the north and east of the country.

From what Dixon could see, the two dozen or so men had parachuted into a black void of nothingness. And they'd stepped off into it gladly, like ascetics giving themselves up to the spirit world.

Damn poetic way of describing idiocy.

Dixon was startled by a sharp punch to his shoulder. Wincing, he turned to face a fully loaded paratrooper wagging a finger across his equipment as if he were a witch conjuring a spell to keep him safe.

No such luck. Just the communications or "como" specialist, Sergeant Joey Leteri, checking his equipment. Leteri was the squad's jumpmaster.

Leteri gave him an extended middle finger and a grin beneath his mask.

That was supposed to mean he was ready to go. Funny.

In the red night-light tint, with full parachute gear, rucksacks and weapons, thick helmets and oxygen masks, the team members looked more like Star Wars troopers than commandos. On a HAHO—it stood for high altitude, high-opening parachute drop, but sounded like something the Seven Dwarfs would say—the troopers sucked O before and during the jump. Dixon suspected there was something beyond oxygen in the others' canisters. They all seemed positively joyful.

Winston submitted to the check next, exchanging fingers and shoulder-chucks. Then he turned to Dixon and gave him a peace sign.

Not peace. It meant two minutes.

Two minutes to live.

Dixon nodded, then realized the sergeant wanted a more emphatic answer.

He gave him the finger. Not necessarily without malice.

Winston used the SAW for a shoulder-chuck back. If Dixon hadn't been braced against the side of the plane, he would have gone straight to the deck. As it was, he swore he dented the metal.

The C-141 was flying in formation with two B-52's. The idea was to make the mission look like just another high-altitude bombing run instead of a deep infiltration. Which undoubtedly it would, since who would think the Americans were this crazy?

Winston leaned closer to the door. Dixon had to go out before him. Or at least, he was supposed to.

So how much of a coward would they think he was if he stayed in the plane?

Big-time. Better to shoot himself with the MP-5.

Might be less painful actually. Certainly a lot less scary.

Winston turned and motioned him forward. Dixon took a small step, then felt himself being pushed forward by Leteri or some other fool.

Arch. That was what he was supposed to do, right?

Arch. Frog position.

Screw it. As long as he didn't tumble too badly. They'd given him an automatic deployment device; sooner or later the chute would open no matter what.

Or maybe not.

The wind kicked up. Dixon was wearing an insulated jumpsuit, but he began to shake with the cold.

He also began thinking about the possibility of a freak wind current scooping him into one of the C-141's Pratt & Whitneys. Or what would happen if one of the B-52's was out of position.

Oh, boy, he thought, it's dark out there.

Oh, boy, he thought, I got to take a leak.

Oh, boy, he thought, here we go.

And then, he was dancing at the edge of the universe—assisted by Leteri's ungentle nudge.

He was flying.

Holy Jesus, he was outside the plane.

Holy Jesus, he was falling.

Oh, yeah, he thought to himself as his stomach left his body, this is why I dropped out of that skydiving program.

2

King Fahd Air Base, Saudi Arabia
24 January 1991
2200

Colonel Michael "Skull" Knowlington had just decided the time had come to write his sisters letters—he'd promised them both he would do so at least once a week, but hadn't since coming to the Gulf—when a tall soldier in desert camouflage fatigues knocked at the open door of his office in Hog Heaven.

"General wanted to know if you were available, sir," said the soldier. Ramrod straight, every pore of his body sweated respect, though Knowlington never knew quite how to take the Delta Force soldiers. He knew this sergeant vaguely—he was part of the general's personal retinue at the Bat Cave, the unofficial name of the Special Operations command center at King Fahd. Since Knowlington had spent considerable time with the general over the past few days, and since there had been some ballyhoo over Skull's recent mission to rescue one of his men north of the border, it was likely that the sergeant's respectful tone was sincere. Still, Knowlington knew the Delta Force troopers held all officers in suspicion. Those from other commands, let alone other services, were usually considered one notch above the enemy, when considered at all.

The general who headed the joint services mission had himself been Air Force, but the operative word there was "had." Besides, the general had flown Puff the Magic Dragon gunships in Vietnam, and he had lost enough blood in combat to impress even the hard-ass noncoms who filled his ranks.

Knowlington struggled to remember the sergeant's first name as they crossed the air base to the Special Ops center in what had once been a parking garage. It was Jake or James or Jack, but taking a guess wasn't going to cut it. So he merely grunted in appreciation as the trooper faded behind him at the entrance to the general's suite.

Suite was a bit of an overstatement. It consisted of a roped-off area studded with guards. Behind them were walls made of supply boxes. Knowlington found the general inside what passed for his situation room.

"Mikey, great," said the general as Knowlington walked over to the stack of boxes that marked the wall. "We're a go. Apache's underway."

For weeks, the Special Ops command had been lobbying for a more active role in the conflict. They wanted to infiltrate Iraq and help destroy the enemy's supply and command structure, as well as take out Saddam's only long-range strategic threat, Scud missiles. But General Schwarzkopf had steadfastly refused—until Scuds started falling on Israel.

Delta troopers and other allied Special Ops teams had begun infiltrating Iraq some days before. "Apache" was even more ambitious—it called for establishing a base more than a hundred miles inside Iraq to support the commando teams. A-10As—specifically, Colonel Knowlington's A-10As—had been tagged to provide air support.

The base would be called "Fort Apache." Deep in the heart of Injun country.

While Colonel Knowlington had helped prepare the plan, he remained slightly skeptical of it and surprised that it had been approved so quickly. "When did this happen?" he asked, sliding over one of the folding chairs that passed for office furniture.

"We got the go this afternoon. We went."

"I'll have your first two planes at Al Jouf tomorrow afternoon," said Knowlington.

"I'm counting on it," said the general. "But I was hoping to have them in the morning."

"The morning?"

"There a problem?"

The squadron had a full frag set for the morning, and nearly everyone who could fly was already assigned. A "frag" was the "fragment" or portion of the Air Tasking Order that pertained to a specific unit, in this case the 535th Attack Squadron (Provisional), which made up its own wing and was under Colonel Knowlington's command. The unit had been thrown together from planes headed for the scrap heap and hustled to the Gulf less than a month before the air war began. So far, it had done a hell of a job bashing Saddam.

But finding a pair of planes—and pilots—to fly two hundred miles into Iraq on less than twelve hours notice?

Not easy.

"I'll see what I can do," said Knowlington. "We were originally talking about forty-eight hours."

"Things change," said the general. "I'm getting your best guys?"

"We agreed on volunteers."

The general smiled. The agreement was that Knowlington would ask his best men first, and both officers knew or at least suspected they would volunteer. They were, after all, Hog drivers.

"I'd like to get a special maintenance team at Al Jouf," added the general.

"Wait a second," said Knowlington. "There are some good people there already. Plenty, from what I hear."

"We want to keep the Apache force separate at Al Jouf. Security."

"Aw, come on. That's just bullshit."

One of the reasons Knowlington was still only a colonel was the fact that he would have said the same thing even if he and the general hadn't been through some butt-wrenching times together over the years. The general gave him just a hint of a disapproving stare, then held his hands out as if he had no choice.

Which Knowlington knew was even more bullshit.

"We don't need your entire squadron," said the general. "But I want people we can count on. Right now we're screwed badly on the helicopter maintenance side. I have one person to keep two helos in the air. That's an accident waiting to happen, don't you think?"

Of course it was, and Knowlington couldn't argue. But it wasn't necessarily relevant. There were plenty of A-10 specialists from other Warthog squadrons out at Al Jouf, which was on the other side of Saudi Arabia and much closer to the border. As a matter of fact, a crew of Al Jouf techies had patched one of his planes together just the other day.

"I don't want one of my pilots flying in a plane that's not one hundred percent," added the general.

"Those are *my* pilots," said Knowlington.

"Our pilots," said the general, his tone about as diplomatic as a Delta Force officer was capable of delivering.

That was a bad sign, thought Knowlington, realizing he was going to have to concede. "What do you need?"

"Well, we can pick up the survival shop out there."

The survival specialists were in charge of, among other things, making sure the pilots had working parachutes. Extremely important—but it was the one specialty he happened to be overloaded with.

"You're kidding, right?"

"Work with me, Skull. I just want to make sure the planes are ready to go."

"I have the same problem here," said Knowlington.

"Ah, your guy Clyston's put together a Super Bowl team. Come on. I'm not asking for everybody, just a few key guys."

"I'll see who we can spare."

The general gave him a look that implied he better spare at least a few of his best wizards, but said nothing more.

"You have up-to-date intelligence on that strip at Apache you want to use?" Knowlington asked, changing the subject as a tactful surrender.

"The last satellite picture shows it there, with no guards, no nothing. Improving it to the point where we can put in C-130's is still a long shot. Now if we had gotten the Js through Congress—"

"I wasn't part of that," said Knowlington, who had heard the pointed lament at least twice in the past three days. He was fudging a bit. Knowlington's most recent Pentagon assignment had included "briefing" Congressmen, and he had been asked—unofficially—to help lobby for the special-edition cargo planes, which could land fully loaded on even shorter strips than the normal models—1,500 feet was the supposed spec. But Knowlington's boss had been opposed to the program because of other funding priorities. The issue was one of the few where the colonel had strictly obeyed orders.

"I better get going," said Knowlington when the general didn't respond. "I have to get your volunteers."

"Thanks for your help." The general got up and walked with him to the boxes that marked the sit-room door. "And thanks for Dixon too."

"What do you mean Dixon?"

"Lieutenant Dixon. The assignment you cleared."

"I didn't clear any assignment. You mean that trip north with the helicopter crew? I'm still pissed at that."

"No," said the general. "The ground FAC assignment. You didn't clear it?"

"I don't even know what the hell you're talking about."

The general stifled a laugh. "Typical Hog pilot." He shook his head. "You didn't tell Lieutenant Dixon to see Jeff Marg in Riyadh?"

Marg was one of the colonels helping plan the infiltration.

"No way," said Knowlington. "I sent him over to Black Hole to cool his heels for a week or two, but I want him back. If only to spank his behind—he got hooked up in that rescue mission on his own."

"Geez, go easy on the kid. Marg told me he shot down a helicopter. And he had a whole platoon of Iraqis surrender to him."

"They surrendered to me and my wingman," said Knowlington. "He got up there by accident. I'm not saying the kid's not a good pilot," he added. "Or that he's not brave. Or stupid. But he's still green. Shit, Dixon's barely old enough to shave."

"Ah. You were young once."

"Not naive, though. Where the hell is he?"

"Parachuting into Iraq."

"Parachuting? Into Iraq? Dixon is parachuting?"

"Well, yeah. We needed someone who could talk to pilots, and he volunteered. Marg thought you cleared it. Dixon's not a skydiver?"

"As far as I know, he's as much a skydiver as I'm a skateboarder."

"Well, I sure as shit hope you're world-class," said the general.

3

The Depot, Saudi Arabia
24 January 1991
2200

Doberman took another swig from the soda can and squirreled his eyes into something he hoped would look like a perplexed squint.

"Hey Dog Man, you betting those threes or what?" asked Shotgun, who was sitting across from him at the poker table.

Captain Thomas "Shotgun" O'Rourke was Captain John "Doberman" Glenon's wingman in Devil Squadron, a Hog driver with considerable experience in the cockpit and even more playing cards.

"Yeah, I'm in." Doberman kicked in a chip to meet the bet. He was showing a pair of threes, separated by a king and a ten. It looked like a dumb move, and truth was, it wasn't a percentage play at all.

The thing was, though, both the king and the ten were spades. And his first two cards, dealt face-down in this game of seven-card stud, were also spades.

An ace and a queen, as a matter of fact. And while ordinarily Doberman would run the odds through his mental computer and reject any possibility of winning with a flush or a straight—let alone landing a royal flush—he was so far ahead tonight that he could afford to play a wild long shot. In fact, he'd been doing that all night—a complete reversal of his usual poker *operandi,* which had brought completely unexpected results: He was winning.

The pilots were playing in a back room of the Depot, an off-base club located in what seemed to have been an old bomb shelter literally yards from the King Fahd runway. Who ran it, let alone who had built it, was unknown. Some people said it sprang whole from the desert after too many GIs had too many wet dreams; you didn't have to take more than a step into the hazy interior to believe that was true. The uniforms the waitresses wore covered less than the average postage stamp. There was a floor show, a cage show, and a ceiling extravaganza—not to mention several rooms that even Shotgun advised against entering.

The official attitude toward the Depot was difficult to gauge. On the one hand, it was the epitome of everything prohibited in Saudi Arabia. On the other hand, at least one two-star general was known to be among the frequent "guests." The Devil Squadron Commander, Colonel Knowlington, didn't approve but didn't censure either. The other squadron commanders seemed equally ambiguous.

"I'll see Wong's raise, and go five more," snapped the player to Doberman's left, Kevin Sullivan. Captain Sullivan had three fours on the table. Normally, his cherubic expression could be counted on to give his hold cards away. But he had worn a consistent scowl from the very first hand, and for the past hour had growled nearly as sharply as the plane he piloted, an AC-130 mean-assed gunship armed with a variety of cannons and a very nasty temper. Sullivan was a particularly poor loser, and like everyone else at the table except Captain Bristol Wong, was down heavily to Doberman.

"You guys are too rich for me," said Shotgun, folding. Richie Stevens did the same. Wong, who was showing two pair, aces high, pushed forward five chips. The intelligence officer—on loan from the Pentagon G2 staff—had been advertised as the night's pigeon. He'd proven anything but; only Doberman's incredible string of luck had held him check.

Not that Doberman thought it was luck exactly.

"Out," said Hernandez, throwing down his cards.

The bet was back to Doberman. Statistically speaking, his best hope was to land another three, and that wouldn't even beat what Sullivan was showing. The way he read the table, Sullivan and Wong were both riding full houses; with his best shot a flush or straight, all he was doing was making the pot fatter for them, something he'd been doing all night.

And yet, if he pulled a jack of spades, how sweet that would be. The odds on getting a royal flush were astronomical—well into the millions. On the other hand, since he had been dealt the four cards to start with, the odds really weren't that ridiculous. In fact, they were no worse than 1 out of 32, since Doberman already knew the card he needed wasn't lying face-up on the table.

Still a long shot. But he'd never had a night like this before.

"Call," he said, pushing forward a five-dollar chip.

"Feeling lucky?" mocked Shotgun. "Oh, I forgot—you don't believe in luck. So how come you're in?"

"Just deal the cards," Doberman told him.

"For someone who doesn't believe in luck, he's sure riding high," said Sullivan.

"I got the luck of Job," said Doberman.

"Anybody want a beer?" Hernandez asked.

"I'll take one," said Shotgun. "See if you can get some of those scorcher wings. I showed Manny or whatever his name is in the back how to pep them up with that hot sauce I got the other day."

"When did you have time to do that?" asked Hernandez. Like Shotgun and Doberman, he was a Devil Squadron Hog driver. "Don't you sleep?"

"Shit, I sleep all the time," said Shotgun. "Hell, we're flying and things are slow, I take a nap in the cockpit. Right, Dog Man?"

"The snores are unreal," said Doberman. "Now deal the fuckin' cards."

"You want a beer, Wong?" asked Hernandez.

"He ought to pay for a round," suggested Sullivan. "He's the new guy."

"I am not drinking beer," said Wong. "And I will not contribute to your dereliction by purchasing any. It is against the custom and law of the country."

"Shit, Wong, are you for real?" asked Hernandez.

"He's busting your chops. Go ahead, it's on him," Shotgun said. "He's got a tab."

"Why does everyone on this base think I'm making jokes?" Wong asked. "And since when do I have a tab?"

"I set it up," said Shotgun. "You can thank me later."

"Hey, are we playing cards or what?" demanded Doberman.

"You're pretty antsy for somebody who's showing bupkus," said Sullivan. "Or did you trade some of your flying luck for card luck?"

"Fuck you."

"Dog Man ain't lucky at planes or at cards," said Shotgun.

"Shit, yeah, he is," said Sullivan. "Nobody in the world could take so many bullets and keep flying."

"Hell, that ain't luck. Hog loves to take bullets," said Shotgun. "Holes in the wing make it fly faster."

"Just because I know what I'm doing and you don't, doesn't mean I'm lucky," said Doberman.

"Yeah, right," said Sullivan.

"You ever fly your crate home without hydraulics?"

"Last card down," said Shotgun, dishing Wong's card to begin the final round.

The plastic beads walling off the room parted, revealing Lieutenant Jack "Happy Face" Gladstone—who, contrary to his nickname, perpetually frowned.

"Colonel needs to see you right away, Captain," he told Doberman. "Wants you, too, sir," he told Wong.

Wong immediately pushed his chair back and rose.

"Whoa—wait a second. We got a hand to finish here," said Sullivan.

"Guess I might as well come too," said Shotgun, putting the deck down and standing. "What's going on, Smile Boy?"

"Hey come on, let's finish the hand," said Doberman. "Where are you guys going? Wong, get back here. Shotgun."

"Colonel's pissed about something," said Gladstone. "The capo told me he was over in the Bat Cave a little while ago. That's all I know."

"Uh-oh," said Shotgun. The "capo" was the wing's top sergeant, Chief Master Sergeant Allen Clyston, a man wise in all things and with more sources than the CIA. Shotgun scooped up the pot.

"Hey," said Sullivan. "We can finish the hand."

"Colonel wouldn't be asking to see us this time of night unless it was real important," said Shotgun. "I'll cash out everybody on the way over to Hog Heaven."

"Shit, he doesn't want all of us," said Doberman. He suspected that this was an administrative thing—the squadron DO or deputy for operations was due to be shipped home, and Doberman was among those in line for the job.

Not that he wanted it.

"You ain't goin' nowhere without your wingman watching your butt," said Shotgun. "I'm trusting you guys to remember what you bet that last round," he added, stalking away.

Sullivan cursed and tossed his cards down. Doberman took a deep breath and rose, the last one at the table.

His last card was lying face-down on the top of the pile.

He hesitated for a second.

More than likely, it was a five or a seven or even another king or queen, something in diamonds or hearts.

More than likely, Gladstone had just saved him from losing a bundle.

He started to walk away, got as far as the beads that formed the doorway, then turned back.

Doberman reached down and flipped over the card nonchalantly.

Jack of spades. Son of a shit.

4

Over Iraq
24 January 1991
2203

The first thing Dixon felt was overwhelming numbness.

The next thing he felt was a severe yank against his chest.

The chute had opened.

Already? It should have taken at least twenty seconds to fall down to thirty thousand feet. He'd only just stepped out of the plane.

Dixon glanced upward, aware that he was supposed to check the canopy to make sure it was properly deployed, but damned if he could remember how the hell he would know.

It was too dark to see anyway. He had a flashlight somewhere, but he wasn't supposed to use it unless it was an emergency.

Or was that the flares?

Fuck it. If the chute was screwed up he'd be tear-assing downward. And he didn't seem to be.

Dixon actually felt himself relax a little. Now that the chute was open, all he had to do was steer to his landing spot.

Which wasn't necessarily impossible. Hell, all he really had to do was land. Let the commandos worry about finding him.

They would, wouldn't they?

Dixon reached up for the steering togs in place on the rig above each of his hands. He was so surprised to find them that he pulled down a hell of a lot harder than he'd intended.

His chute flared, exactly as the tug told it to. Unfortunately, since the still-deploying chute hadn't had enough time to adequately slow his momentum and he was swaying besides, the canopy began to wrap.

Which, in layman's terms, meant things started to get pretty screwed up. Dixon was in danger of becoming a QPO—a quickly plummeting object.

Whether it was the shock of the spin, instinct, or his forgotten skydiving lessons, Dixon managed to ease back and open the ram-air chute enough to stabilize. But before he did, every muscle in his upper body went ballistic; his arms became more rigid than a corpse's.

He tried relaxing by thinking relaxing thoughts. But all Dixon could thing of was how pissed Colonel Knowlington was going to be if he pancaked into the Iraqi countryside.

Somehow, the image of Knowlington's furling lips relaxed his muscles—or scared them into pliability. Dixon began to feel almost comfortable, finally confident that he was gliding and not falling. He turned his head to read the night-glo altimeter strapped to his left wrist.

Instead, his attention was grabbed by the dark shadow of a large rectangular parachute just beyond his arm, nearly close enough for him to touch.

Dixon held his breath and tried to keep his arms relaxed, worried that anything he did to steer away would only take him closer. He lifted his legs—remembering at the last second to keep them together, so he wouldn't change his momentum abruptly.

Gradually, the distance between him and the shadow opened. The other parachute slipped three, then four and five yards away, barely visible. It seemed to hang there, as if kept close by magnetic attraction.

Dixon was damn close, way too close for safety in the dark.

On the other hand, it probably meant he wouldn't be lost when he landed. And nudging gently on the togs didn't seem to help.

Dixon was supposed to yank off his oxygen mask at twelve thousand feet. He looked again at the altimeter, but couldn't make out the reading. In fact, he wasn't even sure he could see the dial.

What he could see were green-yellow streaks off to his right.

Pretty things. Delicate and thin, flares in the night.

Tracers.

Guns being fired at someone or something.

Maybe even him.

The colors told him who was firing. NATO guns almost uniformly packed red tracers. Russian-made weapons usually carried green.

Green means bad, red means good.

Oh.

Actually, it wasn't that hard to steer the chute, once his arms flexed and he got used to it. And Dixon finally figured he wasn't going to suffocate if he just went ahead and yanked off the O, no matter how high or low he was.

Granted, it was pitch black, he had no idea where the ground might be, and he was colder than an icicle on a polar bear's nose. But the lieutenant managed to put a few more yards between himself and whoever was piloting the nearby chute, while still staying close enough to make it out in the dark.

All he had to do was land and this nightmare would be over. He had finally realized that his altimeter had gotten twisted around on his arm during the jump, and for some reason wouldn't stay put where he could see it without gyrating contortions. But he knew he was getting close to the ground. He figured he'd see something when the time came.

If nothing else, his rucksack—hanging off his rig below his feet—would hit the desert a second or so before he did. That was probably all the cue he needed. Or wanted.

Dixon knew how to land. That was easy. You relaxed and

you walked, as if you were coming off the last step of an escalator.

No, that was the way the pros did it. He was still a newbie. Newbies relaxed and walked and *rolled.* The roll took all the energy out of the jump. You went down easy so you didn't break something.

Yeah, right. What about the rucksack tied to his butt? What if it bounced and smacked him in the head?

Serve him right for volunteering.

Dixon looked over and realized that he had lost the other parachute. He saw a much longer shadow, a blanket almost, in its place.

The ground. Must be.

He pushed his left tog down, starting to turn into the wind. Then he realized he'd set it too hard and backed off, but not before his body and the parachute had pitched sharply to the right. Trying to straighten himself out, he flared the chute hard, once again hitting the brakes in midair. His legs whipped forward unexpectedly, and he felt like a kid about to fall out of a swing.

Dixon knew that nine tenths of what he had to do was just relax his arms and shoulders, but his muscles weren't cooperating. The parachute suddenly seemed to have a mind of its own, and his neck felt as if it had a steel boxcar spring wrapped around it.

Somehow he got his arms loose enough to regain some control. And then he realized that the shadows in front of him weren't moving anymore.

The ruck hit behind him, his left leg hit the ground, and the next thing he knew he was twisting his face in the dirt.

Dixon's first thought was that he had broken every bone in his body, neck down.

His next thought was—hot damn, I made it.

He rolled his legs under him and then released the parachute. He got to his knees—and nearly fell over as his head spun like an out-of-control carousel.

It was still shooting around when a short man with a very

large gun materialized directly in front of him. The gun barrel poked into his shoulder.

"Hey, Lieutenant, shit, why didn't you land into the wind?"

It was Sergeant Winston.

Dixon's head finally stopped spinning. He stood slowly. His ribs felt crushed but not quite broken. There was a stitch in his lungs, and his left knee felt wobbly. But otherwise he felt perfect.

"Were you trying to show off?" asked the sergeant.

"Show off?"

"Trying to beat everybody to the ground?"

"No."

Winston obviously didn't believe him, and made a sound halfway between a snort and a laugh. "Well, you did," said the team leader. "And you scored a perfect bull's-eye. Come on, let's round up the rest of the team and get our butts in gear." The sergeant helped Dixon pull in his parachute. "I thought I saw something moving on the highway just before we landed." He shook his head. "Shit. I figured you'd be off a mile at least. Fucking Hog pilots. You think jumping out of a plane in the dark's fun, huh?"

5

Hog Heaven
24 January 1991
2230

"The kill boxes are here," Knowlington told Doberman, Shotgun, and Wong, pointing to a map on an easel in Cineplex, Devil Squadron's multipurpose ready room, hangout space, and briefing area. It was called Cineplex because there was a large-screen TV with a satellite hookup on one end, courtesy of Sergeant Clyston and his unending supply line.

"You're pointing at the Euphrates," said Doberman.

"I know," said Knowlington.

"Pretty damn far for us to be flying in daylight," Doberman told him. "Going to drain time on target to nothing. Be there for what, ten minutes, then have to go home?"

They'd have more than ten minutes—the colonel had figured it at nearly a half hour and maybe more, depending on their load configuration—but it was just like Doberman to complain about that, rather than the problem of actually flying so far behind enemy lines in an airplane built to stay close to the front. Even from Al Jouf—a small forward operating area on the other end of Saudi Arabia—it would take about an hour at nearly top speed for the Hogs to reach the area where the commando teams were operating. That was an hour of flying through some of the best antiair defenses in the world. Granted, allied Weasels had whacked most of the SAM batteries pretty hard. But all it took was one to nail you.

"Hey, time on target's no big deal as long as they got the targets picked out," said Shotgun. "What we need is a good ground controller calling the shots. Somebody who's familiar with Hogs, you know what I'm talking about?"

"Well, we'll have one," said the colonel. "In fact, he's one of our guys."

"One of our guys? No shit," said Shotgun. "Who?"

"Dixon. He parachuted in with one of the commando teams a few minutes ago."

Both men couldn't have looked more surprised if he had told them the world was actually flat.

"Dixon?" said Doberman.

"The lieutenant apparently volunteered," said Knowlington. "The Special Ops command thought it had been cleared with me, which it wasn't."

"He's just a fucking kid," said Doberman.

"No shit," said Knowlington.

"Hey, BJ'll do fine," said Shotgun. "He knows what it's about."

"He's a fucking kid," Doberman told him.

"Whatever he is, he's on the ground in Iraq now," said Knowlington. "And it's too goddamn late to get him back. Wong, you've been awful quiet. What's your opinion?"

Knowlington felt lucky to have snagged Wong for his team, hijacking him after he had come to Devil Squadron on a weapons assessment for CENTCOM. Wong was the self-professed world expert on Russian weapons. Knowlington thought he might well be—but his real asset was the drollest sense of humor the colonel had seen since Vietnam. Sometimes it was so subtle only Knowlington could pick it up, and it wasn't that easy to tell when Wong was goofing or being serious.

He was serious now, definitely.

"The entire operation is a waste of time," said Wong. He

gave a sigh so deep that it sounded like it came from a draft horse. "The so-called Scud or Russian-made SS-1 presents a minimal military threat, even if fitted with chemical warheads. As we saw during the Afghanistan War—"

"You were there?" asked Doberman, about as sarcastic as a reporter questioning a Congressional junket.

"For a time," said Wong without missing a beat. "Even when massed with the most accurate targeting radars and intelligence available, the SS-1 family was of scant use against the rebel insurgency, with an ineffective damage ratio and a destruction envelope that is frankly less intimidating than the average grenade attack. The Iraqi targeting and launch capacity is even less organized than the Russian brigades'. The parabola of probable destruction has the slant of an inchworm at rest. Given the infrastructure and resources necessary to support the Special Ops infiltration, targeting, and disposal of these minor annoyances, it would make much more sense to —"

"It's not our job to argue yea or nay," said Knowlington. "We just have to hit what they want us to hit."

Wong's mouth and throat contorted, as if the rest of what he was going to say had been written on a sheaf of paper and he'd swallowed it whole.

"Yeah, all right, what the hell. I volunteer," Doberman said before Wong could continue.

"I wasn't going to ask you to volunteer," said Knowlington.

"I volunteer anyway."

"Me too," said Shotgun. "There's your two-ship. When are we leaving?"

With Mongoose due to be shipped back to the States, Doberman and Shotgun were, at least arguably, the best two pilots in the squadron; by asking them, Knowlington had fulfilled his promise to the general.

Now he proceeded to try to talk them out of it. Both had seen more than their share of action in the past few days and were due serious rests. Doberman looked especially ragged around the edges. And with Mongoose going home, the squadron needed a temporary DO—one who was here at the home drome, on the other side of Saudi Arabia.

"That's no argument to get me to stay," said Doberman. "Listen, Colonel, no offense intended, but I want to fly, not sit behind a desk."

"Major Johnson didn't sit behind a desk," Knowlington told him. "Mongoose flew as much as anybody."

"Yeah, but I can do without the bullshit, you know? Besides, it screws up your head. And I'm just a little captain."

Knowlington nodded. Doberman was a captain—and part of Devil Squadron—because he had made a career of mouthing off to the wrong people, but otherwise he was more than qualified to handle the critical job of the squadron's number-two man. Still, the pilot was more right than he knew. The downside of the job wasn't paperwork or bureaucracy or even so much the dealing with the personnel matters that inevitably fell in the DO's lap. It was the worrying. You felt responsible for everyone, and it weighed on you, began to eat you away. It had only been as a commander that Knowlington himself had come to feel real pressure; only as a professional worrier that he had fallen into despair, and worse.

And truth was, he knew he couldn't talk these guys out of going. Especially with Dixon somewhere up there.

"All right," Knowlington told them. "Go get some sleep."

The two pilots left, but Knowlington was surprised to find Wong following him down the hall.

"Captain?"

"Begging your pardon, sir, but I wonder if we could discuss an aspect of my transfer."

"Which aspect is that?" Knowlington asked.

"The aspect of its existence. I'm of no use here," continued Wong. "My role is reduced to fetching people and pointing out the mistakes in incompetent estimates. I'm better off in Riyadh or Washington."

Knowlington started to dismiss him when a light flashed in his head: Wong was angling to get involved with Fort Apache.

He should have realized it immediately. Poor guy probably

felt insulted that he hadn't been asked to volunteer. For someone with Wong's record and abilities, it was a real put-down not to be included. But what the hell could he do at Al Jouf? Help coordinate the bombing missions?

Probably. Actually, he'd do an excellent job. But the commandos had their own intelligence guys. Not as good as Wong, but damn good. And probably prickly.

Still, it might make sense to have Wong out there, scoping the air defenses for Doberman and Shotgun. Special Ops people weren't going to be experts on SA-6's or Rolands, and there were plenty of them where the Hog drivers were heading. Wong knew his shit, even if he used phrases like "parabolas of probable destruction" and compared missiles to inchworms.

Damn ball-buster.

"I need you around, Wong," Knowlington told him. "Your insights are important. Seriously."

"With all due respect, sir, a trained monkey could perform the services you require."

Typical Wong-style exaggeration. The whole reason Knowlington kept him around.

But didn't his guys deserve the best?

"All right, Wong. Look, I have to go talk to Sergeant Clyston. Hook up with the team he puts together and get out to Al Jouf ASAP. You have my blessing. Just remember, you're still my guy, not theirs."

Wong turned purple, or at least reasonably close.

"Al Jouf?"

"That's where they're running this from."

"Colonel—"

"Yeah, I know," Knowlington said, slapping him on the back as he started away. "You owe me big-time."

6

King Fahd Air Base, Saudi Arabia
25 January 1991
0005

Chief Master Sergeant Clyston's quarters at the home drome were a testament not merely to the role of the squadron's first sergeant, but to the entire institution of the noncommissioned officer. For Clyston's tent was located in the heart of Tent City, placing the top sergeant in the very midst of the people he supervised. Outwardly, it was unostentatious to a fault, a billboard that said to the entire squadron of techies, specialists, ordies, candymen, crew dogs, and wizards that their premier sergeant, their first among firsts, their man, their capo di capo, their SERGEANT (as he preferred to be called, capitalization included) was, on some admittedly imperceptible level, one of them.

Inside, it was better equipped than a Pentagon suite, and a hell of a lot more comfy.

Some noncoms, having reached the exalted heights that Sergeant Clyston had, let it get to their heads, thinking that, just because they really ran the show, they had to make sure everyone, officers especially, knew it. Some sergeants, having extended their careers into the rarefied air of chiefdom, not only lorded it over their airmen and lower NCOs, but let their commanders know who was really in charge at every turn. But a major part of Clyston's success was his subtlety as well as his efficiency; just as he was approachable by the lowliest of airmen—assuming, of course, the capo di capo had had his first cup of morning coffee—so the ostensible commander of Devil Squadron, Colonel Knowlington, felt he was entering the tent of an old friend, albeit an extremely important one, as he knocked at the door. And in truth, he was. The two men had been a pair since Clyston had helped get Knowlington's Thud ready for a flight over the Ho Chi Minh Trail in the Dark Ages—a flight that had earned the then-lieutenant his first air-to-air kill.

"Disturbing you, Allen?" Knowlington asked Clyston, who was sitting in a recliner, eyes closed, stereo headphones on.

"Colonel. You surprised me." Clyston took off the headphones and pushed the recliner closed. Knowlington plopped himself into one of the overstuffed chairs nearby. How Clyston had managed to get such decidedly non-military furnishings into the middle of Saudi Arabia hardly ranked among the greater Clystonesque achievements. "I was just listening to Chopin," said the sergeant. "London Symphony bootleg."

Knowlington nodded.

"Root beer?" Clyston asked. "I have some from Schmmy's."

Schmmy's was a small, old-fashioned soda fountain in a small upstate New York town where a friend of the sergeant's lived; it was, in the opinion not merely of the capo but of half the squadron, the creator of the world's best root beer. Knowlington found himself agreeing, despite his intention to go grab some sleep as quickly as possible. The sergeant reached into one of his refrigerators—he had several of various sizes and purposes—and retrieved a small hose and spigot. He then took a frosted mug from an ice chest and pumped the colonel a glass.

"You just wanted to talk?" asked the sergeant as he handed him the glass.

"I wish. We need to send a few people over to Al Jouf."

"How many?"

"Enough to keep two Hogs in the air indefinitely."

"Geez, I don't know if I can spare anybody."

"It's important."

In theory, Clyston wasn't on the very short list of people with a need to know about Fort Apache, and so the colonel had not told him about it. But the sergeant was a five-star member of the Pipeline, and the look and slight nod that he gave the colonel confirmed that he knew all about it—quite possibly in greater detail than the men who had planned it.

It was also obvious, his complaint about being short on people notwithstanding, that he had already given the matter some thought.

"Going to have to send Tinman," said the sergeant. "I hate to, but there's no one who knows metal better than him. He'll take three places."

Knowlington nodded, as he did at the other names—until the last.

"Rosen? Again?"

Clyston shrugged. "Colonel, she's the best on the base at all the avionics crap. And not just on Hogs."

"She's a pain in the ass."

"True. But the thing is, she knows what she's doing. I've seen her make radios work that had half their parts. Besides that, she can strip and reassemble three quarters of the engines we got in half an hour, and that's not even her specialty. She's also a certified parachute packer. Hell, I saw her take an f'ing OV-10 Bronco completely apart and put it back together last year. You know, when she first joined the Air Force—"

"It's not her ability I'm worried about," said Knowlington. "She's an Einstein. But she's got the personality of the Wicked Witch of the West."

"That's not precisely fair," said Clyston. He nodded to himself, as if considering his words, though Knowlington had heard most of this speech before.

Several times.

"She just gets involved in difficult situations," said Clyston. "People try to hit on her."

Knowlington rolled his eyes. In fairness to Rosen, some male officers did make unwanted advances toward her; it was a problem for all women in the military. But Rosen wasn't particularly discriminating about what constituted an "unwanted advance." And her way of dealing with them wasn't exactly by the book. A few days before, a captain had shown up in Knowlington's office sporting a badly bruised kneecap and ribs.

Rosen's defense? She was wearing new shoes or she would have broken them.

As a general rule, Knowlington didn't interfere with Clyston's "suggestions" on personnel. No one in the Air Force knew their people better than the capo.

Still . . .

"You sure, Allen?"

"I'll kick her butt around a bit and make sure she keeps her f'in' nose in line," said Clyston. He crossed his heart with his finger.

"It's not her nose I'm worried about. She slugs the wrong person over there and even I won't be able to get her out of it." Knowlington drained his glass and set it down, then got up to leave. "Somebody ought to stick a gun in her hands and send her after Saddam."

"Hey, you never know," said Clyston, putting his earphones back on.

Aside from one of his sisters, about the last person Skull expected to be waiting for him as he walked back to Hog Heaven was Major James "Mongoose" Johnson.

"You're supposed to be back in Buffalo by now, aren't you, Goose?" he asked.

"I missed the plane," said the major. "Mind if I talk to you a second? It's kinda—I'd really appreciate it."

Even though Mongoose had served as the squadron's Director of Operations, the two men hadn't known each other very long and had never gotten along particularly well. Knowlington couldn't imagine why he was suddenly being called on as a confidant, even though he had risked his neck—and Shotgun's—to snatch the major out of an Iraqi troop truck only a few days before. But he led the major into his spartan quarters anyway, waving him toward the only seat in the small room—a trunk at the foot of the cot. Knowlington sat on the cot.

"What's up?" he asked.

"I don't want to go home," Mongoose said.

Knowlington laughed, thinking there was a punch line.

There wasn't.

"I'm serious," said the major.

"Why don't you want to go home?"

"I belong here. There's a lot to be done."

Nearly thirty years in the Air Force, including a shitload of time in Vietnam, and this was a first. Major Johnson had an arm in a cast, to say nothing of a few other less visible injuries. He was in line for umpteen medals and due some major R&R. Knowlington shifted uncomfortably on his cot. "Major—listen, Goose, you deserve to go home. You earned it."

"I didn't earn anything. I got shot down."

"Bullshit. You did a kick-ass job in that airplane. Hell, you took out those bastards who captured you."

"No, you guys took them out. I got lucky."

Knowlington shook his head. "Orders are that you're heading home."

"You can get around them, though. I know you can. You've got connections coming out your—"

He stopped short of saying "ass," which struck Skull as funny, though he didn't laugh. "I don't know if I have enough connections to get around that. Hell, Major, don't you want to see your little baby?"

"Yeah, I do. More than anything. But I belong here. It's my job. You need me."

"No one's irreplaceable, Goose."

"Come on, Colonel. Don't send me home."

"You can't fly. What are you going to do, saw that cast off?"

Johnson ignored the question. "There's a lot I can do. Please. I've never asked you for anything."

What the pilot didn't say—though he clearly implied—was that Knowlington owed him big-time. Major Johnson had taken care of a lot of things—a hell of a lot of things—before Knowlington had finally managed to get control of himself and put himself on the wagon.

The grand total time of which now amounted to twenty days, twenty hours, and fifteen minutes, by his watch.

Of course, tallying it made him want a drink more than ever.

"I really think you belong with your family, Goose. You just had a kid."

"Colonel, I want to do my job."

Tired, surprised by a request he hadn't expected, Knowlington searched his mind for something to say. He'd never been good at this kind of thing. He wasn't a person people usually confided in.

Johnson was nuts. But he did owe him.

Maybe the guy knew something he wasn't saying. The colonel had never pegged Johnson as a drinker or a druggie, but maybe that was what he was afraid of. Or maybe there was something with his wife. Or the kid. Some sort of personal thing that needed time or something. Knowlington had never married, and he really wasn't good at figuring that kind of thing out, except to know that for some guys, a lot of guys, it was important.

But damn. The Air Force had an interest in making sure pilots who'd gone through Hell got a decent reprieve.

Even if they didn't want it?

"Colonel?"

"You know what, Major? I'm going to have to think about this. I just don't know."

"I do know, sir. I belong here."

"I'll talk to you about it tomorrow."

The major's face lit with an enormous smile. "Thanks."

"Hey, I haven't made up my mind yet," said Knowlington.

"I know that," said Mongoose, but he was still smiling as he left the tent.

7

KING FAHD AIR BASE, SAUDI ARABIA
25 JANUARY 1991
0245

Lying in his cot after volunteering to go on the mission, Doberman found it impossible to sleep. It wasn't because he was worried about flying so far into enemy territory. He was thinking about the stupid card game.

He had nearly been dealt a dream hand, unarguably the best seven cards he had ever had with a pot fatter than he could have wished.

No, he hadn't come close to being dealt it—he *had* been dealt it. He just hadn't had a chance to play the damn thing.

The dream hand to top off the dream night. Over four hundred bucks was tucked under the mattress.

What a run. Too bad it had been cut off.

And that was the problem. Because if things had gone on, the odds would have balanced out. He would have started to lose. That was the law of averages, the way statistics worked, the way of probabilities. You could describe it with math. Bing-bang-bam.

Unless there was something else involved, like luck. And

what did Sullivan say—lucky at flying, unlucky at cards, and vice versa.

Bullshit. He didn't believe in luck.

Except a little.

But if he had any luck, it was all bad. Luck of Job. Bullshit luck.

Doberman hadn't believed in luck or any such superstitious bullshit until the war started. Now he did kind of believe—a little. He had to admit he'd been just a little lucky to make it back the second time his plane got hit.

And the first.

The sergeant who saw his plane had called him the luckiest dead man alive.

More skill than luck was involved getting those planes back. Way more.

Though he had found a lucky penny.

Bullshit. He had a goddamned engineering degree, for christsake. There was no such thing as luck.

If he hadn't gotten the stinking card—or if he hadn't peeked at it—he'd be sleeping by now.

Did the fact that he had been stopped from playing the hand mean anything?

Maybe he had only a certain amount of luck and couldn't use it up on cards. So God or Fate or the Easter Bunny had stopped him from playing it.

Right.

Or maybe his luck was running out.

There were X number of possibilities such a hand would come up; he had played Y times. He'd had a million crappy hands. The pendulum had to swing back at some point. The two curves of probability met at the axis point, bing-bang-bam, the best round of poker of his life. No luck involved. Only probability.

Was there another curve that had to do with flying?

If there was such a thing as luck, if he had been lucky, he'd have to admit something was going on. Fate or some other superstition that he didn't believe in. Because if there was such a thing as luck, then there would be things like omens, and then the hand might mean truly that he was screwed.

Or not. Because it was all bullshit and superstition. A man succeeded because he busted his ass. Doberman had learned that lesson from his Uncle JR, the guy who'd taught him everything important. Taught him damn straight about cards. Luck was bullshit.

There were only two kinds of pilots. Guys like Shotgun who were somehow naturals, who just kind of fell into things somehow and made them work. Those guys could fly no matter what happened.

And then there were guys like him, who studied it like a book, worked and worked themselves until they had it so precise you could describe their flights with mathematical models.

If somebody like Shotgun wanted to be superstitious, well, what the hell—the guy was already so whacked out one more thing wasn't going to make any difference. But a pilot like Doberman, a pilot who relied on being exact in everything he did—throw superstition into the equation and that pilot was in serious trouble.

There was no such thing as luck, only probability.

But Doberman couldn't get the stinking idea out of his head. As desperately as he needed sleep, the best he could do was play the game in his head, over and over.

8

Near Fort Apache, Iraq
25 January 1991
0355

Captain Kevin Hawkins stopped and checked the geo-positioner in his hand. They were allegedly less than a quarter mile from the abandoned stretch of concrete the Bat Cave planners had designated Fort Apache, but he couldn't see it. Like the other members of the team, Hawkins had a set of AN/PVS-7 night-vision goggles—NODs or night-observation devices—attached to his helmet. The high-tech devices gave a dim green glow to the surrounding terrain, making it possible to see large objects several hundred yards ahead. But the Iraqi desert was real desert here, with shifting dunes and blowing sands. While they were working off satellite photos little more than thirty-six hours old, Hawkins was worried that the concrete had been swallowed whole.

He was also worried that the flat surface nearly a thousand feet long was simply a mirage. The intelligence folks had not been able to come up with a plausible reason why the Iraqis would start an airport here, nearly five miles from a highway, nor had they explained why the Iraqis had suddenly abandoned it.

Not that Hawkins really cared what the explanation might

be. He only cared that he found the damn concrete, secured it, and then made it into an airfield. If he succeeded, a pair of Special Ops helos would fly in tomorrow night with supplies, and stay for more than just dinner. He'd also start getting serious parachute drops with enough equipment to turn this little sidewalk in the middle of the desert into Saddam's worst nightmare.

Assuming he could find it. Hawkins double-checked the positioner again. The line display on the unit—dubbed by its makers "Magellan"—told him his target lay straight ahead.

His eyes told him there was nothing there. What should he believe?

The positioner relied on information supplied by a set of dedicated satellites high overhead. The system had not been completed before the start of the war, and there were grumbles about its accuracy. But it had always worked perfectly for him.

So he trusted it. More or less.

"All right, we move north. Let's go," he told his team of Delta Force troopers. His voice sounded confident, and he knew anyone hearing it might think he had spotted the base.

Or not. Most of these guys were pretty much on to his style, which was straight-ahead, no-turning-back, no matter the insanity.

"Captain, building at two o'clock."

Sergeant Nomo's warning—which somehow managed to sound like a whisper though it was nearly as loud as a shout—stopped the team. Hawkins trotted up to his position on the northeast flank of the unit.

A jagged wall stood over a low dune two hundred yards ahead. Nomo had found Apache's lone structure, a twenty-by-twenty poured-cement foundation the analysts said stood about three feet high.

Quickly, Hawkins had the team reorient into groups to surround their target. The team's lone infrared viewer—they were more precious than gold in the Gulf—revealed no warm bodies in the chilly night, but this deep in Injun country, they were taking no chances. The men moved out slowly, the lead troopers in each group armed with silenced MP-5's. While not absolutely silent, the submachine gun was difficult to hear more than a few yards away.

Which was one reason why the loud report of a gun a few minutes later sent every member of the team diving into the dirt.

The shot came from the left flank, near the end of the runway. There was no possibility it had come from the troopers, at least as far as Hawkins was concerned. When no other shots followed, he began making his way in that direction, one hand on his viewer as he scanned to see where the Iraqis were positioned.

"What do we have, Vee?" Hawkins asked as he reached the flank team leader without spotting anything.

Sergeant Olhum Vee pointed toward a ditch with the end of his M-16A2. The rifle had a grenade launcher attached to the barrel. "Got to be in the ditch," he said. "Teller and Garcia are swinging around. We have them covered."

"How many?" Hawkins asked.

"Don't know," said Vee. "Nobody saw anything. There's no place to hide besides that ditch—can't be more than four men, tops. Maybe just one or two."

"There's a culvert on the other side," Hawkins told him, gesturing toward the other end of the runway. "But it's empty. We'll move in slow."

It took Teller and Garcia five long minutes to get into position. By then, the rest of the team had the area well covered; nothing else was moving.

Hawkins watched as Teller and Garcia bolted upright behind the ditch where the shot had come from. They jumped into it without firing.

Were they trying to take the Iraqis alive? Hawkins and Vee leapt up, running to assist their men—whom they found leaning against the edge of the ditch, laughing their butts off.

There were no Iraqis.

"What the hell?" said Vee.

"Relax," said Garcia. "It's a crow banger." He held up a handful of spent cartridges and pointed to a small device near his feet. "See the wires? One of us must've got the last one, 'cause it's empty now."

Hawkins bent down to examine the device as the rest of the team gathered at the top of the ditch. Similar to ones used on some American farms, the miniature cannon was intended to scare off animals—crows, or more likely camels in this case. Activated by trip wires in the desert, it fired blanks.

"Damn fucking lucky it wasn't a mine," said Hawkins, which stopped the laughter. "Let's make sure this place is secure. And watch where the hell you step from now on. You may end up with more than camel poop on your boot."

9

IRAQ
25 JANUARY 1991
0455

Dixon's legs felt like they were going to fall off. He dragged them forward, desperate to keep his momentum up. The number-five man in the team, Jake Green, kept looming behind him, and Dixon felt him sneering every time he had to cut his pace to keep from running the Air Force lieutenant down.

The thing was, Dixon thought he was in excellent shape. He had run and won a 10K race just before coming over to Saudi Arabia, and had managed to work out nearly every day since the deployment began. He thought he shouldn't have any trouble keeping up with them.

But the Special Forces soldiers practically galloped through the desert, even with their overstuffed rucksacks. Each member of the team, Dixon included, carried more ammo on him than a good-sized gun store. Dixon's brown desert camo suit was covered by a vest stuffed with smoke grenades and clips for his MP-5; his pockets were so jammed with extra bullets for his Beretta that he couldn't sit properly. Each trooper had a gas mask in a leg pocket; a full chem suit sat at the top of his ruck. The rest of the gear varied, depending on the team member's assigned role. The point man and the tail gunner both carried silenced Berettas and MP-5's. The team's pathfinder worked with a geo-positioner from the number-two slot in the line. All but Dixon carried a pair of night eyes—AN/PVS-7 goggles, which could be attached to a helmet and turned the terrain a fuzzy but viewable green.

Maybe there was something in the goggles that made them move so damn fast, Dixon thought to himself, struggling into a trot to keep his place. He was behind the jumpmaster turned communications specialist, Sergeant First Class Joey Leteri, the number-four man in line. The trooper packed an M-16 with a grenade launcher, and humped not only his own ruck but the satellite com gear as well. But just like the others, he moved along like a racehorse threatened with the glue factory.

Suddenly Leteri stopped short. Before Dixon could react, he was pushed into the ground by Green.

"Tents," whispered Green, who was the team medic. He pointed over Dixon's shoulder toward the left; in the dim twilight the only thing Dixon could see was the shadow of hills that were part of an old quarry some miles away.

Sergeant Winston came back to them. "Aren't supposed to be any Bedouins this far north," he told them. "But we think that's all they are. They got camels. We have to take a jog east near here anyway. Cornfield's about four miles on. That okay with you, Lieutenant?"

It was the first time anyone had made even a glancing reference to the fact that Dixon, though an observer, technically outranked everyone here. There was no question from Winston's tone that it had better be okay.

"You take us where we're supposed to be," said Dixon. "That's more than fine with me."

"Yeah," said Winston, pulling his SAW to his chest before moving down the line to tell the tail gunner what was going on.

Resentment mixed under Dixon's fatigue as the team got back under way. He didn't need to be in charge—didn't want to be, because frankly he had no damn idea what the hell to tell anybody to do. But he wanted to be respected, or at least accepted as an equal.

Which they didn't. At best, they thought he was nuts—and not necessarily good nuts. Staffa Turk, the demo man who was bringing up the rear, had practically sneered at Dixon earlier when he'd assured him he could handle an MP-5.

Granted, it had been an exaggeration, since he'd never actually fired one before. But they didn't know that.

The Delta warriors were all older than Dixon—much—and all were NCOs, a tribe not especially known for tolerating junior lieutenants. And Dixon could only guess what they thought of the Air Force. But heck—he'd already shot down a stinking helicopter in combat, and survived some of the thickest antiair fire of the war. Not to mention herded a platoon's worth of Iraqis into the back of a Pave Low.

Not that he could tell them that, or even hint that he was angry. Saying anything would have exactly the opposite effect that he wanted.

Actually, what he really wanted wasn't anything more than sleep, and plenty of it. He was so tired the marrow was draining out of his bones. Sooner or later he was going to stumble face-first into the hardscrabble dirt in front of him.

Which was the last thing he wanted to do. Dixon concentrated on his steps, tightening his grip on the MP-5's metal stock to keep himself awake.

About an hour after they had seen the Bedouin camp, Winston had the team stop. He told them to eat while they rested; Dixon fished out an MRE and wolfed its contents down in a breath.

"Got a candy bar if you want it, sir," offered Leteri, who was crouched nearby. It was the nicest thing anyone had said to him since boarding the plane.

"I'd love it,"said Dixon. "Hey, uh, you can call me BJ. Most people do."

"I'm Joey."

"That's Joah-ee," said Winston in an exaggerated Italian accent.

Leteri tossed Dixon a Snickers bar.

"I haven't had one of these since I was in grammar school," said Dixon. He played it up, holding it to his nose like a connoisseur sniffing at a glass of expensive wine.

"You're going to want to take the paper off before you eat it," said Leteri.

"Why lose the calories?" Dixon said, unwrapping it. "Maybe I'll just snort it up my nose."

He had just enough self-control to offer Winston half the bar, but not enough to save it for later when Winston waved him off.

"You keepin' up okay?" asked the team leader.

"It's a good hike. You?"

Winston laughed.

"Be honest with you, BJ," said Leteri. "No braggin' or anything, but compared to some of our training gigs, this is like a guided tour of Lincoln Center."

"Where's Lincoln Center?" Dixon asked.

"Shit, you serious?"

Dixon felt his face start to tinge. "You mean the Monument?"

"No shit." Leteri thought this was the funniest damn thing he'd ever heard. "You never heard of Lincoln Center? You serious?"

"Yeah, I'm serious."

"Where'd you grow up, Lieutenant?" asked Winston.

"Wisconsin."

"No shit," said Leteri. "Lincoln Center's in New York City. Every schoolkid in the state's got to tour it before they're twelve. The law." Leteri waited a second before adding. "That's a joke, sir."

"He got it," said Winston. "If it was funny, somebody would have laughed."

"So where in Wisconsin?" asked Leteri.

"Little town called Chesterville. About two hours away from Milwaukee. More cows than people. Nobody's ever heard of it."

"No shit. I come from a town called Chester like an hour north of New York. We got cows there too."

"You have cows in New York?"

"Hell, yeah. It's pretty far from the city. Just nobody believes you when you tell them."

"I thought you were from Brooklyn," said Winston.

"Nah. I was *born* there. I mean, my grandma still lives there and shit. But we moved out of the city when I was three." Leteri turned back to Dixon. "People look at me funny when I tell them I grew up across the street from a farm. Hear New York and they figure, you know, it's all city."

"All right, break time over," said Winston, standing up. "Here's the deal. We got the streambed just over that rise. We follow that into an open area near the road. Obviously they knew we'd have some farm boys with us when they called it the Cornfield. Makes me feel right at home." The sergeant obviously loved sarcasm; he practically broke his jaw twisting his face into a smile. "My signal we shake out. Lieutenant, you want to stay kinda near Leteri here until we know what we got. Leteri, you got my ass."

"I always take the dirt road."

"Yeah, fuck you too, bugger boy."

"Better to be the bugger than the buggee."

The troop was soon moving again, stretching into a long line as they proceeded carefully up the side of a large ditch. Shallow water filled the bottom. Shards of ice had formed along the surface, in case any of them needed reminding about how cold it was. Two dry irrigation ditches ran off at right angles ahead; there were others as the main wadi or streambed snaked around a shallow rise with a good view of the highway a half mile beyond.

That was the Cornfield. The rise not only gave them a decent view of the road, but there was a good space between some of the ditches that could be used by helicopters if they needed to be evacuated.

Not that they were planning on being evacuated anytime soon.

By the time they reached the foot of the hill, Dixon's legs, arms, and upper body had congealed into a numb mass. The soft campaign hat he was wearing felt like a curtain around his brain, a permanent static emitter jamming outside reception.

Sleep would revive him. Sleep would warm his frozen bones, wet his parched lungs. Sleep would fill the hole in his stomach.

Sleep was a woman waiting for him just a few feet ahead, wrapping her legs around him, her open palms and long fingers sliding slowly across his chest. Electricity sparked as she touched him, soft and warm. Her fingers slipped into the crevices behind his ears, around and across his temples, down his cheeks to his neck, to the thick skin beneath his chin, up to his mouth. She spread herself back on the bed and pulled him into her, open and ready.

"We stop here," said Winston.

Damned if the sergeant wasn't part ghost, disappearing and reappearing at will.

"Use the slope here for cover. Hey, Lieutenant, you still with us?"

Dixon grunted an answer as he collapsed butt-first in the dirt.

"Maybe you ought to get some sleep, sir," said Winston. "Catch a nap before the show. We'll wake you up when we need you."

Dixon nodded, then pushed himself prone.

"Uh, BJ?"

Dixon looked up to find Winston grinning in his face. "You probably want to undo your ruck first."

Nodding, he fumbled with the straps, barely getting it off before slipping his head back to the ground.

10

King Fahd
25 January 1991
0455

His nose tickled.

Shotgun bolted upright in the bed, senses at full alert. He took a sniff, then another; quickly, deliberately, he got up and put on his boots. Shotgun slept in a flight suit for just this sort of emergency; he grabbed his jacket and hustled out of his small tent, threading his way through Tent City to follow the faint but aromatic scent. Shotgun veered right, heading in the general direction of "Oz," the Devil Squadron's maintenance and hangar area.

It was before dawn, but Fahd was in full gear. Many of the more than one hundred planes quartered here had already left on their missions north. Shotgun sensed he was closing in as he ducked past a gutted F-16—served the pointy-nose Viper right for wandering onto a Hog base. He soon found himself standing in front of a coffeemaker that had just finished spewing a full pot of black gold. The capo di capo and the Tinman, the squadron's resident Ancient Mechanic, stood nearby, already sipping from cups.

"Jamaican," said Shotgun, nodding approvingly.

"Jamaican it is," said Clyston. "Go ahead, have a cup."

Shotgun realized there would be payback involved, but he was too committed now to stop himself. He grabbed one of the sergeant's porcelain buckets and filled up.

"Except for Dunkin' Donuts," he said, three sips later, "this is the best joe I've had since the air war started."

"Hess privake stack," said Tinman.

Like everyone else on base except Clyston, Shotgun couldn't understand a word Tinman said. "Excuse me?"

"He says it's his private stock," said Clyston. "I hear you and Captain Glenon are flying pretty far north today."

"Yeah. Gonna play hopscotch with some Special Ops guys."

The capo nodded, then took a long sip of his coffee. "Far to go in a Hog."

"We can handle it."

"How's Captain Glenon doing?"

"Doberman?" Shotgun was genuinely surprised by the question. "He's fine."

"Luck holding out?" said the sergeant.

Shotgun laughed. "Dog Man doesn't believe in luck."

"What's with that penny he keeps in his boot then?"

"You know about that?"

The capo just smiled.

"I think it's along the category of, hey, couldn't hurt," said Shotgun. "Course, knowing the Dog, he may have figured out some sort of weight-ratio thing on the rudder pedal or something. Doberman's got a number for everything. But he ain't superstitious."

"Are you?"

There was a serious note in Clyston's voice, a hint that he wasn't just making conversation. Shotgun realized the time for payback had come.

But what the hell. This was real joe.

"Shit, yeah, I'm superstitious as hell," said Shotgun, chugging. "What's the matter, Sergeant? You worried we're going to break your planes?"

"You guys? Nah." Clyston nodded at the Tinman, who bent

over an old toolbox below one of the workbenches. He opened it and removed a small silver cross.

"Es got, no hurt," said the Tinman, holding the small piece of metal in front of him as if it were a holy relic.

"What's that?" asked Shotgun.

"Kind of a good-luck charm the Tinman wants you to give Doberman," explained the capo as the Tinman carefully handed over the small medal to Shotgun. "St. Christopher's Cross. Came from St. Peter's. Blessed by the Pope in 1502."

"No shit. Were you there, Tinman?"

The Tinman said something unintelligible to Shotgun. Clyston only smiled. "I wouldn't be surprised if he was," said the sergeant.

Shotgun turned the small cross over in his hand. It was tarnished and worn smooth. It had definitely been around. "What's the deal?"

The capo gave him a half wink. "Karma thing. Morale."

"Iff will kept him wholk," said Tinman.

Clyston was still grinning. Obviously, this was all for the Tinman's benefit, part of an elaborate capo plot to keep the old-timer churning.

The things you had to do to be top sergeant.

"He wants you to make sure Captain Glenon gets it," said the capo. "Go ahead, have some more coffee."

Shotgun eyed the pot, but stayed where he was. "That's going to be a problem," he told them. "Doberman gets kind of touchy about superstitious stuff. You know, 'im, Sergeant. He won't even take souvenirs, right?"

The Tinman's face had begun to grow red, and he looked obviously agitated. He started to say something, but Clyston put his hand up, silencing him immediately.

"Thing is, Captain," said the capo, "I'd appreciate it if you talked to him about it."

"I can't make him do something he doesn't want to do," said Shotgun.

"If you say you'll ask him, that would be enough," said Clyston, glancing at Tinman to make sure he was in agreement.

The old-timer nodded.

"I'll see what I can do," Shotgun told them. Tinman nodded some more. Obviously satisfied, he drifted off to another part of the shop while Shotgun helped himself to another cup of coffee.

"So where's my cross?" he asked Clyston. "Don't I need karma too?"

The capo made a face. "You don't believe in that superstitious crap, do you, Captain?"

"Nah," said Shotgun. "All I need's a good cup of joe. Mind if I fill my thermos? This is the kind of stuff you want to be drinking when you blow something up."

"You're out of your fucking mind," Doberman told Shotgun when he mentioned the cross an hour or so later. They were suiting up for their mission.

"See, the thing is, Tinman's kind of superstitious is what I think," said Shotgun. "And Clyston has to keep him happy because the colonel's sending him to Al Jouf—"

"Why does he have to be happy?"

"Dog, Tinman pretty much bends metal with his eyes, you know what I'm talking about? The guy really knows his shit."

"He's a fucking loony bird."

"Yeah, but he's gonna keep us in the air. Maybe he's a shaman or something. Yeah, gotta be."

"It's all superstitious bullshit," said Doberman. "Luck. Bullshit. I don't believe in that crap."

"How about that penny you carry around?"

As the words left his mouth, Shotgun realized he had made a major mistake, but it was too late to take them back.

"That's different." Doberman's face was so hot his bristletop hair seemed to flutter with the heat. "That's fucking different."

"Hey, I didn't mean nothin'."

"You think I'm lucky? I got the fuckin' luck of Job. I busted my ass learning to fly. I studied and practiced, that's what I did."

"That's what I'm talking about."

"Haunted crosses. Shit."

"Hey, I'm just trying to keep Clyston happy," said Shotgun. "He gave me this thermos full of coffee. Want some?"

Doberman zipped his flight suit. "Next thing you know we're going to have some fucking voodoo priest dancing on the wings. How the hell do you get involved in this crap anyway?"

"Just lucky, I guess."

11

KING FAHD
25 JANUARY 1991
0755

Doberman ran his eyes over the Hog's instrument panel for one final make-sure-I'm-ready-to-go pass. He wasn't rushing anything, especially today. Laying his hand gently on the throttle bar, he flexed his fingers and loosened the muscles in his shoulders, willing himself into something approximating a relaxed state. He swung his eyes back around the cockpit, inspecting the paraphernalia of his office, the desk accessories—altimeter, fuel gauges, radio controls—no Warthog executive could live without.

At spec and ready to rock.

The plane whined gratefully as he fed her engines a full dose of octane and began galloping down the runway. Doberman blew an easy breath out of his lungs and pushed the Hog into the sky. His mind was in full-blown flight mode and—while he could feel the penny beneath his toe—he'd finally stopped worrying about cards and luck and superstition.

Designed in the 1970s', the A-10A was conceived as a close-in ground-support plane, built to give a lickin' and keep on tickin'. Partly inspired by the success of the A-1 Skyraider in

Vietnam, the plane was an excuse to dump serious iron on an enemy. The two Mavericks—AGM-65B's—and four cluster bombs—SUU-30's—tied to Doberman's wings represented one of several dozen ordnance variations typically carried by the Hogs. The Mavericks were guided with the help of an optical (in this case) or infrared camera in the missile's nose; once locked on target by the pilot, the missile flew itself, leaving him free to play with others. A small screen on the right side of the dash was devoted to the Maverick's display. While originally designed as an antitank weapon, the missile was effective against a variety of targets, as it had proven since the first day of the war.

"SUU" stood for Suspension Underwing Unit, a nod to the fact that the sophisticated weapons were more like dump trucks than conventional iron bombs. Popularly known as cluster bombs, they packed several hundred explosive and fragmentation devices, releasing them at a preset altitude after being dropped. The CBUs were an optimal weapon against "soft" targets, which included unarmored vehicles and tasty treats like radar vans and dishes. The SUU could accommodate specialized loads depending on the mission; Doberman's were CBU-58's—which hosted a total of 650 BLU-63 fragmentation/antipersonnel bomblets.

Besides the AGMs and cluster bombs, the Hog could carry an assortment of conventional iron—unguided, straight-at-you blowup bombs. But in the opinion of most Hog drivers, the plane's fiercest weapon wasn't strapped beneath its wings. It was the GAU-8/A Avenger cannon that sat in the plane's chin. The Gatling gun could deliver as many as four thousand rounds per minute; during a typical three-or-four-second-burst more than a hundred uranium and high-explosive bullets darted from the revolving barrels. The plane had been designed around the huge gun; the weapon was so awesome it could literally make the Hog stand still in the air as it was fired.

The one thing the Hog couldn't do was go fast. Doberman had the stops out and he was barely making 350 knots. And without an autopilot, the plane demanded at least a modicum of attention at all times.

Still, as he climbed through the Saudi sky en route to a pit stop north at King Khalid Military City, the pilot's mind started to wander. This part of the mission—staging out to Al Jouf before heading into Iraq—was very plain-Jane, as close to boring as you could get in a war zone. Inevitably, his thoughts shambled back to the card game—and to Tinman's idiotic cross.

A lot of the crew members and more than a few pilots were heavily superstitious, he knew, but you had to draw the line somewhere.

Luck. Luck was some magic BB with his name on it sailing out from Iraq a zillion miles away and managing to nail him. Luck was something flaky happening with the engine in level flight, which in his experience was almost as likely as the magic BB shot.

He thought about that, he frowned, and in the next second the right engine stopped winding its turbine. He saw the indicator zeroing out of the corner of his eye as he tightened his grip on the stick, his body jumping to work the plane and compensate for the loss of power. Something unconscious took over, something that felt rather than thought.

His head sawed through contingencies. It would be best if he could make it back to the home drome, but he had plenty of divert fields closer if he couldn't. His heart pounded and Doberman felt his scalp tingling, as if his brain had gotten a quick shot of adrenaline.

He also felt himself suddenly out of kilter in the cockpit.

Not because the Hog had slumped from losing the engine. All 120 pounds of his compact body were compensating for something that hadn't happened.

The engines were humming perfectly. There hadn't been a malfunction. In fact, everything was at operating manual specification.

Son of a bitch.

Doberman twisted backward in the seat, craning his neck to look out the cockpit glass. He couldn't actually see the GE turbofans mounted on either side of the fuselage in front of the Hog's double tail. But he had to look anyway.

Just as he had to tap each one of the engine instruments when he turned back and saw they were claiming he was fine.

Maybe they had flaked out for a second.

No. Everything was perfect. It was all this thinking about superstition and luck and that crap that was putting him over the edge.

"Devil Two, this is One," he said, calling Shotgun. His wingman was flying about a quarter mile back, off his wing in a loose trail. "How's our six?"

"Clean," said Shotgun. "You ducking flies?"

"Negative. Just staying awake."

"Ought to drink more coffee."

Air speed, altitude, rpms, fuel—everything at spec. No way his engine had even burped.

It was just that he was tired. Damn royal stinking flush had cost him a good night's sleep.

"Something up?" Shotgun asked.

If he didn't know better, Doberman would swear this was something Shotgun and the capo had rigged up to teach him a lesson.

But which lesson would that be?

"Just wanted to make sure you were with me," Doberman told his wingmate. He glanced at his watch and did some quick math. "We have ten minutes, twenty seconds to the Emerald City."

"Yeah, I'm unwrapping my last pocket-pie now."

12

Fort Apache
25 January 1991
1157

A dried-out but very deep wadi formed a semicircle around the abandoned runway. Hawkins, kicking at the erosion at the southeastern end of the runway, theorized that the Iraqis had found the tributary too rough to deal with, the seasonal rains eating at the ground they needed to stay solid under the long expanse of concrete and asphalt. Why they wouldn't have realized that before laying out a thousand feet of concrete, though, he had no idea.

It was nice of them to tear up the road leading out to the highway, though. That made sneaking up on Fort Apache a little more difficult.

Hawkins's men had set out a good defensive perimeter and studded it with a variety of weapons; still, a concentrated armor attack could easily overrun them until they got their AH-6G gunships in. With luck, they would get them in tonight.

Hawkins turned and began walking carefully down the center of the cement. Except for minor crumbling around the expansion joints, the concrete was smooth and seemingly solid. He could certainly land his helos.

He wanted a lot more. Like an MC-130, loaded for bear. But to get the big four-engined gunship in and back up in the air again, they needed two thousand feet.

Six of the twelve men who'd come in on a parachute drop after the base was secured were combat engineers. They'd landed about ten minutes before dawn; a few seconds later he'd gotten them to work plotting an extension that would add nearly six hundred feet to the northwest end of the runway. Steel mesh was due to be parachuted in as soon as the sun went down. But that would get them only to the edge of the streambeds. Without a bulldozer and cement culverts, the runway wasn't getting any longer.

Still, all things considered, Hawkins had only relatively minor problems at the moment. One of the men on the second team—an inexperienced jumper who really had no business on the mission, volunteer or not—had broken his leg and arm during the drop. He was their only casualty so far. He was in decent enough condition to stay, but he was their lone helicopter mechanic.

Team Blue, operating north of the Euphrates since the night before, hadn't checked in on schedule, though that might just be due to problems with the satellite communications system. But the team he'd been most worried about, Team Ruth, was in position and ready to work several hours ahead of schedule.

Sent to an area thought to be one of the main Scud highways, Team Ruth would be vectoring in bombers by late afternoon—assuming they found something to target. Hawkins had put some of his best men on the squad, including Master Sergeant Eli Winston, who was leading the team. And Ruth included the lone Air Force officer assigned to the Injun country operation, a ground FAC who was supposed to sweet-talk the iron onto the Scud trailers. A pair of A-10As had been attached to Apache; for now, they were at Team Ruth's beck and call, though Hawkins could change that if he needed to.

The captain took a wistful glance down the runway. It was

good to know the Warthogs were on the job, but he couldn't wait for his own helicopters to get there.

He turned back for the command bunker. There was just enough time for a cup of Earl Gray before the scheduled call to his colonel at Al Jouf.

13

Over Iraq
25 January 1991
1540

Doberman glanced through the clear Perspex bubble overhead, scanning the light blue sky. Somewhere above him, a pair of F-15C Eagles flew like guardian angels, swift police dogs ready to nail any Iraqi who dared take flight. Just to the southeast, the backseater in a Phantom F-4 Wild Weasel scanned his radar warning screen, ready to point a homing missile into the dish of any air defense system foolish enough to turn itself on. To the north, a package of attack planes and electronic jammers streaked toward the outskirts of Baghdad, loaded with bombs and defensive weapons. Far to the south, an Air Force E-3 Sentry AWACS plane coordinated the entire air war, scanning for threats and potential threats, moving planes to meet them like a chess champion throttling an opponent.

And yet, Doberman felt alone in the cockpit, accompanied only by Shotgun flying now a half mile back. Both Hogs were at 17,110 feet. The ride up from Al Jouf had been free and easy, but it had been long, and they still had nine and a half minutes to go before they flew in range of the Special Ops unit they were tasked to assist.

If you were waiting for a stagecoach in the middle of town, nine and a half minutes wasn't that long. If you were riding into Dodge with all kinds of bad guys eyeing you from the roadside, it was an eternity. While not completely defenseless, the planes were hardly bullet- or missile-proof. The A1Q-119 radar-jamming pods on their right wings were near-revolutionary dual-mode jammers—when they were introduced back in the Stone Ages. While the pods still provided protection against the older elements of Saddam's multilayer air defense, they were hardly an invincible shield. The A-10A's somewhat more robust radar-warning receiver or RWR could find and track more than a dozen threatening radars in several bands, telling the pilot that he was starring in his own radar show. But that was hardly a guarantee that he wouldn't be shot down.

Among Saddam's varied arsenal, his Soviet-made SA-6's and German Rolands were particularly effective weapons, posing more than a theoretical threat even to the fast-movers. While the Devils had been briefed on the known positions of the SAM batteries throughout Iraq, both the SA-6—NATO code-named "Gainful"—and the Roland sat on mobile launchers that could pretty much be moved at will.

A pair of Sidewinders sat on a double rail on Doberman's left wing. Excellent heat-seeking weapons, they were meant for close-in air-to-air defense. They'd be handy if an enemy plane managed to get by the Eagles—but any MiG that could do that was a pretty damn serious threat. It would also have probably already launched missiles from beyond visual range, well outside the Sidewinder's scope.

But maybe nobody even knew they were here. The A-10As were far too high to be heard from the ground. Most Iraqi radar operators who had survived the first day of the air war had realized that the best way to stay alive was to leave their knobs in the off position. Besides, the desert and scrubland below the Hog's wings were mostly empty—and hardly worth protecting.

Doberman checked his position on the INS, then worked himself slowly through a routine check of his instruments. He was like a Western marshal, buckling his gun belt before the big showdown, checking each bullet in his gun carefully, spinning the revolver more for luck than to make sure it was working properly.

Luck.

Doberman flushed his brain of trivia, concentrating on his mission. Once on station, they'd take it down closer to the ground and look for Scuds. The missile carriers were supposed to move along the highway in mid- to late afternoon, en route to their launching spots. The commandos—Dixon—would spot them; the A-10's would blow them up.

There were only so many highways the Scud trucks could use. That was one curve of probability. Time was another. Even assuming the intelligence was good, their small time on target because of fuel considerations meant there was a bit of luck involved.

Luck again.

I am an engineer, Doberman told himself. Planes do not fly on luck, bridges are not built on luck, Scud carriers are not splashed on luck.

He checked his instruments and tightened his hand around the stick, precisely on course and on time.

14

IRAQ
25 JANUARY 1991
1540

Dixon woke up with a kink in his neck the size and shape of New Jersey. Both hands were numb. He had to take the worst leak of his life. And as he got up, he felt something hard and heavy push him back down.

"Truck."

Leteri's hoarse voice brought Dixon back to reality. He rolled over, scooped his gun from the ground, and began following Leteri up the hill on his hands and knees to a dug-out position just below the crest of the hill.

"What do we have?" he whispered as Leteri peered over the top of the ridge they were using as a lookout post. "Should I call in the planes?"

The sergeant shook his head, holding up his finger to tell Dixon to wait. Turk and Winston lay against the top of the ridge, watching the road through binoculars. Dixon heard the distant sound of a truck approaching. The sound got louder, and then began to fade.

"Just a pickup," said Winston, slipping down. He gave Dixon his binoculars.

The Steiner 7x40's brought the roadway into sharp relief, making it somehow seem more real. The yellow-gray haze of the distance melted into crisp shades of brown and blue. The moving finger with its trail of dust sharpened into a white pickup.

A Chevy, as a matter of fact. About ten years old.

"They may be checking the roadway, scouting it to see if it's safe," Winston said.

"This deep in Iraq?" asked Dixon.

The sergeant shrugged. "*I* would. Then again, it could be nothing. We've seen three trucks since you fell asleep."

The sergeant resumed scanning in the direction the pickup had come from. Dixon followed Leteri back down the hill to a small dug-out position at the foot of the slope.

"Latrine's anywhere in that direction," said Leteri, pointing a few yards beyond.

"You have ESP?"

"Yeah— ESPP, extra sensory pee perception."

Dixon took care of business, then returned to check out the communications system, which Leteri had put together while Dixon was sleeping. It consisted of two parts. One was the unit itself, contained in a rucksack; the handset and controls lay at the top. The other part was a small folding radar dish that looked something like the folding circular clothesline Dixon's mom used to use in her backyard. The sergeant had oriented the dish so that its signal could be picked up by an orbiting satellite. With the push of a button, they could talk with Apache or the air support units or a command center in a Riyadh bunker, and from there, literally to the world. The short-burst transmissions were nearly impossible for anything but the most sophisticated equipment to intercept.

"Here we go," said Winston above. He chortled a bit, as if he had laid a long-shot bet that was now paying off. "Yeah, here we go."

Dixon climbed back to the top of the ridge.

"It's a truck, but I don't think it's a Scud carrier," said Turk.

"There's another truck right behind it," said Winston.

Dixon could hear the engines now. Two tiny ants approached, winding their way across the distant highway.

"Just trucks, Sarge," said Turk.

"Here, Lieutenant, you take a look," said Winston, handing him the binoculars. "You got pilot's eyes, right?"

Dixon's pilot's eyes took a · econd to adjust to the glass, then shaped the silver and green blurs into a pair of tractor-trailers. He caught a Mercedes emblem on the front of the leading vehicle as it took the long curve toward them.

"Sorry," he said. "They're not missiles."

Winston frowned and took the binoculars back. The trucks might be carrying military supplies or they might not. In any event, there was no sense telling the Hogs to hit them.

"Bus or something coming the other way," said Turk. His dark mahogany cheeks began glowing cherry red. "Hey, now, here we are. That, my friends, is a Ural 375 flatbed, built by Ivan just for our obnoxious friend. That's a crane, I do believe, and here we go—you tell me, Lieutenant, what's under those tarps? Huh?"

Dixon took Turk's binoculars and quickly focused on the road. The lead truck was a common Warsaw Pact export, as ubiquitous as a U.S. M-35 6x6. On its back was a long crane, the type that could be used to erect a derrick or even a modular house in the States. But the two tractors following behind it indicated the crane had a much more sinister purpose—the Zil-157 long-haulers were know Scud ferries, and there were large tarps curled around suspicious shapes at the back of each truck.

"Aren't they going in the wrong direction?" asked Dixon. "They're going east."

"Don't worry about what the intel people told us," said Winston. "Damn—get your guys on the horn. Now. Uh, sir."

Dixon was already scrambling down the hill to do just that.

15

Over Iraq
25 January 1991
1552

"Devil Flight, this is Ground Hog. Are you up?"

He'd been expecting to hear Dixon eventually, but even so, Doberman actually turned and looked out the cockpit canopy, as if BJ were gunning a Hog next to him.

"We're here," Doberman told him.

"Captain Glenon? Doberman? Is that you? Geez, how the heck are you?"

"I'm fine," said Doberman. There was no need for an elaborate authentication procedure—only Dixon would say "heck" instead of "hell." The kid was way behind in the mandatory cursing unit of Hog training.

"Yo, War Hero," said Shotgun. "How the fuck are you? Blow up any helicopters today?"

"Listen, Devil Flight," snapped Dixon, suddenly all business, "we have three targets for you. Proceeding east on the highway, uh, two, three miles now from Point Super Zed-Three. You copy?"

Doberman glanced down at the grid map on his knee, which showed the Special Forces checkpoints against the Iraqi terrain.

Zed-Three was a point along the highway. They were, by his quick calculations, exactly 8.75 miles southwest of it.

"I have the position," said Doberman. He swung the Hog back toward the north, calculating an intercept with the vehicles, which he figured would be moving along at fifty miles an hour, or thereabouts.

Doberman spotted the highway about a minute later. As he began to close, he saw a vehicle. But the truck was moving in the wrong direction. His eyes strained past the bullet-proof Perspex glass of the canopy, working the grains of sand into lines and ants.

Nothing except for the truck going the wrong way. Zed-Three was ahead to the northeast, about two o'clock. He pushed on, the plane level at 8,550 feet; it was somewhat high for ID'ing moving targets, but their instructions were to fly no lower than eight thousand feet unless absolutely necessary, which would keep them safe from all but the most persistent antiair guns. Doberman had a clear view, and figured once he spotted a likely candidate for Dixon's trucks they could move lower.

But at the moment, he couldn't see anything. He double-checked the map to make sure he had the right highway—not that there were many choices—then asked Shotgun what he was seeing.

"Nothing but camel turds."

"Let's take it this way another forty-five seconds, then crank back," Doberman told him.

"Forty-five seconds? Why not forty-four? Or forty-three."

Doberman was just about to tell Shotgun to fuck off when the AWACS controller shouted a warning over the radio.

"Devil Flight, snap ninety south!"

Doberman jerked to comply, putting the Hog almost literally onto a right angle. As he juiced the throttle, the AWACS operator filled in the reason for the emergency evasive maneuver—a pair of MiGs had just taken off from an air base to their north.

With pedals to the metal, the Russian-made interceptors

could reach the Hogs in under two minutes. And splash them soon thereafter.

A flight of Eagle interceptors scrambled to fry the MiGs. Doberman's instinct was to punch the Hog into the ground fuzz at twenty feet, then say screw the MiGs and get back to Scud hunting. But this far inside enemy territory that wasn't a particularly wise thing to do. Instead, he and Shotgun settled for a wide turn a good thirty miles south of the action.

By then the MiGs had disappeared from the AWACS radar—probably by landing back at the base they had started from, though the controller wasn't immediately sure. Doberman angled back toward the highway, but he knew that by now the trucks would be long gone. Worse, the Hogs were down to ten minutes of loiter time, thanks to all the maneuvering.

"What's going on up there?" Dixon asked over the ground radio just after Doberman and Shotgun had crossed over the road—without, of course, spotting the Scuds.

Tersely, Doberman explained that they had been shunted off the trail by the AWACS. And that they were almost bingo fuel.

"Did you pass the location on to the AWACS?" BJ asked.

"Fuck, no," said Doberman. "We fucking couldn't find them."

"Aw, shit."

"Yeah, copy," said Doberman. "Shit-fuck and cum-sucking hell in a whorehouse."

"Bad news, Dog Man. I'm bingo," said Shotgun. "Bingo" meant he had used up the fuel allocated for loitering. He now had only enough left to get home, with a modest amount left over for emergencies.

"Yeah," muttered Doberman. The two planes had to stay together and in any event, he was nearly at bingo himself. He blew a deep sigh from his mouth, cursed some more, then reoriented the Hog for the long, dreary trip home. He was so pissed he didn't bother answering when Shotgun joked that Special Ops obviously agreed with Dixon—the lieutenant had used a four-letter word on the radio.

16

THE CORNFIELD, IRAQ
25 JANUARY 1991
1621

"Son of a shit. We could have blown the goddamn things up ourselves," said Winston. He looked at Dixon as if Dixon had been the one flying the planes. "Son of a shit. How the hell could they have lost it?"

"I don't know that they ever saw it."

"Well, fuck. They're in goddamn airplanes, right? How the hell hard can it be?"

The truth was, it wasn't that easy picking out moving targets from the altitudes the brass had the Hogs flying. And the planes weren't carrying super-enhanced videos or extra-perceptive radars or anything beyond Mark-One standard-issue eyeballs. The MiGs had been the real problem. Since the A-10's were sitting ducks against any interceptor, their only defense was to run away, and even that hardly guaranteed safety.

But it was tough to explain all that to someone on the ground—especially when the ground was in central Iraq.

"What the fuck is the sense of our being here if they're not going to squirt the damn things when we point them out?" Winston insisted.

"They'll get them," said Dixon. "Give them a chance."

Winston grunted, and turned his binoculars back toward the highway. Dixon slid back down the hill to the radio, though there was little reason to at the moment. It would take the Hogs close to two hours to refuel and return. By then they would be limited by the available light as well as their fuel.

Dixon had just decided to brave an MRE when Leteri came sliding down the hill, nearly landing on his back.

"Patrol," hissed the corporal. "They're on the side of the road and they're moving slow. Stay down."

Dixon spun back around, pressing himself into the dirt and pulling his gun under his arm. If they came under fire, his job was to stay with the radio; they might need air support, which he could get through the AWACS controller. But holding the MP-5 felt like the right thing to do.

Leteri continued to the very base of the hill, crawling into a shallow trench the commandos had dug and camouflaged so it could be used as an observation post. The far end of it gave him a good view of their flank as well as the road. Dixon watched him work along it slowly. Moving slowly must be an exercise in great willpower, Dixon thought; the temptation to rush would be almost overwhelming, but doing so might expose you to the enemy. Patience was such a difficult thing in war—in life, for that matter. It was a trait he didn't have.

Leteri reached his post, stayed flat against the side of the trench a minute, then leaned back and gave a thumbs-up. The others had relaxed as well. Curious, Dixon scrambled up the hill, flopping between Winston and Turk.

"They're staying put, at least for now. They're on the other side of the highway," said Winston, handing the binoculars over. "Got their backs to us."

Dixon peered through the glasses. Four men in tan fatigues were walking a staggered line beyond a troop truck.

"What are they doing?" Dixon asked. "Looks like they lost something."

"They may have seen the planes," said Turk. "The idiots

probably think they mined the road. They did the same thing about a mile north."

Winston took the smallest of sips from his canteen, rolling the water around and around the inside of his mouth before swallowing. "Crazy fucks."

"They use their own men to trip mines?" Dixon asked.

"Saddam doesn't give a shit. And hell, most of those guys probably think they'll go straight to heaven," said Winston. He screwed his canteen closed. "We're going to have to move off this hill."

"Why?" asked Dixon.

"It's the tallest feature on the landscape, the most obvious place to check the road from. If they really are looking for mines, hell, even if they're fucking picking up litter, they're paranoid enough to figure out that someone on the ground brought the planes here. Besides, maybe one of the trucks turned off down the road a bit. They may be setting up to bomb Tel Aviv right now."

"Trucks were headed east," said Turk. "We going to follow them to Baghdad?"

"Shit, why not?" said Winston. "Let the lieutenant get a chance to practice his Arabic."

"I don't know Arabic."

"Fuck, no," said Winston in mock horror. "And here I thought you went to college."

Turk laughed. Dixon couldn't think of a comeback. He waited a bit, and when Turk changed the subject, he slid back down the hill. When the time came to move out, he told Leteri he'd take a turn humping the com gear, then did his best to ignore the trooper's surprise as he shouldered the ruck and got into line.

17

APPROACHING THE IRAQI BORDER
25 JANUARY 1991
1752

Two hours and one record-time tanking later, Doberman found himself clicking his mike button and getting nothing but a steady stream of static. They'd been trying to find Dixon for the past five minutes without any luck. He was about to try hailing the Delta unit again when Shotgun beat him to it.

"Devil Flight to Ground Hog. Yo, Dixon, where the fuck are you?"

"Real military," Doberman told Shotgun over the short-range fox mike radio, tuned to the squadron's private frequency.

"Yeah, well, you try."

"Just keep their frequency open. I'm going to have Cougar double-check for us, in case we're out of range or something."

Cougar was the call sign for the AWACS. The controller told them—as he had only a few minutes before—that the ground unit had not come back on the air after signing off to change position. This wasn't unusual, implied the operator, who all but directed the Hog drivers to just chill.

"Man, I'll tell you something. I'm getting a little fed up with Cougar," said Shotgun. "Kinda like havin' my fourth-grade teacher lookin' over my shoulder. Hang out. Break. Run away. We need somebody back there who's a Hog driver, you know what I'm talking about? Like, here's a couple of tanks to splash while you're waiting. That's what I'm talking about."

Doberman let Shotgun rant on as he examined the map unfolded in his lap. The two Hogs were at 16,675 feet, flying a wide, perfect circle around the coordinates where the ground team had spotted the trucks earlier. As they swung through the northern arc, the Euphrates edged into their windscreens, a thick brown line in the distance.

Doberman had read somewhere that civilization started along the Euphrates. The Sumerians had built an impressive empire well before the Egyptians, taming the wiles of the river with massive irrigation projects. They had enjoyed tremendous wealth, building cities of gold.

Hard to imagine that now. This was supposed to be part of the country's fertile area, but the terrain looked blotchy at best. Doberman had flown over Iowa cornfields—now those looked like something, orderly lines of green extending out as far as you could see.

Part of the problem was, they were too stinking high, as per their orders to maintain a safe altitude. Safe for whom? Might just as well be on the moon as far as he was concerned. He couldn't get a clear view of the highway, let alone make out what exactly might be moving on it. Scud launcher or a milk truck looked the same from here—smaller than an ant's behind.

"Getting kind of dark," Shotgun hinted.

"Copy," said Doberman. "Let's take a run over the highway down where we can see something smaller than a fucking battleship."

"That's what I'm talking about," snapped Shotgun.

Doberman pushed his wing over and threw the Hog into a tear-ass dive, plunging so quickly even the A-10 was caught by surprise. He moved his stick until the gray line of the road fell into his windshield. He was below five thousand feet before he started to recover, pulling the Hog level in a smooth, precise arc. The GE power plants hummed behind almost gently, their steady rhythm a subconscious sound track as he flew.

Some pilots flew by making the plane an extension of their bodies. They moved their arms and legs and the plane moved. They felt the wind curling in a slipstream around their bodies and their eyes were part of the radar nosing ahead. At some point the line between man and plane blurred; they flew as much by instinct, by stomach or gut, as they did by carefully accumulated knowledge and deliberate action.

Doberman considered himself more a director, or maybe a sitter—he sat on top of the plane, pushing its levers the way an experienced heavy equipment operator might move a bulldozer through a construction site. The plane went where he wanted it to, not the other way around.

No luck involved in that. You knew the data, worked with it. Wind had a certain effect, depending on the altitude and angle of attack; you calculated it, you compensated for it, you pushed the button to drop your load. Anything else was bullshit.

"Six is clean," called Shotgun.

Doberman eased his stick right, following the road's curve northward. Now he could see damn well. A bus appeared ahead—a matchbox-sized vehicle with a light brown color. A half mile in front of it was something that looked more military—grayish-brown waves of camo flopped over the back of a medium-sized truck. Might be a troop carrier.

Drawing closer, he saw that the tarp was pulled up over some ribbing, and the exposed bed was empty. But his disappointment melted as he saw two flatbeds further along—carrying tanks. They were behind two long tractor-trailers and a tarp-covered flatbed. A pair of armored personnel carriers cruised in front of them. Further ahead, something similar to a Land Rover led the procession.

Hot damn. Something worth hitting.

Doberman banked to the right, parking out of the target's sight in a quick orbit while he consulted his map. The two A-10's were a few miles east of the point where they had lost the Scud carriers—or whatever they were—earlier. It seemed to him possible, if not entirely probable, that these vehicles might be going wherever the Scuds had gone. He checked his fuel. He and Shotgun had about a half hour more of linger time—more gas than light, which was fading steadily now.

"Let's follow these guys for a ways and see if they take us anywhere," he told Shotgun. "Peg your altitude at seven thousand feet where they can't hear us. We'll give Dixon ten minutes to come back on the air. They're still sleeping, we take these guys."

"I'm counting the seconds," replied his wingman.

Doberman walked his eyes slowly across his instruments as he rode his Hog back around to the road. He had good fuel and a clean threat indicator.

Doberman put the road just above his left wing-root. He lowered his neck slightly and drew a long breath, gathering himself exactly as if this was an exercise over Germany. The tail end of the Iraqi convoy nosed into the corner of his windscreen, a small blur the size of a cockroach's foot. Gradually, it began to grow. He thought he recognized the roadway, and figured the trucks were now beyond the point where they had started looking for the Scuds; the road curved and straightened for nearly two miles in an arrow toward the river. Then it came almost due east, heading in the direction of Iran.

No way the damn Scud carriers could have outrun them earlier. They had to have turned off somewhere. On the other hand, the briefings had the Scuds going the other way, so who knew what the story was. He wondered if Dixon had dished him the wrong location or marker.

The convoy was now the size of fat cockroaches. Doberman hesitated a moment, scouting ahead, rechecking his compass heading and then the altimeter, making sure his gas was still good. He couldn't see a turnoff, and certainly no Scuds.

"Stay with me," he told Shotgun, marking his INS for a reference point before tacking north with a tight turn. This time he kept his eyes trained on the ground, trying to sort the shadows and shades into something—anything—that would tell him where the Scuds had gone. He saw a rock quarry and beyond that a group of buildings that seemed to be abandoned, but nothing thick enough to be a missile. From the air, simple Scud carriers looked like longish milk trucks; the dedicated launchers looked like soap dishes with turds on top. He saw neither.

The shadows were starting to play tricks; it was getting too dark to play up here much longer.

"Our friends must have seen us," said Shotgun.

Doberman pulled the Hog around and saw the vehicles kicking up a storm of dust to their south. They'd left the highway.

"How's your fuel?" he asked his wing mate.

"Twenty-something years to bingo, give or take," replied Shotgun. "You still want to wait?"

"Fuck it. Let's shag 'em," Doberman told him. "I have the tanks."

"Just leave something for me," said Shotgun.

The procession had stopped about three hundred yards off the roadway. The two tank carriers—long, narrow crickets on broken leaves—sat on the western flank. Doberman eyeballed them, then pushed his face almost into the Maverick's targeting screen, where the cursor was already flat on a turret.

The long shaft of a 125mm smoothbore pointed down from the back of the tank, the stick of a lollipop stuck to the cockroach's back. Doberman flicked his thumb back and forth over the stick—it was a habit he'd picked up just a few days before, a tick that was now part of his routine before pushing the trigger. Bing-bang-bam, he told himself, and pickled. As one AGM-65 dropped from his wing he quickly dished up the second, hurrying the cursor into the meat of the second tank as the screen filled with Saddam's latest hamburger special.

Bing-bang-bam. The second Maverick clunked from its firing rail, the Tikol motor catching with a whomp that sent the missile in a direct line toward the image burned into its brain. As it neared the T-72, the Maverick suddenly pulled up, arcing so that it could nail the target at the exact weak point of its armored hull, the turret top.

By then, Doberman was no longer paying attention to the tanks or the trucks near them. For Shotgun had shouted a warning about something much more interesting—one of the armored personnel carriers had stopped and set up a position on a slope near the highway.

Except that it wasn't an armored personnel carrier; it was a four-barreled ZSU-23 antiaircraft gun, an old but effective flak dealer, and it had already started to fire at him.

18

OVER IRAQ
25 JANUARY 1991
1758

"That's the kind of thing that really pisses me off," said Shotgun as the ZSU began chewing up the air in front of Doberman. The Iraqi gunner was firing without his radar, but in some ways that made him more dangerous, since nothing short of a high-explosive sandwich could jam the bastard's eyesight. A second unit began spinning its turret two hundred yards to the west, and Shotgun whistled—he might be peed that anyone dared fire at a Hog, let alone his wingmate, but he had to admit that the scummers at least had some balls in their pants, trying to go after the A-10's without using their radars and in a nice, isolated, and easy-to-hit spot besides. Granted, their flak was falling in a useless though artistic pattern across the desert as Doberman jinked away, but you couldn't hold that against the towelheads.

Well, actually he could and would. Shotgun fell into the attack, adrenaline pumping. For the briefest second he contemplated taking the Hog all the way in and using the cannon; this was exactly the sort of down-in-the-dirt no-holds-barred mud fight the A-10 was built for, flying into Abdul's 23mm shells, tickling proximity fuses, and laughing at the shrapnel spiking the air. Mano a mano, sweat versus sweat, my dad can take your dad, and your mom's ugly too. It had been almost twenty-four hours since Shotgun had revved up the gat, and he felt like he was going through withdrawal.

But truth be told, that would take too long and might give the Iraqis the idea that firing at a Hog was an acceptable thing to do. So he sighed, dialed in his Mavs, and push-buttoned the mobile antiair batteries to Hell.

The AGMs' flights to target were short and sweet. The penetration of the flat, tanklike turrets and the all-too-thinly-armored bodies of the ZSU-23's was a thing of beauty, erotic in a way, shaped-charge warheads slicing in and the guns bursting in an orgasmic riot of flames, smoke, and debris.

Shotgun loved art as much as anybody, but he pried his eyes away, turning his attention to the long trailer in the middle of a group of vehicles beyond the tanks. He pushed his Hog into a hard, sharp angle downwards, near sixty degrees—the theory being that the closer to straight down the less chance for error. This was actually a math thing, having to do with cosines and angles, the sort of problem Sister Carmella had made such an issue of back in high school. Shotgun had a soft spot in his heart for Sister Carmella, but didn't particularly like math, so he fudged the wind correction and just let the cluster bombs go when the feeling struck. He pulled his stick back hard, recovering from the dive and pushing to track back into the figure-eight Doberman ought to be cutting above their targets.

In the meantime, the vehicles disappeared in a flash of black and red, the four bombs smashing perfectly on target.

"Good shooting," said Doberman as Shotgun reached altitude. "You leave anything for me?"

"Tried to," said Shotgun. "See now, you could shoot like this if you had that medal."

"What medal?"

"Tinman's cross."

"You still pushing that?"

"Told him I would."

"I can shoot better than you with my eyes closed."

"Oh, man—you mean we're supposed to fly with them open?"

After dodging the triple-A, Doberman emptied his CBUs on the two clumps of vehicles at the far end of the party. Shotgun took his plane in an arc around the pluming smoke. Nothing was moving.

"Everything's good and broke," he told Doberman.

"I think that Rover or whatever it was stayed on the highway."

"Nah."

"Let's find out."

"Got ya," said Shotgun, reaching into his customized flightsuit to pull out a celebratory Twizzler. Nothing like licorice to top off a good bomb run.

Doberman led him back along the road. They spotted a bus and some sort of small truck, but not the Land Rover. Then Cougar cut in.

"Break ninety degrees," the AWACS controller told them. "Bogies coming off A-1. Break."

Shotgun echoed Doberman's curse as the jets snapped onto the new coordinates south. He could tell he wasn't going to get to use his cannon or his cluster bombs, which was a damn shame really.

The two Iraqis were quickly ID'd as a pair of F-1 Mirages, and just as promptly chased back to base by F-15's. By then the Hogs were into their fuel reserves; Doberman told the AWACS crew that they were heading back to Al Jouf for the night.

Shotgun's mood always grew reflective as he headed for home. He decided to treat himself to a second Twizzler, then clicked his CD changer to dish up Guns N' Roses.

19

IRAQ
25 JANUARY 1991
1825

The commandos waited until dusk to cross the road. They chose a spot near a short run of rock outcroppings, which would give them a staging area and some protection in case of traffic. The last fifteen minutes of waiting were the worst—Dixon's eyes were weighted with the fatigue of slogging the rucksack and communications gear on his back, not to mention the long day and night before. Two or three times he felt his mind wander off into the null space of pre-sleep. If it hadn't been so cold, he might have fallen into a slumber and not woken up for at least a week.

Two vehicles passed during that time—a Mercedes panel truck—probably, though not necessarily, civilian—and a small car that bore a red crescent, the Muslim symbol of the Red Cross organization.

Dixon wondered about the Red Cross car, thinking that maybe it might be carrying a prisoner. At least one allied pilot had gone down over Iraq during the last two days.

For a fleeting moment he wondered if he should give the order to stop it, and then he wondered whether the troopers would have obeyed it.

It was their job to find Scud transports and launchers, nothing else. They had already let a score of other military vehicles go.

But rescuing a pilot was different. That was worth blowing their mission for, wasn't it?

Shit, yeah. He could explain it to them—he'd have to, since they still thought of him as an outsider. They wouldn't automatically do what he said, even if he was an officer.

But it was too late now—the vehicle was by them and gone.

In the dull blueness of the fading day, the countryside looked vaguely familiar, almost American, a desert scrubland just beyond farmland. Look carefully and the illusion evaporated, but no amount of staring showed how dangerous their position truly was. At any moment, an Iraqi troop truck or tanks or helicopters could materialize and kill them. They had a ton of ammo, but it was finite. Eventually they would be outgunned—they were, as Jake Green had said three times during the last hour, in the ragheads' backyard.

It would be better, infinitely better, to die fighting than to be captured, Dixon decided. If captured, he would surely be tortured and killed anyway. Better to go quickly.

Besides, if they didn't kill him, it would be worse. He'd be used for propaganda. That was his real fear. To be tortured to the point where he would agree to anything they said—that was the worst horror.

In survival school, they told pilots it was no disgrace to go along if you had to. Bend so you didn't break. The people who counted back home would realize that you were being coerced. Your mission was survival, not playing hero.

But Dixon didn't entirely accept that. The shame of being a prisoner, of being helpless—it would be more than he could stand.

He'd learned that lesson flying in combat the first time. Bitterly. He remembered how failure felt.

"Lieutenant? You coming?"

Dixon jumped as Leteri tapped him. He followed across the open ground to the roadway. After two strides he felt the weight of his two backpacks balance him; by the fourth he felt as if he could run forever, adrenaline surging. He gripped his MP-5 with both hands, trotting with it before him as if it set out a force field of protection.

"You're looking like a goddamn Delta trooper now, BJ," said Winston as Dixon approached the team leader's position beyond the roadway.

Dixon was too tired to tell if he was mocking or admiring. Probably both. The lieutenant slid down on his knee and waited as the rest of the patrol crossed and scouted ahead.

"Okay," said Winston after his scouts reported back. "Here's what I'm thinking. We got the old quarry a mile ahead. If those trucks stopped anywhere around here, it was there."

"I'll go with whoever's scouting it," said Dixon.

"Not so fast."

"I got to be close to call a bomber in. I can use this, don't worry," said Dixon, holding out his gun.

"Relax. We're staying together."

"I can take care of myself."

"It's not you I'm worried about," said Winston. "I don't want to lose the radio."

"Yeah, I thought you sounded a little sentimental."

The comeback surprised Dixon as much as Winston. It was the sort of thing he would have expected Shotgun or Doberman to say, something that would have come out of the mouth of a guy who'd seen Hell a few hundred times and learned to laugh at it.

Winston laughed lightly, shaking his head. "Fuckin' Hog pilots. You guys think you're going to win the war all by yourselves, don't you?"

"If we fucking have to," said Dixon.

"Yeah, well, you're not going to. We're moving forward as a team. Stay close to Leteri, okay?" Winston gave him a chuck and moved out.

Fucking? Had he said *fucking*? Dixon pulled himself to his feet, moving ahead on sheer amazement alone.

20

Al Jouf FOA, Saudi Arabia
25 January 1991
1900

No question about it: Wong was definitely allergic to something in the desert. He sneezed into his handkerchief, at the same time muffling a curse that the half-dozen officers assembled around the table pretended not to hear.

Had to be an allergy. Sand maybe. Or the air.

Then again, it could be Major Wilson, who insisted on punctuating his briefing on the Fort Apache mission with historical notes on the formation of Delta Force and commando operations in general. Wong wouldn't have minded this so much if the major didn't get every third fact wrong.

Captain Wong had actually served with Delta Force twice, once as a tactical advisor on Russian weaponry, and briefly, as something called an "attached adjunctive administrative officer." This was a cover for an assignment to handle a clandestine drop into the northern Vietnamese jungles, a CIA-inspired mission where he went along to assess the wreckage of what was supposed to be a Chinese superweapon—and which turned out, as Wong knew it would, to be merely the latest version of the F-7, a Chinese copy of the MiG-21. The base model was an antiquated death trap Wong wouldn't allow even his worst enemy to fly, and his inspection showed that the Chinese had succeeded in making the newest version even more hazardous.

During that mission he had worked with several outstanding troopers, including a Green Beret captain named Hawkins, who encouraged him to believe that occasionally the Army bureaucracy lucked into choosing the right men for the right job. But in general, Wong held almost as low an opinion of the Special Ops bureaucracy as he held of the rest of the defense establishment, Air Force partly excepted. Major Wilson, droning on about "clandestine implants," was doing nothing to disabuse him of his opinion. The man's knowledge of enemy weaponry and the role of air support was rudimentary, in Wong's opinion, though he at least recognized that the Hogs would be operating beyond their preferred parameters. Wong started to second the point when his nose tickled again; he barely managed to pull a fresh handkerchief from his pocket and cover his face in time.

"You wanted to say something, Captain?" asked Colonel Klee, who was in charge of Apache and the infiltration teams associated with it.

Wong nodded as he finished blowing his nose. He had reserved opinion on Colonel Klee; his khakis were fairly crisp, no small accomplishment in this wilderness.

He was also admirably short on patience.

"Well?" asked the colonel. "What is it?"

"I was going to suggest that if we want the Apache forces to work in conjunction with our attack planes, we institute combat-area refueling procedures. A pair of C-130's flying over Iraqi territory—"

"That's on hold," snapped the colonel. "Go on, Wilson. And skip the history bullshit, will you? These people can get to the library themselves."

The major unfolded a large map across three easels at the front of the room. Fort Apache had been sketched in about a third of the way from the top left corner; various Iraqi air defenses and other installations were diagrammed in below.

"We want to add a lifeboat contingency," said the major. "As well as local firepower."

Between sneezes, Wong listened as Wilson updated the plan to base a pair of "sterile" Little Bird McDonnell Douglas AH-6Gs at Fort Apache. Descendants of the Vietnam War era Loach, the Defenders were special "black" versions of the versatile helo known in official circles as the Cayuse. The small, light choppers were equipped with machine guns and rocket packs; they were excellent support aircraft, could greatly extend Fort Apache's operating area, and—this was where "lifeboat" came in—could possibly be used to evacuate teams and even the base if necessary. There was only one problem: The choppers' loaded range was barely over two hundred miles, and the plan called for them to be loaded to the gills when they went north. And for reasons the major suspiciously did not specify, there were no available ferry tanks to help extend the range. Even with a stop to refuel right at the border, the trek to Apache was a stretch—and not even the Special Ops people thought they could make it in a straight line.

A big Pave Low could make it, of course. But no way anyone in their right mind would authorize flying an aircraft that valuable that far north. In fact, nothing valuable could go up there.

Which was why the Hogs had been assigned the overall support role, obviously.

Finally, thought Wong, the reason I am here. He raised his hand, sneezed, stood, blew his nose, and then cleared his throat.

"You want a safe route to Fort Apache, I assume," he said.

"I have a route to the airfield," bristled the major, pointing to the line.

Wong took Wilson's pen and began drawing parabolas around some of the defenses.

"Besides sneezing, what are you doing?" asked the colonel.

"The different performance envelopes of these defenses have not been adequately charted," he explained. "And I notice that several of these sites are misidentified. This here is an SA-2 battery, a problem for an older support aircraft flying at medium altitude and above, but it should be essentially oblivious to a helicopter running at night, which I assume is how penetration is planned. Additionally, some of your information is incomplete and/or out of date. You have not noted the defenses in this sector, as per the latest briefing. This GCI site was listed as only thirty percent destroyed in the last assessment. Experience shows that it is best to assume that is optimistic."

"Meaning?"

"A halfway competent operator would have no trouble frying your helicopters," said Wong. "Approached from this angle, however, the detectable envelope shrinks dramatically."

"Are you sure?" asked the major.

Wong sighed. "I assume I was asked to come to this sand trap because I am the world's expert on Russian defense systems. If you are willing to take great risks, fly in a straight line. I haven't done the math, but it undoubtedly offers no lower a coefficient of probable success than your course does. And with wing tanks—"

"We don't have wing tanks and even if we did, there's not enough weight left for them," said one of the helo pilots, a warrant officer named Gerry Fernandez. "We were supposed to be refueled en route."

"I did not see that contingency outlined on the map," said Wong.

"That's on hold as well," said the colonel without further explanation.

"We've already dropped fuel at Apache," said Major Wilson. "There's plenty of fuel for you, once you get there."

"We're going to have to lighten the load to get there," said Fernandez. "A hell of a lot. And carry fuel with us besides. With all due respect to the major, I'd like to hear what course this captain recommends."

"Go ahead, Wong," said the colonel.

Wong went back to sketching a safer course. Wilson started to object again, but this time was stifled by an impromptu dissertation on the effective range of the pulse-band radars emitted by the Roland mobile batteries.

The secrecy of the mission imposed a further constraint on Wong's planning, because it was necessary for the helicopters to avoid not only known antiair defenses, but places where any sizable number of troops might congregate. Wong's final route, to be flown about six feet off the ground, minimized the helicopters' exposure to everything but sand mites.

It also totaled close to four hundred miles and was more convoluted than a drunk's stagger.

Which the pilots promptly pointed out.

"It is necessarily intricate," said Wong, intending to suggest that if the pilots couldn't follow it, he knew several who could. But he was cut off by a sneeze.

"We can follow it," said Fernandez. "The question is range. Even with ferry tanks we couldn't do that."

The colonel leaned over to hear some advice from one of his lieutenants. Major Wilson whispered on the other side. Finally, the colonel nodded reluctantly.

"There's no sense taking this kind of risk if we're not going to deliver usable supplies and get up there fully armed," said the major. "It makes no sense to fly them all the way to Fort Apache without enough bullets and rockets to fend off an attack. We won't be able to arrange for a new drop until tomorrow night. By then, we ought to have a C-130 cleared as a tanker. And if not, we'll rig something similar to what we did to get the fuel down at Apache. The prudent thing is to wait."

"What if they need us before then?" said Fernandez.

"I'm not going to send you up there empty," said Klee.

Wong sighed. He glanced at the colonel, who could only be waiting for him to point out the obvious. Surely both he and the major had realized the solution by now. This charade could only be meant to make him feel more comfortable and withdraw his transfer request. A worthy gesture on the colonel's part. Perhaps there was hope yet.

Wong walked back to the map and marked an X roughly halfway through the course he had laid out. "There. They can land and pump the gas in themselves."

"And just how do we get it there?" said the major. "That's a hundred miles due south of Apache. Our troops there have no way to deliver it. Not to mention that they'd have to go through at least one known Iraqi troop placement."

"Two additional helicopters, with fuel drums—"

"Unavailable," said the major. "It's impossible unless we cut the supply load. The whole thing has to be scrubbed."

"Air-drop it," said Wong.

"How? I don't have any planes, Wong."

Wong shook his head. No one could be quite this dense. Clearly, Wilson had adopted the role of devil's advocate.

"You could use the same method you employed for dropping fuel at Apache," said Wong. "Now of course, you would wish to have some redundancy, so I would suggest—"

"We won't have those planes again for another two nights," said the major smugly.

"Then adapt other planes for the role," said Wong.

"What? The A-10's?"

Wong shrugged. "The configuration will require creative thought, but if we examine the—"

"That doable, Captain?" asked Klee quickly.

"Of course."

"I like you, Wong, I really do," said the colonel. He turned to a lieutenant. "Jack, get the captain some antihistamines, then go find the A-10A maintenance people and tell them to get this thing done. Better yet—Wong, go with him. Get as creative as you can before you sneeze your brains out."

21

Al Jouf FOA, Saudi Arabia
25 January 1991
1900

They were calling it Oz West, but compared to the Devils' maintenance area at the home drome, the facilities at the forward operating area were bare-bones at best. Still, even without the Clyston-supplied amenities of elaborate test benches and gourmet coffee—Sergeant Rosen wasn't sure which she'd rather do without—she and her "boys" could completely strip down and rebuild a Hog in under twenty-four hours. Twelve, if she broke into the Tinman's special coffee brew. Hell, with that coffee and the Special Ops people as inspiration, they could probably do it in under six, and wax the landing gear to boot.

The Hogs were designed for battlefield maintenance. Rosen had to hand it to the engineers for keeping things very basic. But it was also true that her skeleton crew—Jimmy, Elephant, and most of all the Tinman—were the best crew-dog technical-expert ground wizards in the Air Force. The fact that the capo had put her in charge of the operation made her determined to bust twenty more guts than normal; she was good and damned if she wasn't going to be better.

So if the truth be told, when the two Devil ships came back

to base looking like they'd spent the day in an auto dealer showroom, she was a little disappointed. It wasn't that she was looking for something to do—they were going to be here for a while and had a ton of organizing to do, not to mention the fact that their talents could always be used helping the base detachment with other planes. It was just that Tech Sergeant Rosen felt like there ought to be something more challenging.

And, since she'd heard that Lieutenant Dixon had been assigned to this mission, she was more than a little disappointed he hadn't shown up.

Which was part of the reason she went to report the detachment status to Captain Glenon personally. Glenon and Captain O'Rourke—Shotgun to everyone, including Rosen—were still debriefing in the makeshift intelligence area—a sandbagged tarp not far from the runway.

"Captain, just wanted you to know, both Hogs are good to go."

"Jesus. We landed ten minutes ago," said Glenon.

He seemed annoyed; Rosen was used to that, having dealt with the squadron's DO, Major "Mongoose" Johnson, a world-class ball-buster. Still, they'd just busted their butts getting the planes ready. She'd worked with Glenon a few times and never had any trouble with him before; for an officer, he'd seemed all right.

But that was then, this was now. Stinking officers were all the same.

"I'm sorry if you expected them sooner, sir," she said, her lips pressed together tightly.

"No, that wasn't what I meant. Hell, relax, Sergeant."

"Relax, sir?"

"Yeah, you don't have to kill yourself," said the captain. "We won't be flying until tomorrow morning."

"Speak for yourself," said Shotgun. "I was thinking of going camel hunting."

Rosen recognized that that was supposed to be a joke. She laughed politely, and looked back at Glenon.

All right, so he was okay. For an officer. Short guy, all muscle, quick temper, but okay. Kind of guy you could trust.

"The planes will be ready the second you want them, sir."

"Okay. Get some sleep or food or whatever."

"Thank you, sir," said Rosen, but she didn't move.

"Something up?" asked Glenon.

"Oh, um, nothing sir, just—I was wondering about Lieutenant Dixon."

"Dixon? What about him?"

"I haven't seen him, but I heard he was assigned to this mission."

"BJ's uptown with the commandos," said Shotgun. "Crazy fuck parachuted down with them last night. They went out at like thirty-five thousand feet—you believe that?"

Rosen nodded and stepped back to let the men pass. She felt her side stitch up, as if she had been running for a half hour. She massaged it gently, but knew it wasn't going away.

22

Al Jouf FOA, Saudi Arabia
25 January 1991
1920

"You want to drum up a card game after dinner?" Shotgun asked Doberman as they walked from the briefing area.

"Nah," said Doberman. He was feeling tired and a little beat-up from the two long runs north. About the last thing he was going to do was play cards. "I'm just going to bed."

"Bed? Shit, you kiddin' me? Bed? Instead of cards?"

"Screw off."

"Oh, man, you're making a big mistake," insisted Shotgun. "I'm tellin' ya, that cross of Tinman's gonna be hot shit at the poker table."

"I'd be careful about playing cards with these Special Ops types if I were you," said Doberman. "You win too much they may bury you in the desert."

"Yo, look who's here," said Shotgun, spotting Wong walking toward them. "Hey Brainiac, where's the food at?"

"Food. Right," said Wong.

"Seriously, there a place where we can get something to eat?" Doberman asked.

"There are several, though I wouldn't advise any of them,"

Wong told them. "Before you eat, Colonel Klee wants to see you."

Doberman listened with disbelief as Wong relayed the scheme to drop fuel for the helicopters.

"That's impossible," said Doberman.

"Merely difficult," said Wong. "If it were easy they wouldn't be interested."

"How's that airstrip up north coming?" asked Shotgun. "You think we can use it soon?"

"Don't be crazy," Doberman told his wingman. "It's just about in Baghdad."

"Baghdad is quite a distance away," said Wong. "Given the layout of the Iraqi defenses as well as their overly centralized command structure, to say nothing of their competence, the base might as well be in Riyadh. This is a classic outgrowth of the Soviet philosophy, the inherent flaws that were first pointed out by Herman Dedorf in his 1951 report and subsequently demonstrated by a little-known project entitled—"

"Spare me," said Doberman. "No matter where it is, a thousand feet isn't long enough to land anything. Let alone take off."

"Shit, Dog, that's doable," said Shotgun. "What do you say, Brainiac?"

Wong seemed not to understand why he had suddenly been nicknamed after a character in the Superman comics. But it didn't prevent him from spewing forth.

"They wish to double the length and land C-130's there. That will require considerable work and earth-moving equipment, a most inefficacious contingency, though they seem undeterred by such considerations," Wong told them. "If they can achieve that, then by all means your planes could operate there as well, assuming reduced weights and combat schemes. In fact, with the modest extensions to the present configuration that are already planned, the Fort Apache strip would be theoretically accessible to an A-10A, as you already undoubtedly are aware."

Doberman thought Wong sounded like a kid on a quiz show who wouldn't shut up. And Shotgun egged him on, bobbing his head up and down like a toy on a dashboard and gesturing like a windup toy with an overwound spring.

"If you operated at forward combat weight of approximately 32,771 pounds, you would need just 1,450 feet to take off," said Wong. "Of course, there are several contingencies, including the wind and, in Captain O'Rourke's case, how much candy he happens to be chewing at the time."

"And whether I got the stereo cranked," said Shotgun.

"But the idea of placing American warplanes so far behind the enemy lines where they would be open to a concerted ground attack is itself insane," said Wong.

"Thank you," said Doberman.

"It's not that crazy," Shotgun told Doberman after they finally managed to get Wong to point them in the colonel's direction. "If we could refuel there we wouldn't have to go home every time the AWACS calls out a snap vector. Shit, we're flying so goddamn far north as it is, what difference is landing going to make?"

"Strip's only a thousand feet," said Doberman.

"Yeah, but Wong said they're extending it."

"Wong."

"Guy's a brain, Doggie. He's the world's expert on Russian weapons."

"What does that have to do with lengthening airstrips?"

"Hey, you look at him, you say: There's a guy who knows concrete."

"Only because he's going to end up buried in some."

Even though the idea of landing a Hog two hundred miles deep in Iraq sounded crazy, Doberman realized that there was a certain logic to the insanity. It would immensely increase their time on station—hell, they would *always* be on station. And while the actual bomb runs were no picnic, the most perilous parts of their missions were actually the long legs to and fro. Flying high made them immune to triple-A, but if the wrong SAM site picked the wrong second to come on line, a dozen Weasels couldn't take out the radar quickly enough to protect them. Even the old SA-2's—flying telephone poles that had been around since Vietnam—were potent weapons against a slow, heavily laden Hog. And a Roland or SA-6—forget about it.

So Doberman didn't immediately punch Shotgun when he mentioned using Apache to the colonel in the command bunker.

Actually, the reason he didn't was the fact that Shotgun was across the room and out of reach.

Even the Special Ops colonel could tell the idea was crazy. His mouth and cheek worked up and down, as if he'd gotten something caught in one of his back teeth.

"You know, son, I used to fly Hueys up Ho Chi Minh's butt," he told Shotgun. "You don't have to impress me."

"I'm not pushing a permanent home drome," said Shotgun, oblivious as always. "What I'm talking about is a fuel depo, and maybe get some gun dragons up there, load up the cannon between shows. Dump in a few hundred iron bombs while we're at it. Nothing big. That's what I'm talking about."

The colonel gave Doberman a look that said, *He's crazy, right?* Before Doberman could answer, Klee turned back to Shotgun. "You boys just do this fuel drop tonight, all right?" said Klee, his tone as dismissive as a drill sergeant's.

"Excuse me, Colonel, can I get a word in here?" said Doberman.

"I wish you would, Captain."

"I'm not saying we can't do this fuel-drop thing, as long as those tanks don't explode when we drop them."

"They won't," said Colonel Klee. "We've made similar drops from MC-130's. Assuming your people rig them right."

"If they can be rigged, our guys will do it," said Doberman.

"Then it's in your court."

Doberman clamped his teeth together, trying to choke back his bile. He didn't like being treated like a flunky. The colonel's dismissal of the problems involved in the mission was, in his mind, reckless.

But it was difficult for him to say that without exploding. It was difficult, at the moment, to breathe without exploding.

"Damn straight it's in our court," he finally managed. "Damn straight. We're going to do a kick-ass job and you can count on it. But realistically, Colonel—realistically, the A-10's are not equipped for night fighting, and their navigational systems are not exactly state-of-the-art. This drop has to have a pretty wide margin of error. Unless we use flares, we'll be bombing blind. And—"

"No flares," said Klee. "We'll live with whatever margin of error you give us."

"Skull and I used Maverick Gs when we rode up and grabbed Goose," said Shotgun. "If we can round up a couple of those suckers, we'll be able to see the ground at least."

"Get them," said the colonel. "You have to put X-ray machines in those planes, do it. But nothing that gives the helicopters away."

Doberman blew another long breath, this one calm enough to exit through his mouth without rattling his teeth. He told himself he was just pissed about the colonel's personality, which wasn't an important thing to be pissed about.

The gig was impossible, but what the hell. They'd done harder shit. As long as it was him and Shotgun taking it, they'd figure something out. And if it weren't for the fact that Dixon's neck was on the block up north, he wouldn't give a flying turd's crap what happened to this jerk-ass of a colonel's command. If he wanted to risk stranding two helicopters so deep in Iraq that it took the entire Army and Air Force and maybe the Marines to rescue them, what the hell.

"When are the helos taking off?" Shotgun asked.

The colonel glanced at his watch. "They should be in the air by now. They're refueling at the border. According to Wong's timetable, they needed a good head start. You have a little over three hours to meet them. You miss them, don't bother coming back."

23

On the ground in Iraq
25 January 1991
1920

It was Leteri who realized the ground between the two quarry hills was mined. Something about the neatness of it tipped him off just in time to grab Dixon's arm and yank him physically backwards.

"Stop!" yelled the sergeant. "Everyone freeze right where you are."

He didn't use the word "mines." He didn't have to.

Winston and Green were nearly twenty yards deep. Staffa Turk was five yards behind Dixon and Leteri, who were maybe seven or eight yards deep. The others were stretched out in a jagged line either ahead or over toward the road on the rocks, apparently safe.

Maybe. It was fairly dark and difficult to tell.

"What we're going to do is go back exactly the way we came in," Winston told the others. He pulled the flashlight from his vest; the others did the same. "We're going to do it one person at a time, and we're going to move slowly no matter what happens. Turk, you go, then the lieutenant. Use the lights to check your marks on the ground. Watch for mine nubs, if you can."

It seemed to take forever for the trooper to back out. Finally, he shouted for Dixon to come.

Dixon had only the roughest idea of where he had stepped. He started to turn, but Leteri yelled at him to stop.

"Exactly the way you came, BJ. Backwards if you can. Lean back with your right foot. That was the step you took." He directed him with his light. "I can tell by the way you're standing. See that mark there?"

"You're right. Thanks." Dixon put his leg backwards, trying to pretend he was a character in a rewinding video. He found a foothold, shifted his weight, and took the backwards step. Whether he had found the exact footfall or just got lucky, nothing happened.

Three more steps and he was still intact. It would take four or five more to reach the boundary, where large boulders strewn on the gentle slope showed they'd be safe.

Probably.

"Go as slow as you want, Lieutenant," said Winston. "No rushing here."

Dixon flexed his upper leg muscles, studied the ground. He resisted the urge to dash back to the line that was supposed to mean safety, tried to remember how he had walked, saw the shadow of a boot print.

Or was it the top of a mine?

He moved his foot at the last second, planted, moved back another step, then another.

When he was finally far enough away, he let the com gear and his rucksack slide off his back in a heap. Dixon rolled his head backwards on his neck and let out a breath of air so huge he nearly fell over.

Leteri came back next. Only Green and Winston were left. Green was ahead of Winston, but the team leader insisted that he come back first.

"Just do what I fucking tell you to do," he growled when Green protested. "Can't you hear I'm getting hoarse?"

Dutifully, the medic began to retrace his steps. The arc he had followed took him near Winston's position; they exchanged a sardonic glance as he passed. Green took a step back, then rested, flexing as much as he could without moving his feet. He was about ten yards, no more, from safety, near where Dixon had been.

Practically home.

He took another step back, and exploded.

24

ON THE GROUND IN IRAQ
25 JANUARY 1991
1927

It was a movie he was watching. The camera panned back from a wide shot, moving away from the brief flash and burst of dirt. Two dark bodies jumped against the dull shadows behind them, one twisting forward in a macabre dance, the other falling straight over from the side, like a tree axed by a woodsman. As the dust and smoke settled into the heavy twilight, a figure ran toward the dancer. Its steps were awkward and fitful, as if following an unheard music score.

The camera view changed, zooming on the second body, closing in on the sand-colored motley of his uniform, the odd shapes of brown and yellow and tan blurring as the lens momentarily lost focus. The camera swirled, and then showed the ground, hard-pressed dirt and sand galloping by in an artistic effect, pitching in a way that made him slightly seasick, and seemed at the same time to weigh down on his back. Finally the lens fell on a black boot stained with a spatter of blood brighter than the red of a poppy. It stayed there for a moment, drinking in the color, then moved to another spot of red, another perfect splotch, this one on a dull yellow and black fabric. The camera moved forward and the fabric was revealed to be an arm, the hand gripping something, its long, slender fingers curled so tightly the small veins popped greenish-blue against the knuckles. And then the camera moved back again; something fell slowly through the frame, another body, the same body the shot had begun with. The lens moved up and found a thick, pained face, creased with lines and the stubble of a day-old beard. The mouth moved with a groan or a curse; it was impossible to say.

"Green's dead," said Leteri, still huffing.

Turk was leaning over Winston. "Don't talk, Sarge. Let me get this around your leg."

Winston's protest contorted into a groan as Turk pulled the bandage around the open wound. Bits of muscle and gore splayed out; Dixon saw what he thought was the thigh bone, white gray amid the sea of blood.

"He's trying to tell you that was a stupid thing, running into the minefield," Leteri told Dixon.

"If I only did smart things I wouldn't be here," said Dixon.

Turk rolled Winston onto his side. The back of his uniform was already dark black with blood.

"We're gonna have to look at this real careful," said Turk.

Dixon realized the others were looking at him, expecting him to say something, even if it was the most obvious thing.

Which was?

"We're exposed here," Leteri said. "Let's find some cover."

"You think we ought to move him?" asked Turk.

The sergeant's moans had faded into one continuous semi-screech. Dixon knelt next to him and gently placed his two fingers along the sergeant's neck.

"Weak pulse, but with us," Dixon said.

For a moment, the words jangled in his mind, reviving a memory of the last time he'd felt for someone's pulse. It was his mother's, nearly four months ago, and the result had been very different—he'd been feeling for himself, the last time, to make sure what the machines were saying, what the doctor and nurses were saying, was true, that she was dead.

"We shouldn't move him, probably." Dixon stood up quickly. "But we have to have better cover than this. Those rocks up there—Leteri, can you check them out? Mo, Staffa, scout the road and then cover us. Bobby and I will move the sergeant as gently as we can, once Leteri gives us the all clear."

The men jumped into action. It was only later, after they set the sergeant down, that Dixon realized he had given orders and they'd followed them without question.

25

Al Jouf FOA, Saudi Arabia
25 January 1991
2050

They looked like Warthogs with tits.

Two five-hundred-gallon tanks—with elaborate airdrop chutes and what looked like accordion baffles custom-welded around them—had been slapped to the number-five and -seven hard-points beneath the A-10As' wings. The basic drop tanks had been borrowed from RAF Tornadoes—an accomplishment in itself since as far as Doberman knew there were none at the base. Tinman had worked out the modifications himself, with a little help from Wong and Rosen. They were equipped with parachutes that worked off altimeter settings; apparently these included a pair of more-or-less-standard Special Ops chutes and three smaller drag "foils" from British bombs ordinarily used to crater runways.

Rosen had explained the mechanics of the chute-and-baffle system to Doberman, but the setup seemed as much of a marvel as the MRE Shotgun was wolfing down. The bottom line was that she said it would all work.

Probably.

Wong agreed. Which was almost enough to make Doberman nervous.

"You really ought to try one of these MREs," said Shotgun. The planes had been pitted and except for the customary walk-arounds, were ready to go. "This sole in vermouth with a touch of lemon—it's what I'm talking about."

"Sole in vermouth?" asked Rosen.

"Sorry, finished. I got lobster bisque with crabmeat and a squeeze of saffron left. You want it?"

"I don't think so."

"You got to buddy up with the Special Ops guys if you want decent grub," said Shotgun, opening the plastic packet and pouring it into a drab green cup. "They got connections."

Doberman nearly fell over from the thick odor of simmering soup wafting across the desert.

"I know what you're thinking," said Shotgun. "Should have gone with the soup course first, right?"

"Yeah, that's what I'm thinking." Doberman shook his head. "You ready?"

"I was born ready."

Doberman turned and started to inspect his airplane. Rosen followed. One thing he had to give her—damn planes couldn't have been in better shape than if they'd just rolled out of the factory.

"Listen, Captain, don't forget—you have to drop from exactly thirty-five hundred feet so the chutes fully deploy and the landing is soft. That's the one cludge. All right?"

Rosen was about the only crew member in the squadron—maybe the only person in the Air Force—who physically looked up at the five-foot-four Doberman. Maybe it was just the dim base lights that made her look less severe—call it bitchy—than she'd ever seemed before.

For just a second.

"I'll give it a shot," he told her.

Rosen smiled. "Kick butt, Captain."

She chucked him on the shoulder harder than a linebacker.

• • •

Forty-five minutes worth of butt-grinding Hog driving later, Doberman checked his map against the INS and his watch. They were thirty seconds off, close enough for anyone but him. He edged his power forward infinitesimally, recalculating and adjusting until he had the thing nailed.

Wong had sketched the Hogs a route to the fuel drop point that was considerably more direct than the path the helicopters were taking. Even so, the timetable was tight and the course was not the easiest; they still had one known Iraqi position to overfly.

The Air Force had once planned to upgrade the A-10A with things like ground-avoidance radar and night-seeing equipment—reasonably desirable items, given the Hog's primary mission to work with ground troops. But the A-10 was always treated like a forlorn stepchild at budget time; the pointy-nose fast jets got all the fancy gear, and the Hogs had to make due with leftovers, hand-me-downs, and wishful thinking.

Still, even something as basic as an autopilot would have been nice, Doberman thought. For one thing, it would make it easier to pee, which he suddenly had to do.

No way he was braving the piddle pack until after the drop.

They went over the Iraqi position without drawing any fire—without, in fact, a hint that there was anything besides sand beneath their wings. Doberman adjusted his course as planned at the next way-marker—he had it tight this time, and he edged the plane's nose below five thousand feet, angled perfectly to hit 3,500 feet in exactly two minutes and twenty seconds at the drop point.

He checked the Maverick screen; as a primitive night-vision device it was far from perfect, but at least he could make out the road Wong had X'd on the map south of the target.

Perfect. Doberman keyed his mike to make sure Shotgun hadn't fallen asleep.

In the next second, the sky in front of him erupted orange-green, the flak so thick it looked like a psychedelic waterfall.

26

On the ground in Iraq
25 January 1991
2050

They dug a shallow grave at the edge of the minefield and buried Green, making sure to get a good read from the geo-positioner so they could retrieve the body when the mission was over. The men looked to Dixon to say something, or at least he thought they did; he stepped up and asked them to bow their heads. Standing solemnly at the head of the medic's grave, he remembered his mother's funeral, and a chunk of a reading flew into his head from Job, God's justification for mankind's trials:

> Gird up now thy loins like a man: I will demand of thee, and declare thou unto me.
>
> Wilt thou also disannul my judgment? wilt thou condemn me, that thou mayest be righteous?
>
> Hast thou an arm like God? or canst thou thunder with a voice like him?
>
> Deck thyself now with majesty and excellency; and array thyself with glory and beauty.

That was as far as the passage had gone at the funeral, and Dixon's voice fell silent. But after a few seconds Staff Sergeant Staffa Turk, demolitions expert and tail gunner, filled out the verse:

> Cast aboard the rage of thy wrath, and behold every one that is proud, and abase him.
>
> Look on everyone that is proud, and bring him low; and tread down the wicked in their place.
>
> Hide them in the dust together, and bind their faces in secret. Then will I also confess unto thee that thine own right hand can save thee.

Winston's back had been peppered with shrapnel and bits of Green. The damage was difficult to gauge, and Dixon worried that some of the wounds had hit his spine and the nerves around it. They made him as comfortable as they could, hiding him in a crevice along the rock ledge that gave them a reasonably good view of the road, the minefield, and the next hill, though not the interior of the quarry. They could fight from here, if they had to.

Each trooper carried a syringe of morphine. They debated whether to give Winston his or not. He was moaning and certainly in some pain, but if they used it they'd have nothing else to give him except their own. And they couldn't be sure how long it would be before they could be evacuated.

Once again, the men looked to Dixon to decide. It seemed to him that the best thing to do was call Fort Apache, the forward base that was supposed to be their support link, and see what could be arranged. Once they knew helos were on the way, they could give him the shot.

"If he starts screaming, then we absolutely have to knock him out," said Leteri.

"Definitely," agreed Dixon.

The radio had been hit by something when the mine exploded. Leteri set up the antenna, sure that he could get it to work somehow. The other members of the fire team began carefully searching the quarry, trying to figure out why the mines were there and if there were others. Dixon, meanwhile, looked after the wounded man, trying to make him as comfortable as possible.

There wasn't much he could do, except wad a shirt as a pillow and cover him with a blanket. Dixon felt as helpless as his last days in the ICU, watching his mother fade into the night. Weird thoughts had gone through his head then. One moment he'd see himself yanking out the tubes; another moment his eyes would flood with tears and he'd conjure wild promises and deals with God to keep her alive.

"Radio's pretty screwed, Lieutenant," said Leteri. "It's the power, I think. The battery got whacked. I'll keep trying."

"Makes sense," said Dixon.

"How's Winston?"

Dixon shrugged. He wanted to be objective—he wasn't a doctor and he had no idea what the extent of the wounds were. The sergeant's pulse was strong. But there were at least three big wounds in the middle of his back.

Turk appeared at the ridge before Dixon could find a way to diplomatically say he was afraid the sergeant might be paralyzed. "Hey, Lieutenant, you want to come look at this right away," he said. "I think I found what those mines are all about."

27

Over Iraq
25 January 1991
2155

Doberman whacked the Hog hard left as the fingers of fire seemed to reach for his windshield. He twisted the plane back, feeling her buck because of the unfamiliar tanks tied to her wings. He lost his balance, felt his left wing coming around, and got down on his rudder pedals, muscling the plane stable with his nose still pointed toward the ground. He started a gradual recovery, then realized the altimeter was winding down faster than he thought. His engineer's brain spat a series of equations with bad variables; he pushed them away and pulled back on the stick, leveling off at two thousand feet, headed in the wrong direction and damn-shit confused.

To say nothing of pissed. He wondered where in hell the flak guns had come from, and felt his bladder backing up into his kidneys.

"Hey," said Shotgun.

"Hey back."

"You hit?"

"Nah." Doberman gave the instrument panel a quick once-over just to doublecheck.

Shotgun read him his position, but Doberman had already figured out where his wingman would be. He brought his plane back into a slow bank north, sliding around in an arc that kept the flak—still firing intermittently—well off his right wing. He was still low—3,500 feet—but since he had to get low to make the drop, decided to keep it there.

"You got screwed up?" asked Shotgun.

"Fucking fuel tanks threw me off."

"Still got them?"

"Shit, Shotgun, what do you think?"

"Man, you're testy. You know what it is, you didn't have anything to eat. Blood sugar's all whacked out. You got to take better care of yourself. When you eat's as important as what you eat. That's what I'm talking about."

"What the fuck was shooting at me? I didn't get a radar warning or anything."

"I couldn't get it on the screen, but it probably was something dug in near the road. Shot real high. Got to be a bunch of ZSU-57's, don't you think? Would of taken a lucky shot to nail you."

"Lucky for who?"

"Good point. Want to go back and waste 'em?"

"Hold on."

Doberman checked the positions out on the map. Wong's course had the helicopters coming in from the northwest, which meant the battery was well out of range. Besides, the helos would be almost at the refuel point by now. The Hogs were better off saving the guns for the return flight, if they even bothered.

The guns stroked up again. There had to be several of them, and Shotgun was probably right about them being ZSU-57's or something similar—their tracers seemed to extend fairly high. The guns were usually mounted on vehicles like the ZSU-23's; they might be attached to a convoy or positioned to defend something intel hadn't yet picked up. In any event, they were firing blind and almost straight up. Most likely they had heard the Hogs approaching in the distance and gotten spooked.

Firing blind in the night was stupid, since it gave your position away and was unlikely to bring any results, but Doberman could understand the ground crews' frustration. You could only sit and get pounded for so long before you lashed out.

"Looks like your friend Wong missed some pretty serious guns," said Doberman as he plotted a new course to the drop point.

"Hey, I didn't say Brainiac was perfect. Besides, those old suckers, shit, it would have taken a really lucky shot to get you. One in a hundred, you know what I'm talking about?"

"All right." He gave Shotgun the new course and got back into gear. He was back in control; even his bladder eased up a little.

"You could go Italian, you know."

"What are you talking about, Shotgun?"

"Pasta is very high in carbohydrates," said the wingman. "Instant energy. And versatile. All sorts of shapes and sauces. You got your marinara, your Abruzzi, your Alfredo—"

"Just watch my back."

"Six is as clean as pasta right out of the pot," said Shotgun.

28

Over Iraq
25 January 1991
2200

Shotgun eased his Hog back, giving Doberman plenty of room to make his drop cleanly. While he had a huge amount of trust in the ground crew's ability to improvise, even he was curious about whether this fudge would really work.

It better. He had the choppers coming on now four miles away, so low they could be trucks.

Shotgun's Maverick viewfinder was selected at what passed for wide-field magnification, six degrees. The ground battery that had made things interesting was well off to the rear, and no longer firing; they'd either run out of bullets or hit themselves with their falling shells.

The Hogs' "target" was a set of coordinates that translated into a hunk of sand about a half mile beyond an impressive collection of bushes; the brush was probably considered an oasis, though Shotgun was hardly an expert on that sort of thing, as the only oasis he was familiar with featured topless dancers. The gray shadows of the bushes looked like an undulating test bar in his screen as he banked to follow Doberman on his approach.

One of the test bars morphed into a mountain.

The mountain changed into bodies.

A couple of dozen bodies. All running west right into the drop zone.

"Hold off, hold off," Shotgun shouted into his radio, alerting Doberman. "Shit. Cisco freeze. Cisco Freeze," he added over the frequency the helicopters were monitoring. The code words ordered the helicopters to stop immediately.

Shotgun thumbed the Mav's screen down to a narrow angle, which magnified the scene. He waited for the viewer to flash up an entire herd of Iraqi infantry.

That or some very strange bushes.

"Devil Two, this is One. What's the problem?" asked Doberman.

"Don't you see them?"

"See what?"

"Hang tight." Shotgun banked his plane, temporarily losing his angle. The Maverick screen showed nothing but empty desert.

A malfunction?

Hell, no. The screen filled as he came back around—but now Shotgun saw that the bodies streaming westward weren't Iraqi troops or weirdly mobile fauna.

They were camels. At least two dozen of them.

He might have laughed, except it wasn't funny. The animals were moving right into the area where the tanks were supposed to be dropped.

Doberman cursed in his headset. Obviously he had seen them too.

Shotgun made out a man's shadow, and what might be a tent. Some Bedouins were putting up for the night at the oasis. In fact, they were the oasis he'd seen.

Geez, you'd think they lived here or something. And wasn't there a leash law? The damn camels were tramping all around the target area.

"All right, I'm going to set up a course toward Cisco," said Doberman. "Let them improvise."

"I got a better idea," said Shotgun, pushing the Hog down toward the dirt.

The big warplane hesitated a moment, then realized what her pilot was up to. She snorted, and answered Shotgun's whoop with one of her own. A salvo of flares, ordinarily used to defeat heat-seeking missiles, burst from her wing-tip launchers.

Startled, the camels turned their heads as one and stared at the meteor that had appeared from nowhere.

Then they ran like hell, their masters in hot pursuit.

29

Over Iraq
25 January 1991
2210

"Yee-fucking-haw!" shouted Shotgun over the radio. He had the camels on the run.

Doberman slipped the Hog into the proper coordinates for the tank drop. His thumb danced back and forth—*bing-bang-bam*. He pickled, and felt the plane jump beneath him, glad to be free of the unfamiliar tanks.

Doberman banked and pushed forward in his seat, anxious to see how he had done. But it was far too dark outside and at the moment there was nothing but a bleary blankness in the Maverick's screen.

He keyed his mike and told the helicopters they could proceed in zero-one minutes; in the same instant he saw the outline of a small parachute in the corner of the TVM, then another, and finally a third, all holding up the same fat canister of fuel.

Finished spooking the camels, Shotgun pulled off and swung in for his own drop. Doberman began to climb in a spiral intended to keep himself away from both the helicopters and his wingman; in the dark good flight discipline was particularly important and he hit his course precisely, climbing quickly—

for a Hog—to ten thousand feet. The straightforward plan called for the two Hogs to remain in the area for thirty minutes, which hopefully would be long enough for the two helos to refuel and get under way.

Once the helicopters cleared, the Hogs could waste the triple-A battery and go home. Where bed was waiting. Doberman's body ached for rest, even if it was on a cramped cot stolen from the Special Ops troops.

There had been no fireballs. That was a good sign.

If you believed in luck, this was exactly the sort of gig that depended on it. Rigging a bizarre plan, flying to a point on the map with a notoriously inefficient INS system, then hooking up with helos that had already been flying for hours on a course so convoluted they were headed south—only to have the whole thing almost screw up because of a group of wayward camels.

Luck?

Bullshit. How about tons of skill—great technical people coming up with a creative solution to an impossible problem. Great navigational skill on his part, making mid-course corrections and dealing with an unexpected glitch in the shape of an antiair gun. And even impromptu finesse from Shotgun, scaring the crap out of the camels to herd them away from the drop zone.

Luck was bullshit.

Of course, he did have the penny in his boot.

Doberman felt his leg starting to go numb from inactivity. He danced it up and down, twisted his muscles, and shook his knees around, trying to ward off the pins and needles.

Rosen and Tinman had done a hell of a job, conjuring up this drop-tank thing. Of course, Tinman had probably done this sort of thing before, like maybe for the Wright Brothers.

Silver crosses. Jeee-zus.

Rosen, though, she was pretty damn smart for a girl.

Check that. For a woman.

She was a woman. There was something sincere in her eyes, something warm, as if she really cared if they made it on their mission.

The refuel took longer than planned, and Doberman decided to wait until the helicopters were in the air before moving on. He played with the variables, but couldn't quite squeeze enough time—and fuel—to allow the A-10's to splash the batteries after the choppers left. Reluctantly, he spun the Hogs onto their go-home course.

"Six is clean as a scared camel's rear," said Shotgun.

"Very funny. You watch I don't put you up for a medal for that."

"Hey, I got the only medal I need, courtesy of Tinman. You notice that gun opened up on you, not me."

"How's your fuel?" asked Doberman.

"Not a problem," said Shotgun. His words were almost lost in what seemed to be an uncontrolled chortle.

"You laughing at me, Gun?"

"Hell, no," said Shotgun. "I'm just thinking of those helicopter crews when they landed. There must have been a ton of camel shit everywhere. Got to be more toxic than anything Saddam could load into a Scud."

30

On the ground in Iraq
25 January 1991
2210

The more he walked, the less tired he felt. Whether it was because he was so far beyond fatigue that he'd become numb or something biological was kicking in, Dixon couldn't say. All he knew was that he was more awake and alert than he'd ever been in his life. The night was a little lighter than last night had been, and whether because of that or some shift in his senses, he could see Turk and the way down to the road almost as if it were high noon.

The sergeant led him back to the road, then across and parallel to it. After about a tenth of a mile, he pointed out a rock that marked the edge of the minefield on the other side. Just beyond it was a dirt road that curved between two crags in the hills.

"The entrance off the road is down further," the sergeant explained. "But this is shorter."

Dixon followed silently. They came to a pass and walked about twenty yards into the quarry. A rock face loomed ahead; they'd seen the top from the position where they'd taken the sergeant, but had not been able to see all the way down to the base because of the angle.

And the base was definitely worth seeing. There was a large metal door, the kind that might be used on a factory or warehouse.

"Old mine?" Dixon asked.

"Check it out," said Turk, handing the lieutenant his NOD. "Brand-new combo lock. Got to be hiding something, don't you think?"

It wasn't just a combo lock—it had a high-tech digital face and a massive panel.

"Probably booby-trapped," said Turk. "Got a slot for a key, so you can't just fudge the combination either."

Dixon's mind conjured up different possibilities—the Mother of All Scud Bases, Saddam's own secret palace, a vast underground base for the Revolutionary Guards. He saw the same end for each—a raid by Devil Squadron to send the bastards to hell.

Another vision mixed with the others—the memory of his mother's funeral. It had been a bright, sunny day, perfect in every way but the most important.

She'd chosen the Job reading herself. For years his mother had cared for his dad, suffering as the Biblical figure. Cancer had long ago left him an invalid; by the time Dixon was twelve he had reconciled himself to his father's death.

Yet his father hadn't died, and in fact, as of a few nights ago, was still living at the nursing home Dixon had put him in when his mother suffered her first stroke.

His mother never talked of death, not the countless times it seemed likely that his father would pass away, and certainly never of her own. And yet he'd found the passages all noted in her top drawer, written perhaps years before, too long for any premonition, surely.

"What do you think?" Turk asked.

Dixon handed the viewer back.

"Underground bunker, or some sort of storage facility," said Dixon. "Way out here, my bet would be a chemical or biological warehouse. Maybe even nuclear. NBC."

He started to take a step forward, but Turk caught him.

"Could be mined," said the trooper. "The way I'm thinking about it, that minefield we stumbled into is set up for defense, so they don't need too many men to guard the place, see? Things get tricky, you send a team in. You can locate your posts there and there, not worry about your flanks. And this way too."

Dixon nodded. He took the viewer back and began scanning the rocks, looking for a ventilation pipe. As he did so, he remembered that the trucks had been heading in this direction.

A coincidence?

You couldn't drive them through the door; it was too small. The shadows thrown by the rocks might hide them temporarily, though.

Hard to tell. He scanned first for another entrance, then for a ventilation system. Finally he spotted a thin pipe a good forty yards back on the hillside, around in the opposite direction from the hill where they had placed the sergeant. He oriented himself, realizing that the bunker's hill was connected by a long ridge to theirs.

"Intelligence people don't know about this," said Turk. "Otherwise they'd have told us. Hill wasn't even named on our maps. Nothing special to them."

"Yeah," agreed Dixon. "But it's real special now."

PART TWO

SUGAR MOUNTAIN

31

In Iraq
25 January 1991
2230

They moved down from the rocks so slowly and carefully that Dixon felt as if he were walking backwards. He held his submachine gun in front of him like a stubby balancing bar. Twice they stopped because vehicles were approaching on the nearby highway; each time they retreated back to the rocks, waiting until trucks sped by.

Turk's explanation that the mines were placed as part of a pre-positioned defense scheme made sense; logically, Dixon knew that if that were true, the road itself wouldn't be booby-trapped or mined. But twice his foot slipped in the dirt and he felt an electric jolt in his muscles, part of him sure he was about to be blown up.

The door was metal, twice as wide as the front door to a house and about half again as high. A normal-sized truck probably couldn't quite fit through. The locking mechanism had both a mechanical key and the combination—as well as what seemed to be a booby-trapped wire that Turk pulled Dixon back from.

"This doesn't look like anything I've worked on," said the

demolition expert, after pulling out a small penlight flashlight to look it over carefully. "But my guess is that you fiddle with the key and it sets off a charge. Maybe under there." He pointed the light at rocks just above them. "Drop a little avalanche on you. Or there could be a charge beneath us."

Dixon put his hand on the steel door, feeling the surface as if his fingers could somehow tell how thick the metal was behind it. There were no straps, no bolts, just smooth metal.

"Safest thing to do is get back to the road there, shoot up the lock, and see what happens," said Turk.

"You think that'll do anything besides telling the Iraqis we're here?"

Turk thought about it. "Probably not. We might be able to get through the door with our C-4. Depends on how thick it is."

"Riyadh will probably want to bomb the site," Dixon told him. "I think we're better off talking to them first. If we do anything, the Iraqis will know we're here. Maybe they'll empty the site before the bombing, maybe they'll find us."

"I ain't arguing with you."

Dixon took a step back. Turk caught him.

"Listen," he said, pointing back toward the road.

A low cough rasped against the hills. Dixon and Turk sprinted up the road back into the rocks. They climbed a few yards up the hillside, taking cover as the truck approached. Dixon watched from his crouch, expecting it to speed past like the others.

But it didn't. Instead it stopped dead in the middle of the highway, not ten yards from them.

It was a Mercedes truck, a simple cab in front of a boxy back; nothing remarkable. A million similar trucks were driving in a million similar places at that very moment, delivering a multitude of things to a multitude of places.

But this one was here. Dixon had a clear line of sight, and took the NOD from Turk.

The driver and his passenger were debating something. Then the passenger got out of the truck. The two Americans hunkered against the rocks as the man shone a flashlight across the darkened landscape to find the path to the mountain entrance. Once he found it, he waved at the truck, which followed slowly as he began walking toward the rock face.

When he reached the door, he bent over the lock. He worked it very slowly. His back blocked Dixon's view, but the lieutenant saw there was a second panel behind the electronic lock; that one took even longer to deal with. Finally the Iraqi bent over and pushed something with his foot. A metal lever rose from the dirt.

But not even this opened the door. The man returned to the panel and punched more keys before the door finally popped free. He gripped the edge and pushed it open; a dull red light turned on inside.

"You get all that?" asked Turk.

"Oh, yeah, I got it memorized," whispered Dixon.

"Fuckers spent half their defense budget on locks. Cheaper just to post guards."

"Maybe they're inside."

"Yeah. Could be," said Turk.

The Iraqi walked quickly to the back of the truck. He came out with what looked to be a large suitcase.

"Door's damn thick," said Turk, examining it through the NOD. "I don't think we got enough C-4, unless I can figure out a weak spot."

After the soldier had been inside for quite a while, Dixon realized he ought to have timed his disappearance; it might tell them how large the facility was.

Or maybe not. He noted the time on his watch, then took the NOD and looked back at the driver, who was shifting nervously around in the cab.

Most likely the man had only a pistol, if that. They could take him out easily; Dixon could, simply by lifting the MP-5 and firing. He was ten yards away.

But were there others inside the truck or the mountain?

The Iraqi reappeared from the bunker and trotted to the

back of the truck. He took what seemed to be an identical suitcase from the back before returning to the mountain.

"Boxes of candy," said Turk. "For Sugar Mountain."

"Yeah, Sugar Mountain," said Dixon. "A big candy store."

"We can take out the guy in the truck," said Turk. He lifted his silenced MP-5. "You think we should?"

The truck driver sat upright in the cab as if he had heard them. He turned on the truck lights and a moveable spotlight mounted on the doorway, playing it over the rocks. The two Americans ducked as the spotlight swung in their direction.

Should they rush him? They could take care of his companion when he came out.

If he spoke English, they could find out what or who was inside.

Maybe. More than likely, he didn't speak English.

Hell, they could just go inside and see for themselves. Assuming it wasn't booby-trapped.

Or that there wasn't a guard below. The suitcases could have been dinner.

Even if they got one of the Iraqis and made him talk, could they believe what he said? They could force him to walk ahead if they went inside, force him to reveal any booby traps—but perhaps the people who had designed the structure had anticipated that. Given the elaborate mechanism to open it, surely they had.

Better to call in a bombing raid.

What if they were bombing a gold mine?

Or an NBC—nuclear-biological-chemical—storage site?

What if Saddam himself were inside? Now that would be the kicker to end all kickers.

"Let's get him," said Dixon, rising as the light swung across the opposite hillside.

"Whoa—hold on," said Turk. "Here's our candy man."

The Iraqi shouted—it sounded like a curse—at the driver as the two Americans ducked back behind the rocks. By the time they realized the shout hadn't been meant for them, the thick door had been swung back into place. The truck was already backing onto the highway.

The Iraqi who'd gone inside Sugar Mountain ran to the truck, pulling himself in as he continued to berate the driver. He was most likely angry because of the lights—the driver slapped them off and hit the gas as soon as all four wheels were on the hard pavement.

32

Fort Apache
25 January 1991
2350

They were louder than hell, at least as far as Hawkins was concerned. But the two dark shadows growing in the southern corner of the gray-black haze before him were the prettiest damn things he'd ever seen.

Not quite, but damn, Hawkins felt good about the AH-6G Scouts as they came into the base. Fort Apache was open for business, with its own air force to boot.

No slam on the Hogs. But they had to keep running south to get ammo and gas. The Little Birds were his.

The lead AH-6G blinked. One of Hawkins's men answered with a recognition code, assuring the chopper crews that they had not been overrun. The lead bird flew forward toward the strip.

The civilian MD 530 MG that the AH-6G was based on was itself a variant in a popular and highly successful line of civilian and military utility choppers. An extremely versatile design, the latest version—the MD 530N—came equipped with a NOTAR system that eliminated the rear rotor and made the small helicopter one of the most maneuverable aircraft in the world. Those versions were in short supply in the service, however, and would never have been allowed this far north.

But the AH-6Gs touching down on the Iraqi concrete weren't slouches. Each had a pair of 50-caliber machine-guns and seven-tube 70mm rocket launchers mounted on their stubby wings, and featured forward-looking infrared radar mounted under their chins. TOW antitank weapons and miniguns—not installed but packed in the helicopters' small holds—added additional firepower.

Hawkins trotted forward as the whirlies spun down, hesitating long enough to make sure he knew where the tails were. He had once seen a trooper get his face shaved off by the back end of a helicopter, and the experience gave him a healthy respect for rear rotors.

"Captain Hawkins?" asked the pilot, pushing open the door and pulling off his helmet. His night-flying gear weighed several pounds. He was obviously an experienced flier—he had the bull neck that typically came from years of working with the heavy sights.

"You Fernandez?"

"Yes, sir. Where do you want us?"

"We'll unload you here. We're working on a little bunker and camouflage for you across the way," said Hawkins, gesturing. "Won't be O'Hare."

"Hey, I'm used to LaGuardia. Anything you can do."

"How was your flight?"

"Piece of cake, once I got it off the ground. We're a bit heavy," said the pilot. He turned back to his controls, which were arrayed around multi-use screens, and finished securing the helicopter. "Shit, how much runway you got here?"

"At the moment, just under a thousand feet. Iraqis left it so smooth we don't even have to repatch it." Hawkins pointed toward the far end, where six of his men were laying out metal grids that had been parachuted in a few hours before. "We're extending it. I should have fifteen hundred by the morning, maybe the afternoon."

A frown flickered across the pilot's face; he knew that wasn't long enough for a C-130 to land.

"Hey, Captain!"

Hawkins turned and saw Sergeant Gladis running toward him. Gladis was moving quicker than the helicopters had.

"We got something from Team Ruth you got to hear," said the communications specialist. "Their radio's breaking up big-time, but you're going to want to talk to Leteri or Lieutenant Dixon yourself."

"Leteri? Where's Winston?"

Gladis shook his head. "You want to talk to them yourself. They stepped in a mountain shit."

"Good shit or bad shit?"

"Both. Very big shit. The biggest shit you've ever seen. A mountain of shitting shit. They're calling it Sugar Mountain, but it's a pile of stinking shit."

33

Al Jouf
25 January 1991
2350

The position was vulnerable, certainly. He was definitely overextended, with only a wire-thin defensive chain; if his perimeter were pierced, he would sustain heavy casualties. His opponent was crafty, fortified, and exceedingly cool.

But Wong could tell that the deep penetration of his bishop on his opponent's right flank had left the black commander off balance. The Caro-Kann defense was ordinarily a solid one, fighting white for control of the middle and often, though not necessarily, shifting the balance of power from the attacker to the defender. And certainly the man behind the chess pieces, Sergeant Curtis, was a worthy opponent, a veteran not only of the Special Forces but the Army chess wars. But he had stumbled on the last move, nudging his knight forward unimaginatively and leaving his queen to be guillotined. He was left now with only one move, pushing his queen to the far side of the board—a concession that she was toast.

"Check," said Wong, pulling his knight forward.

"Damn," said Curtis.

Wong nodded thoughtfully. Curtis had no option but to take

the knight with his bishop; the queen would then be taken by Wong's bishop. Besides forcing the exchange, Wong had opened a gaping hole in black's defenses.

"You out-commandoed me, huh?" said Curtis.

"I was inspired by the setting."

"Another game?"

"Of course," said Wong.

If King Fahd was a scorpion-infested, third-rate trailer park, Al Jouf was a burned-out VW microbus in a sand trap. Still, there was no amenity like chess, and even at the Pentagon it was difficult to find an opponent both competent and worthy. So when a runner came to summon Wong just as they turned the board around, he got up with something that actually approached regret. Surely the only reason Colonel Klee wanted to see him at this hour was that he had agreed to entertain his request to be shipped to Washington. He consoled himself with a promise to look up Curtis again.

But Wong's transfer was the furthest thing from Klee's mind—a fact Wong realized when he approached the colonel's command bunker and saw that fully half of the commander's officers were already inside.

"Wong, about time," growled the colonel when he came in. Glowering at Klee's side was the ubiquitously ignorant Major Wilson. "Look at these images."

A bleary-eyed lieutenant passed what seemed to be a fifth-generation copy of a satellite photo to him. Wong's first impression was that he was looking at a pimple on a walrus's nose.

He kept that, as well as his more graphic second impression, to himself.

"Yes," he said finally, giving it back to the lieutenant."

"Well?" asked the colonel.

"A storage facility. Unmanned. High-value-asset facility, limited access, high-grade protection. The viewing angle is particularly poor, which is quite surprising, actually, given the performance specification of the satellite's—"

"You get that from a ventilation pipe?" asked Wilson.

"Of course, there are infinite possibilities in a theoretical sense, and I have to base my assumptions on a best-use thesis, meaning that my theory is based on the facility being fabricated in a manner best suited for its intended use, though as we all know—"

"The bottom line, Wong," said the colonel.

"Dry and secure storage facility," he said. "Originally for inert materials by design. Weapon-wise, I would say it is suited for chemicals, but the Iraqis have demonstrated such ill-informed planning that it could be and probably is for biological assets."

"Give him the description of the door," the colonel told the lieutenant, who passed a piece of yellow paper to him. The paper was an intelligence briefing describing a combination mechanical and electrical lock on an oversized but non-vehicle entry in a natural-feature-enhanced bunker facility.

Pretty much what he'd expected. The Iraqis showed a consistent lack of creativity.

"So?" asked Wilson.

Wong proceeded to the front of the bunker, where a large pad of paper sat on an easel. He drew a big circle, then the small roadway and what had to be a passive ventilation pipe.

"Our key features are the lack of a substantial air-exchange mechanism and the narrow aperture of the doorway," he started. "The locking mechanism clinches it. It was designed for chemicals or perhaps small-scale valuables such as diamonds, though it would now be a prime candidate for the Iraqi dispersal program. I would suspect some agent on the order of anthrax, inappropriate for the facility but completely within our known experience. My reasoning is not complex. The use of existing geographical features to enhance storage systems dates to the Neanderthal period, and thus parallels are naturally hazardous. Still, we have the benefit here of a paper written in 1978 by no less an authority than—"

"All right, I'm convinced," said the colonel. "Goddamn it, five hundred people must have missed this. Is Wong the only officer is Saudi Arabia who knows his ass from a hole in the ground?"

"That would be his ass from a ventilation pipe," quipped one of the officers.

Everyone, even the colonel, laughed.

Except Wong.

"If I may move on," Wong said, clearing his throat. "The configuration of this site, which I assume we are here to target, will present some very unique challenges for whoever is tasked to hit it. I assume that it was not detected during infrared surveillance, from which we may make several deductions, two in particular. First, that it is not continually manned, which of course we know since the ventilation system is so small, but confirming evidence is occasionally useful, if only for morale. There is no heat in the exhaust," Wong added for the men at the side who weren't quite keeping up. "It would have been very obvious. Second, there is probably a thick layer of natural material between the surface and the interior. I predict that the space for the pipe will be found to have been drilled, as unlikely as that sounds to the uninitiated. There will be basically two avenues of attack, the ventilation system and the front door. Going through the front door, of course, has its drawbacks, since it is both thick and protected by several man-lethal devices, more commonly known as booby traps. We don't know what types, though we can make some guesses, including at least two families of chemical derivatives undoubtedly modeled on the KK-37B facility in the Ural Mountains—"

"Hold that thought a second, Wong," said the colonel. "How about the vent? Can we get a smart bomb down it?"

"The shaft is not sufficient for a Paveway-series weapon to fly down," said Wong. "Nor will the vent serve as a sufficient fissure-point for an attack if my guess as to its construction is correct. The probability of the heaviest weapons in the series being effective can be measured in the range of ten to the negative one-hundredth power. Some would argue for a repeating attack pattern taking advantage of wave harmonics to enhance the destructive value, and there are additional alternatives, but beyond what I have said, my discussion would involve possibilities outside the code-word clearance of anyone in the room."

Wong was thinking specifically of an attack by GBU-24/B Paveway III laser-guided bombs, 4,700-pound monsters capable of taking out even the hardened-aircraft shelters Yugoslavia had built for Saddam. The captain's opinion was classified not because of the bombs—fairly well-kept secrets themselves—but because of the way they would have to be used to have any chance of penetrating the rock.

The others didn't quite appreciate that, however, responding to Wong with a variety of predictable curses and mutterings. It was exactly the sort of rumble from the rabble he had put up with all his life. It was the price one paid for being Wong.

"I like the front door myself," said the colonel. "But I know what Riyadh's going to say. You sure the door is booby-trapped?"

"Without a doubt," said Wong.

"Any way around it?"

"Given enough time, there is always a way."

"We don't have time," said the colonel. "They want it hit by dawn, one way or the other. All right, get me Riyadh on the line. Sit down, Wong—someone get him some coffee. Wait," added the colonel as an assistant flew to the door, "better make it decaf. I'd hate to hear him on a caffeine buzz."

34

AL JOUF
25 JANUARY 1991
2350

The way Shotgun figured it, every hour playing poker was worth two hours of sleep. The idea of sleep, after all, was to restore your creative powers and recharge your muscles. Poker did the same thing, only quicker. It was like taking a sauna, and in fact if you played cards perpetually, you'd never grow old.

Doberman nonetheless begged off. If "fuck yourself" could be understood as begging off.

Shotgun eventually found his way into a game with some of Klee's support staff; within a half hour he was twenty dollars ahead in a quarter-limit game. They were conservative for commandos, and had apparently not even heard of Baseball. He was just explaining the intricacies of the poker variant when a youngish staff sergeant appeared and called the officers to a meeting with the Special Ops colonel.

Shotgun immediately decided that he and Doberman belonged at the meeting.

"Screw off and drop dead," grumbled Doberman when he tried to wake him.

"Yo, Colonel Klee wants to see us."

"Why, the war over?"

"Could be."

Doberman turned over, but only enough to determine from the lack of light that it was still nighttime. "Go away," he growled. "Tell the colonel to eat shit."

"He's standing right here."

"My ass."

That was the sort of challenge that made it worth fetching the colonel and bringing him back, just to see the look on Doberman's face when he saw that he actually had cursed out a colonel. But that would take too long, and Shotgun really wanted to check out the meeting. So he settled for merely shaking the cot.

"Hey, let's go," he told Doberman. "Something big's got to be boiling. I was playing cards with half the guy's staff and—"

"You're out of your friggin' mind."

"Nah, they're not that good."

"Good night, Shotgun."

"If there's anything going down, I want to be there. Maybe Dixon's in trouble."

Doberman rolled over. "Oh, fuckin' hell goddamn all right. Shit. All I want is ten goddamn minutes of rest in this country."

"Shoulda come and play cards. Fountain of youth. That's what I'm talking about."

By the time the two pilots got there, Klee was talking with someone on a scrambler phone set. The man obviously outranked him, since he was being almost polite.

Shotgun's attention was suddenly snagged by a half-full Mr. Coffee at three o'clock. He set an intercept vector, jinking past a pair of semi-hostile-looking majors, and arrived at the machine just as the colonel hung up the line.

"All right, I guess you probably heard some of that," the colonel told his officers, handing the phone to an aide. "Riyadh's tasking an F-111. Don't bother, Wong," he added quickly. "I know what you're fucking going to say, but it's no use. Chris, you and Cleso get with Wong here and figure out some sort of backup plan, one that'll work, and one that we can do ourselves. Kelly, get Hawkins on the line at Fort Apache and tell him what the hell is going on. Get our people as far away from there as you can. Ruth will be compromised by the hit, even if they're not poisoned by the fallout. Put those helicopters to work. Charley, find them a new sector to sift."

Shotgun took a gulp of the coffee, then immediately spit it back into the cup.

Decaf. The ultimate war crime.

He looked up and realized everyone was staring at him.

"So what's our assignment?" asked Shotgun.

"Assignment?" asked the colonel. "What the hell are you two doing here?"

"Waiting for an assignment," said Shotgun. "Certainly not drinking coffee."

"You're supposed to be resting." Klee gave a furious glance behind Shotgun toward Doberman—though not nearly as furious as Doberman's own.

"Ah, we'll rest on the way," said Shotgun. "We bird-doggin' for the Aardvarks? Or escorting the helos?"

"Get your butts back to bed," snapped Klee, "or wherever it is you damn Hog pilots go when you're not blowing up things. Shit, what are you trying to do, win the war all by yourselves?"

"Only if we have to," said Shotgun—whose words, fortunately for him, were muffled by Doberman's hand as he was dragged toward the door.

SUGAR MOUNTAIN
25 JANUARY 1991
2355

"Captain's on the line," Leteri told Dixon, holding out the radio handset. "Reception's in and out, but I think it'll hold together."

Dixon glanced at Winston before speaking. The sergeant's face seemed somewhat peaceful; he was snoring.

"This is Dixon."

"Hey," said Hawkins. The line clicked on and off, but the words that did come through were sharp. "We have orders."

The line died for a second. "Cornfield."

"Repeat," said Dixon. When there wasn't an answer, he asked again.

"Solo at four," said Hawkins. He said something else that was lost, then repeated, "Solo at four. Cornfield."

It was the command for an evacuation. Four was 0400, and the Cornfield was the spot where they had first watched the highway.

It was a good location for the helicopters, but would Winston make it?

"You know our situation?" Dixon asked.

There was a long, empty silence. Finally, Hawkins's voice snapped onto the line. "They're flashing the pipe by 0500."

A bombing mission.

"Repeat?" asked Dixon, but again there was no answer. He tried twice more before Hawkins came back with the bug-out command.

"Acknowledged. We copy. We'll be waiting," Dixon told him, signing off.

The scream sounded like something out of a horror movie, only it didn't end.

"Put him back down. Okay, okay," said Dixon. His hands shook and sweat poured from his neck as he and Turk lowered Winston as gently as possible. Leteri was already pushing the plunger on the morphine.

The sergeant continued to scream, then gasped for breath. Dixon fell to his hands and knees. He stooped over Winston, wondering if he should give him mouth-to-mouth.

Or maybe just let him die.

He couldn't.

As he leaned forward, the sergeant's breath caught; he started screaming again, though this time the howl was a little lower. Dixon took that as a good sign.

Twenty minutes passed before the morphine finally took hold. Winston's groans gradually faded into a soft scat song of pain. Finally, his mouth loosened and his breathing became more regular.

As soon as they lifted him, he yelled again.

"Down," said Dixon. He had the sergeant's head, and cradled it gently as they replaced it on the ground. "We're going to have to leave him here," he told the others.

"Leave him?" said Leteri.

"I don't mean alone. I'm staying."

"That's not a good idea," said Turk.

"We're screwing something up just lifting him," said Dixon. "I don't want him paralyzed."

"Better that than dead," said Bobby.

Dixon could tell from their expressions that some of the others weren't so sure.

"You don't think he's paralyzed already?" asked Leteri.

"He wouldn't scream if he was, I don't think," said Turk. "Maybe if we had a backboard or something. You know, keep him stiff."

Winston turned his head into Dixon's knee. His eyes were closed but he seemed to be struggling to say something. Dixon bent to listen, but the words weren't intelligible.

His mother had done that a few days before she died. The monitors and their color-coded lines and numbers right next to her head blurred in his eyes as he leaned over.

What he thought she said was, "Kill me." But he couldn't be sure.

Maybe it was, "Save me." That was what he wanted her to say. That was what he wanted to do.

"Lieutenant?"

"Here's the deal," Dixon said, standing. "I stay with the sergeant. You guys go up to the Cornfield, get picked up, come back for us. We have an hour between the pickup and bomb strike; that's plenty of time."

"I think I should stay," said Turk. "Me and Bobby."

"Why don't we just have the helo pick us all up here?" Leteri suggested.

"Even if the radio were working right, Apache's off the air by now," said Dixon. "They won't be listening for us."

"Fuck, we can get them through Riyadh or the AWACS. We can take a shot at it, at least."

"We don't know what other contingencies there are," said Dixon. "They're going to be coming through shit."

"Yeah, but hell, there's shit and then there's shit," said Leteri. "And splitting up is shit."

Leteri was right, but something made Dixon shake his head. "Let's do it this way. We get in and out without any sweat."

"Lieutenant—let's be realistic, okay? You don't have to prove anything," said Turk. "We already know you're brave. We saw you go into the minefield."

"No, you know I'm nuts. Brave is something else," said Dixon. "Look, it makes more sense for you guys to be together. You can move faster without me, and handle the weapons better. The sergeant and I are safe enough here, as long as you guys make it to the helicopters. That's where the risk is."

There was logic to his argument, but the others insisted that keeping the entire team in one place was the safest plan. Dixon finally agreed to let Leteri take a shot at getting Apache or Riyadh on the line to change the pickup site. But the com gear refused to fire back up.

"All right," Leteri said. "We have to get to the Cornfield. But one of us should stay with you."

Dixon laughed. "You think I'm that bad a shot? I got half the hill covered, and a minefield besides. I can pin a battalion down from here."

"We're not saying you can't shoot straight," said Turk. "We just don't want you in over your head."

Dixon started to laugh. He was so far in over his head that nothing worse would make any difference. "I'm okay," he told them. "Seriously. Look, it makes more sense for you guys to stay together. You're the ones in danger, not me."

"Yeah, but—"

"Look, I outrank you all, and I'm giving you an order."

"With all due respect," said Leteri. "I mean, shit, don't go Rambo, you know?"

Dixon didn't feel quite as nonchalant as he acted, but he wasn't lying about thinking it was smarter for them to go.

"Who's going Rambo?" he told Leteri. "The helicopters will get me after they pick you up. You don't think they're going to leave me here, do you?"

"No."

"You guys gonna forget the way?"

"Fuck you," said Leteri.

"Fuck you back. Think of it this way—they're a hell of a lot more likely to come back for me than for one of you guys, don't you think?"

Leteri didn't have an argument for that.

• • •

Dixon turned over the M-16A2, which had an M203 40mm grenade launcher attached to it. The rifle was still fairly light, though the bulk made it feel a bit awkward.

"You okay with that?" Leteri asked.

"Works just like a shotgun, right?" he said, pointing at the pump action on the launcher's barrel. The grenade mechanism was installed below the rifle's main barrel.

"You got maybe four hundred yards range. Better to put one in front of your target than behind—but not too far in front, if you know what I mean. First time you launch it, your shoulder's gonna kick a bit."

"I won't even need it," said Dixon.

"Good thing to have."

"Oh, yeah, I agree."

The grenade launcher and M-16 combo was a standard configuration, but Dixon had never seen one up close, much less used one. A breechloader that worked, as Dixon had said, much like a shotgun, the launcher was not particularly difficult to use. Still, he wasn't entirely convinced that his first salvo wouldn't land at his feet.

It did make the M-16 look kind of ugly, though. That was comforting. Hog pilots liked things that looked ugly.

"Take care," he told them. "See you in a couple of hours."

"Sir." Leteri stood back and snapped off a drill-sergeant salute.

Dixon gave it back. Then he tried to smile, but either he was too tired or reality was starting to sink in, because he couldn't manage more than an awkward, off-kilter grin.

36

KING FAHD
26 JANUARY 1991
0100

Colonel Knowlington had thought, had hoped really, that his flight north to rescue Mongoose would represent some sort of turning point, that getting back in the cockpit under fire would vanquish some of the demons that had followed him for so many years. But they were still there.

Demons? No, Colonel Michael "Skull" Knowlington wasn't oppressed by demons, but by something much closer to him, much more dangerous, much simpler.

He wanted a drink.

It was nothing new. He'd wanted a drink every day of his life. He'd resisted before. Twenty-one days now in a row.

Or was it twenty-two? He felt something close to panic as he couldn't remember. Not knowing the count was like losing control.

And he couldn't do that. He sat straight up in his cot, casting his eyes around his empty room. There was nothing here except his old trunk and the cot and the plain walls. He liked it that way, spartan. It gave him control.

He needed to drink.

He had to do something. Maybe wander over to Oz. No matter what the hour was, there would be at least a few people working in the maintenance areas; coffee too—Oz always had some going.

Knowlington didn't like to make his men too nervous by hanging around, but on the other hand they liked to know that he took an interest, and something good always came from the few minutes he took to chat.

He was tired. He should sleep. He didn't need to get up. He needed to sleep. He closed his eyes.

He hadn't made a decision on Mongoose's request to stay with the unit yet. Damn Mongoose. Was he out of his mind? Who wouldn't want time off? See the kid, for cryin' out loud. And make love to his wife. Hell, stay in bed for a whole year.

If it were him, he wouldn't want to go home either. But that was different—he didn't have a home, or a kid, or a wife to go to.

And besides, he was sober here. Going back to the States would throw everything back up in the air.

He did have a home—the Air Force. He was a lifer, and way beyond that. His damn skin was blue.

Mongoose was too. In a different way.

Maybe he ought to let him stay. It would help the squadron certainly. And if it helped the squadron, it would help the Air Force, and made sense.

Knowlington felt his eyes closing. He started to drift off.

Mongoose's wife screamed that he had killed her husband.

The colonel bolted upright in the bed.

It had been a dream, or the start of one—but so vivid that he was trembling with it.

He needed a drink.

Knowlington got up, rubbing his arms against the cold and barely pausing to throw on boots before hiking over to Oz.

37

Al Jouf
26 January 1991
0230

Doberman had about as much chance of falling asleep as a butterfly hitching a ride on a Hog. He gave it a decent try—flipping over and over in the cot, pushing his arms into different positions, pulling more blankets on and throwing them off. But it just didn't work.

Klee pissed him off and Dixon worried the shit out of him. The kid was on the team that found the NBC storage site. Which figured. Volunteering to go north with the commandos was pretty stupid, no matter how you looked at it, but it was typical Dixon. The kid reminded Doberman of his brother, reckless in a good-natured, gung-ho, 'scuse-me-ma'am way. Doberman actually felt a little proud of him—but he didn't want to see him hurt.

After a few million rolls, he decided to do something about it. He pulled his clothes on and headed toward the Hog pit area.

Rosen and the rest of the crew had been assigned a large tent directly behind the area they were using to maintain the Hogs. Doberman hovered at the entrance a moment, trying to see if anyone was awake. He couldn't hear anything, but decided to at least step inside and see if someone was stirring.

He got half his right foot across the threshold when something hard, cold, and metallic was shoved into his stomach.

"You're gonna identify your fuckin' self or there'll be a nine-millimeter hole through your colon."

"Rosen?"

"Captain Glenon? Sir?"

Doberman started to explain, but Rosen reached her hand to his face to shush him.

"Outside," she said. The pistol was still in his stomach.

Glenon backed out as quickly and as quietly as he could. The gun and the sergeant holding it followed.

She was wearing a bulky military T-shirt over a pair of sweats. Maybe it was the light, maybe it was the Beretta, but Rosen looked damn good.

Better than that. Absolutely beautiful, despite the scowl on her face.

"I didn't mean to startle you," he told her.

"You didn't startle me. What's up?"

"I wanted to know how soon we can get the Hogs in the air."

Her voice softened just a bit. "Now?"

"There's some sort of trouble north with Dixon's party. I want to be there."

Rosen lowered the gun.

"Look, I don't want you making a big fuss," Doberman said. He explained what he had heard about the NBC site and the need to evac Dixon's team. Technically, the Hogs weren't signed up for the operation—but since he was in charge of the planes, and he was just sitting around . . .

"Sir, we'll have those planes ready to fly faster than you can take a leak. You round up your gear and Shotgun; I'll get some ordies and take care of everything. Hell, I'll slap the bombs on and top you off myself if I have to."

"Thanks, Sergeant, I appreciate it."

"No sweat, sir. Uh, you can call me Becky if you want. Most of the guys do."

God, thought Doberman—she's hot for me.

"Thanks," he told her.

"Kick butt," she said, disappearing back into the tent.

Doberman admired one butt in particular, then got his own in gear.

38

Al Jouf
26 January 1991
0230

Some things you could bluff, some things you couldn't.

A full house, aces over jacks, you couldn't.

But when you were sitting pretty with five aces—three natural, one permanently wild, and one declared in the special version of Hide and Seek Draw Out Shotgun had taught the Special Ops officers—there wasn't much need to bluff.

And while the guys were, in general, good losers, the fact that Shotgun had completely cleaned out the lot of them made for some less-than-harmonious comments.

Which didn't necessarily seem like bluffs either.

Not that he was worried. On the contrary. He had finally arrived at the spot he had been aiming for since joining the game.

"Seeing as how this was your first time playing a Hog pilot," Shotgun told them, pushing the chips back into the middle of the table, "I don't think it's fair of me to take your money. But there is something you can do for me in return."

Which was how, with a minimum of haggling (as those things went), Shotgun ended up behind the wheel of a butt-kicking, desert-romping ratmobile, officially known as an

FAV—for Fast Attack Vehicle. The FAV was essentially a very fast go-cart with two machine guns and an AT4 antitank missile launcher. She was a two-seater; the driver, in this instance Shotgun, sat in the bottom between a light-caliber machine gun and extra gas tanks. Directly behind and above him sat a gunner, in this case Major Wilson, who had drawn the low straw. Shotgun suspected that in normal operations, the man on top actually had the better post, since he got to work both the missile launcher and the 50-caliber machine gun, as well as a lashed-on grenade launcher. But considering that it was nighttime and they weren't technically authorized to shoot anything, and in fact might not be technically authorized to drive at all, Shotgun contented himself with handling the wheel.

And damned if this little buggy didn't move. It reminded him of an old big-block Chevy he'd had briefly; a little ol' Nova that he'd rebored and jacked up. Bottom line on that was that it couldn't hold the road worth shit, no matter what he tried doing with the suspension, and for a little car it sure felt like a truck, but you stepped on the accelerator and she cranked, baby.

Just like this. The FAV spat sand ferociously as Shotgun blasted off into the desert. She had a whole row of headlamps but he figured, there being a war on, it didn't make sense to use them. He could see pretty well with the infrared night setup he'd insisted on as part of the deal.

Damn helmet was heavy, though.

Shotgun veered to the right, narrowly missing either a large rock or a buried tank. He thought he heard the major groan, and felt his boot kicking the chair.

"Yeah, I know I can go faster!" shouted Shotgun. "Hang on!"

He mashed the accelerator pedal. The ratmobile pushed herself down as she picked up speed. They were doing sixty, maybe seventy.

The major's kicks became more violent.

"It's at the firewall now," yelled Shotgun. "Problem is you got that muffler holding the engine back. You take that off, then we're talking speed."

A fence or the edge of the earth loomed ahead. Shotgun

yanked hard right, felt the FAV starting to tip, corrected. Two wheels came off the ground before the go-cart settled down and began accelerating in a new direction.

No wonder Dixon had volunteered to go north, thought Shotgun. He was probably driving one of these right now.

Parachuting *and* driving an FAV. Some guys had all the luck.

For a brief second, he wished it was him and not Dixon who had gone north. Then he thought again about trying to get his Harley into the Gulf. Not the good one, just the '89.

That short moment of inattention caused him to miss the fact that he had headed straight up a dune.

Had he seen it, he would have accelerated.

The FAV flew off the top, launching into the air like an F/A-18 catapulted from an aircraft carrier.

Of course, an F/A-18 had wings, and the FAV didn't. It hit nose-first in the sand, harder than Shotgun would have expected. That didn't stop him from giving a proper war whoop, however.

The major didn't kick. Obviously he'd decided Shotgun was going as fast as he could.

The pilot glanced at his watch as he cranked around for another turn. He really ought to be getting back.

Time for one more try.

This time, he managed to get the FAV to accelerate sufficiently to land on the back wheels. The resulting wheelie wasn't much—barely three seconds long—but it was a hell of a way to end the night.

Doberman was waiting as Shotgun drove up to the Hogs' maintenance area. He hopped out of the vehicle and turned to help the major down. But the Special Ops officer waved him off.

The light wasn't that good, but it seemed to Shotgun the major looked a little under the weather. Probably the homemade hooch.

"Where the hell have you been?" Doberman demanded. "We're going to go back up that helo flight that's picking up Dixon. The Hogs are fueled and armed."

“About time you got out of bed,” said Shotgun, starting to trot toward the shack where his gear was stored. “Be with you in two minutes.”

“Make it one.”

“I don’t think Tinman can brew the coffee that fast,” Shotgun yelled back. “But I’ll have him take a shot.”

39

Over Iraq
26 January 1991
0310

The F-111F had barely taken off from its airfield with the rest of the package on a precision strike deep into Iraq when the AWACS controller broke in with a change in plans.

Captain Jay "Heavy" Muir, sitting in his weapons officer's slot next to the pilot, pushed back in his seat as the new target info came in: a suspected NBC site a few miles south of the Euphrates. Heavy's mind clicked, erasing everything it had stored about the aircraft shelter they were originally tasked.

Among other things, Heavy handled the Aardvark's Pave Tack radar, which guided the big laser-guided bombs strapped beneath their wings. While he didn't consider the new mission itself that difficult—Heavy was rated the best operator in the squadron, which made him among the best in the Air Force—the change in plans put a fresh kink in his already wrenched neck. Especially when he was told that his aim point was a small pipe on the side of a hill in an old quarry. That wouldn't be particularly easy to spot on the targeting screen. He had no photo, no briefing folder, nothing more than a vague description and a set of coordinates to help prompt him.

"Needle in a rock garden," said his pilot, Captain Chris Klecko, as they laid out the new course.

"Yeah," said Heavy. He studied his paper map, letting the details soak in. The pipe was in a rock quarry, above a large metal door. Just a pipe, not a full ventilation system.

Not easy. But yesterday he had put a pair of Paveways down a chimney.

The idea here would be to break the top of the shelter. His Paveways were serious hunks of explosive. He didn't have to hit the pipe exactly.

But he would. As soon as he could see it in his head.

"Doable?" asked Klecko.

"Oh, yeah," said Muir. "Assuming we can find it."

"We have plenty of time. They want it splashed by 0500. We'll be there by 0400 latest."

Muir closed his eyes, clearing everything else away. "I'll get it," he told Klecko.

40

Sugar Mountain
26 January 1991
0340

The first thing Dixon thought when he heard the noise was that his friends in the truck were returning. A half second later he realized it was far too loud to be just one vehicle.

He shifted around behind the rocks near Sergeant Winston, pulling the M-16 and its grenade launcher next to him but not shouldering the weapon. He was so cold he was shivering. They'd left him with one of the nightscopes, and it felt like an ice cube when he held it to his face.

An armored personnel carrier was leading a pair of light trucks on the highway; there was another APC, maybe a second and third, in the blur behind. A tank loomed behind them like a vast battleship on the horizon; it took a moment for his eyes to separate enough detail so he could tell that it was riding on a flatbed.

There were two other flatbeds.

More tanks. No, these were self-propelled guns. Antiair, or maybe tracked howitzers.

Antiair. Four barrels. ZSU-23's.

Dixon glanced down at his watch. The helicopter was nearly a half hour away.

He pushed back against the rocks as the lead elements of the procession rounded the bend. They'd be at the cave in a minute, then start setting up their defenses.

No way the helo was getting in with those guns. Dixon had to leave or he'd be trapped.

Winston rasped gently. He had a smile on his face. The morphine probably.

I'm not leaving him, Dixon decided. Even if it means taking on the whole damn Iraqi Army.

Which it might.

Several trucks in the convoy didn't have mufflers. The roar against the sheer rocks was deafening. The noise surrounded him, shaking every part of his body.

The trucks were all around him.

And then beyond, still on the highway. Still moving.

Dixon scrambled to his feet. Clutching his rifle, he went out to the slope where he could get a view of the highway. He was exposed momentarily, but it was dark and he figured unless someone was looking directly at him, even during the day, he'd be hard to spot.

He saw the thick shadow of an armored personnel carrier speeding away on the road. Then the tank carrier. And the rest.

Dixon couldn't help feeling enormous relief, even though he knew the heavily armed convoy was heading in the direction of the Cornfield.

41

NEAR THE CORNFIELD
26 JANUARY 1991
0345

Captain Hawkins found himself leaning forward in the helicopter, as if his weight might add more momentum to its speed.

The Little Bird was cranking, but it wasn't going fast enough. Hawkins needed it there now, at the Cornfield, his men climbing aboard, the helo taking off.

With the exception of his Air Force FAC, he knew all of the members of the Ruth team. Green, who had been killed, had worked with him just a few days before. The young sergeant was a man of many talents; he filled the medic slot for Ruth and had worked point and como.

Was. Past tense. They'd get his body back when this was over. Maybe there'd be enough time to get it back now.

Hawkins turned to the pilot. Fernandez tapped his watch but said nothing.

He was counseling him to be patient. They were ahead of schedule.

The AH-6Gs were skimming about six feet over the terrain. Hawkins, who unlike the pilot wasn't wearing the night-vision goggles, braced himself against the side of the helo and stared into the darkness. The ground below was patchy scrubland, becoming more fertile the further they went. For him that meant there were more people in the area, more things that could go wrong.

The AWACS told them the bombing attack would now probably coincide with their pickup. Fernandez assured him they'd be far enough away. It would be a good diversion really, in case anyone was nearby or watching.

You planned, you trained, you tried to cover every contingency, but you couldn't. That was part of the excitement of it, part of what made it almost fun.

Except it wasn't fun, because it was way the hell too serious. It was a job, work, something with severe consequences.

Like dead friends.

The helicopter flicked briefly to the right. Hawkins's arm was so tense it felt as if it was going to snap in two against the metal panel.

In-out. No sweat.

They had the mesh units in place, but his runway was still way too short. Tomorrow night, a Herc was supposed to try dropping some motorcycles by parachute. Hawkins wondered if he could somehow arrange to get a bulldozer instead. Move the culvert pipe into place and then fill around it. Cover it with mesh—the runway'd be two thousand, three thousand feet in no time.

Could they parachute a bulldozer?

Sure they could. Goddamn combat engineers could do just about anything. Hell, one would probably ride it down.

"Shit," said the pilot.

Hawkins looked up and saw the bright red tracers arcing ahead. A pepper of green flared from the opposite direction.

"Looks like a problem," said the pilot. "LZ is hot."

Aside from a string of curses, it was the last coherent thing Hawkins heard him say.

42

OVER IRAQ
26 JANUARY 1991
0355

Heavy pushed himself upright in his seat, working his neck around to loosen his muscles. The Vark weapons officer had first gotten the kink from a fall on a 5.12 climb in the Idaho Sawtooths two days before the deployment orders came through. Nothing he had tried—aspirin, massages, home brew—had cured it. Short of sticking his neck in front of his F-111F's radar for half an hour, he was willing to do anything, even see a chiropractor, to get permanent relief.

He hadn't found a chiropractor in Saudi Arabia yet. And the medical doctor he *had* found gave him lousy advice, fortunately unofficial: take a few weeks off.

That he wouldn't do. So, almost anything.

Heavy's job basically came down to pasting his face against a small viewscreen as long as it took to designate and vaporize whatever Black Hole wanted smashed. This magnified the kink into something abominable, since inevitably it tensed every muscle in his shoulder and back. While he knew it would feel better if he relaxed, that was tough to do when the F-111 was cranking at 650 knots two hundred feet above the ground.

Which they had been doing now for nearly ten minutes, thanks to Heavy's detection of some overachieving Iraqi SAM operators in their path.

Klecko gave him a quick tap. The two men had worked side by side in the F-111's unique cockpit for more than a year. They had long ago given up using sentences during the business part of a mission; communication was more like ESP. Every gesture, every word, was densely packed code. The tap meant half a dozen things, including "Are you okay?" and "We're just about there."

Heavy gave Klecko a thumbs-up and got his head back into the game.

The quartet of Paveway III laser-guided bombs beneath the F-111's variable-geometry swept wings were controlled with the use of a revolving laser designator carried in a pod glued to the F-111's belly. Once they found their target, Klecko would buck the Vark upwards and they'd pickle, lofting the missiles toward the NBC facility. Rolling ninety degrees, the pilot would give his weapons officer—aka "you over there" in the Vark community—a nice long look at the target. Heavy would steady the laser designator where he wanted the bombs to hit. The Paveways would fly their two-thousand-pound payload of explosives right to the spot.

The maneuver was called a "ramp toss," as if the plane was running up a ramp and throwing the bomb at its target. It wasn't necessarily the easiest way to hit something, but they had practiced it extensively and used it from the first night of the war.

And despite what it did to his neck, Heavy liked it.

Of course, he also liked 5.12 climbs.

The ground erupted with tracers to their north. Heavy realized immediately that they weren't being shot at, but it took nearly a second for him to wrestle his eyes and full attention back in the direction of their rock quarry, just now coming into view. He scanned carefully but quickly for his aim point, the small pipe on the side of a hill above a shallow rock face. Something inside his brain clicked, and he forgot not merely about the tracers but about his shoulder, the seat, the physical parts of the viewer, the cockpit, the world. He was in full hunter mode, sifting and searching, running his eyes deliberately against the shades of gray, searching for the one particular shade he wanted. He was on the rock face, eyes straining for the infinitesimally small nub that would friction him up two more feet, the handhold that would get him closer to his goal.

Not there.

Patience.

Not there.

He was shocked to see the miniature outline of two men in his viewer.

A hallucination? His neck spiked stiff, pulling every muscle from his ears to his toes into spasm.

Relax.

His eyes climbed the rock, scaling it slowly, looking for the pipe, his pipe.

Patience. He would find it. It was just a matter of working the screen, feeling the rock.

Patience.

43

In Iraq
26 January 1991
0355

Even as he cursed, the helo pilot began firing his 50-caliber machine guns into the Iraqi position. In the confusion and the dark, Hawkins couldn't immediately tell what they were facing, but it was obvious there was serious firepower down there. He tried patching into the AWACS, hoping to get some support. But the helicopter was too low to get the controller directly, and when the E-3 Sentry AWACS operator failed to acknowledge his second try, Hawkins tried his ground team instead.

They didn't answer either. He thought he could tell from their red tracers where they were; he told Fernandez and the pilot behind to roll up the flank of the Iraqis, drawing their attention at least temporarily.

The pilots were a step ahead of him, already sweeping in with a coordinated rocket attack. Hawkins's chopper stuttered with the force of the 70mm rockets gushing from the tubes on both stubby wings; he felt himself buck forward and then wrench violently to the side. The Little Bird's machine guns opened up again, a quick burst that perforated a black shadow 250 yards away. The shadow turned into the outline of an APC, which morphed into red flame. Someone was hailing him on the radio, but in the confusion Hawkins couldn't hear precisely what they were saying. He pointed to the spot he wanted the chopper to fly to, and felt the aircraft complying immediately, as if it and not the pilot were responding to his command. A new line of tracers erupted on his right, arcing away; these were thicker than the others, and green, the enemy. Hawkins felt the AH-6G twist to get a better aim on his new threat, saw the line of bullets beginning to turn as they did.

"Get that son-of-a-bitch!" he shouted, and in the next second something happened to the front of the helicopter; it seemed as if it were a giant tea kettle suddenly bursting. Hawkins looked at the pilot, saw that he was bent over his control stick, and then felt the ground ram against the skis beneath his legs as his head smashed into something hard and very dark.

44

In Iraq
26 January 1991
0355

The first flickers of the firefight looked like a fireworks display, errant sparkles shooting off at odd angles.

Then it turned into green and orange roman candles, rockets flashing, white streaks igniting everywhere.

Then a piece of Hell opened up, volcanoes spitting fireballs into the air.

Dixon watched it all as if it were a movie. This seemed different than combat. Combat was flying a Hog and shacking a target, g's hitting you in the face as you pulled up and whacked yourself the hell out of there. That was real. You felt that. Your head swam with blood and sweat; you struggled to keep your eyes cold and hard and focused; you tried to hit your buttons on time. Everything screamed in your face and was real.

This was far away. He could feel the ground shake with the explosions, but it didn't feel like war.

His friends, Leteri, Turk, the others, were in the middle of it. They were shooting, maybe dying. But it was so unreal it didn't make sense.

Except for this: The gunfight probably meant the helicopters wouldn't be coming for him.

He looked at his watch. The bomber would have taken off by now. He wasn't sure what they would send. Most likely it would be an F-111 or a Nighthawk, something with fat laser-guided weapons. Most likely, they'd aim for the pipe he'd spotted.

Winston coughed.

Dixon trotted back down the hill to the hiding place where he'd left him. The sergeant wasn't smiling anymore. His expression was bland and pasty. Dixon leaned over and checked for a pulse. He didn't find it at first; frantically, he pushed his thumb around the bone at the inside of the sergeant's wrist. Finally, he got a beat.

Not strong, but there.

Odds were, Winston was bleeding internally. Back was all shot up; probably he was already paralyzed. He was coughing. Dixon knew from his mother that wasn't a good sign. Probably meant his lungs were filling up with fluid.

He'd die soon. Certainly if they couldn't evac him.

Dixon cursed himself for not demanding an immediate evac when they got out of the minefield. They should have been out of here hours ago.

Maybe not. They were closer to Baghdad than Saudi Arabia.

Winston knew that when he volunteered for the mission. So did Dixon.

Not really. He hadn't thought it out. He hadn't figured that shooting his mouth off about skydiving would lead him to find a hidden Iraqi bunker in a rock quarry, divide him from his team, get them ambushed.

He hadn't thought that staying with Winston would mean he'd be stranded. He might have known it was a possibility, but he hadn't really played it out, actually pictured it happening.

He had to now. Because without the helicopters, he and Winston were a hell of a long way from anyplace good. Whatever happened next was going to depend a hell of a lot on what he thought out. And more importantly, on what he did.

45

In Iraq
26 January 1991
0405

Hawkins coughed ferociously, trying to dislodge something from his throat. It was big and felt like a Brillo pad, scratching flesh. He coughed and coughed, arms drained of feeling, head spinning.

It flew out. Moisture flooded onto his face and chin. He looked down, saw he had spat up blood.

But he could breathe. He pushed himself up, then remembered he was strapped in the helicopter.

No, he was free. The helicopter was a few feet away. He'd gotten out somehow. He was sitting on the ground. Hawkins stood, reaching to his belt for his pistol, then felt himself yanked back to the ground.

A quick burst of rifle fire ragged the air above him.

"Hang tight, Captain."

The voice was familiar. Leteri or Ziza, one of the New Yorkers. He twisted to see who it was. Instead, he was distracted by the white light of a shell hitting behind them.

"Assholes don't know quite where we are."

It was Mo Ziza. He quickly laid out the situation. The team

had been surrounded by the Iraqis, who had acted like they knew the commandos were there but couldn't locate them in the dark. The Iraqis had mounted the hilltop overlooking the road, posting about a dozen soldiers there while the rest of the heavy stuff stayed between the plateau and the road. Rather than letting the helicopters walk into an ambush, the troopers had opened fire as soon as they heard the helos in the distance; they'd managed to wipe out the bastards on the high ground even before the rest of the Iraqis began to return fire.

"We disabled one of the APCs before you got here but then they got lucky," said Ziza. "Joe Leteri and Bobby Jackson are dead. Turk's still holding them off up there."

"Where's Winston?"

"Sergeant Winston couldn't travel. Lieutenant Dixon stayed back with him at Sugar Mountain."

"What?" Hawkins struggled to clear his head. "Shit. Why the fuck didn't you radio that in?"

"We tried. Radio got hit when we walked into those mines."

"Dixon?"

"He didn't want to leave the sergeant."

"No shit. Why the fuck did you let him stay?"

"He told us it was an order."

"Oh, fuck that, he's a goddamn pilot. Shit fucking hell."

"He's got balls for a pilot."

"The helicopter. Fernandez." Hawkins jumped up and ran back to the chopper. Ziza followed, reaching him just as Hawkins got to the door.

Fernandez was slumped forward in his harness, chest, neck, and head laced with bullets. A line of holes arced up across the top of the AH-6G's front glass. Otherwise it seemed in good shape, though Hawkins was far from a mechanic.

Or a pilot. He didn't even know how to turn the panel on.

A fresh round of gunfire sounded from the Iraqis' position beyond the hilltop plateau. His second helo passed overhead, unleashing machine-gun fire in that direction.

"How the hell did they get Fernandez and miss me?" Hawkins said as he ducked.

"They didn't. The side of your head's bleeding."

Hawkins touched his temple. It was wet. He pushed his finger gently along the skin, felt something small and sharp.

A piece of metal or glass. But it must not be serious or he'd be dead. Unconscious at least. His chest had also been hit, though he wasn't bleeding beneath his vest.

"All right. Let's go get Turk and get the fuck out of here while we still can," he told Ziza. "Show me the way."

Ziza stooped slightly as he trotted. Hawkins huffed to keep up. He had a good feel for the situation now, had it laid out in his head.

His other helo was behind them somewhere, trying to sort out what was going on.

They could retreat and hop in. Swing around and get Dixon and Winston. Go back to Fort Apache. Get their one spare pilot, maybe a mechanic. Bring back the downed helo.

Mechanic had broken his leg. Wasn't going anywhere.

Fuck that. Cart him there in a stretcher if they had to.

Ziza slid in behind the hulked ruins of an Iraqi truck as the enemy began firing mortar rounds. They were way off the mark and their first corrections were in the wrong direction. Hawkins ducked nonetheless, trotting toward Ziza and Staffa Turk. Turk was hunkered over guns on one end of a wrecked Iraqi vehicle. Four or five dead Iraqi soldiers lay on the ground, most still clutching their weapons.

The Iraqi mortar stopped firing. Turk nodded at the captain, then handed his starlight viewer to Hawkins, pointing out the Iraqi forces.

"They seem to think we're still up on the hill," he said, pointing to the rise on his left. "They don't know what they're up against. There, see that APC? It's been there since the choppers opened up with the rockets. It's got a gun and it works, but maybe its wheels are gone on the other side. I can't tell. There's about a squad of men clustered around that truck, and maybe three more over there with that one. Something fired once from there; I heard it but that was it. Sounded like it might have been a grenade launcher. Whatever it was landed closer to Baghdad than to me."

Hawkins scanned the positions. There were two wrecked APCs between them and the main body of the Iraqi force. Further right was a tracked vehicle with a four-barrel turret; obviously an antiaircraft gun, though it would still be deadly against ground forces. The enemy troops were arrayed as if the threat lay on the plateau, which rose about twenty-five yards to his left.

"What's behind these guys?" he asked Turk.

"Out to the road? There's at least one tank. I heard it moving around before. You figure they stopped shooting because they think we're all dead?"

Hawkins laughed. "Yeah, that's what I think."

Both men knew the Iraqis were merely regrouping.

"I'll give them one thing," said Ziza. "They're smart enough not to fire a flare."

"That's only because they don't know how outgunned we are," said Hawkins. "We have to drop back and hook up with the other helicopter before they figure it out."

"Assuming he's still here," said Ziza. "I haven't heard him for a few minutes."

"He's there." Hawkins knew the pilot would take the AH-6G back and watch for them.

Have to move now, though. Any second the Iraqis might get their shit together and realize where the Americans were. Tanks could roll them up.

"Okay, let's pull back in the direction of that helo," said Hawkins. He pointed to the downed helicopter. "We'll go to the helicopter, then move back into that open area. There's a shallow ridge maybe a mile beyond us. That's probably where the other helo is."

He got up.

"Ziza, you lead the way." He pushed him forward, waited a second, then tugged Turk. There was a flash behind them. Truck engines revved. He began to run like his life depended on it.

Which it did. The Iraqis realized they weren't on the hill and were coming across the plain.

"Tank!" yelled Ziza as something whizzed through the air ahead. "Tank's firing!"

Hawkins fell toward the ground, spinning away from a white-red flash that momentarily silhouetted the middle of a large, hulking shadow.

In the next second, a fierce shriek split the earth ahead as a shell from the tank's big gun landed barely out of range to kill them.

And then an enormous white metallic light turned black Hell into bright Heaven, and the air was rent by the concussion of a three-hundred-pound Maverick G warhead smashing open the top of an Iraqi tank and incinerating its crew.

The commandos' guardian angels had arrived.

46

OVER IRAQ
26 JANUARY 1991
0410

Doberman heard Shotgun shout over the radio as his Maverick flashed dead on the turret of the T-72 tank, bursting through the relatively thin coat of armor and exploding inside. Forty tons of Iraqi metal went from an average 37 degrees Fahrenheit to over 300 in a half second; the turret popped up like the top on a boiling pot of water and the only thing that escaped was steam and ashes.

Doberman saw part of the tank begin to burn in the bottom corner of the Maverick's cathode-ray tube as he edged the aiming cursor into the shadow of an APC. But he couldn't set it—the damn pipper wouldn't stay pipped. He cursed and relaxed his fingers, trying to feel himself into the target, lost it completely, felt the plane starting to buck as an antiaircraft gun on the edge of the Iraqi position finally figured out where the hell he was. He yanked to throw the gunner off, saw the cursor slap into place, steadied the plane, but lost the target again. Doberman took a hard breath and got it back, did his thumb thing quick—*bing-bang-bam*—and nailed it down tight and pickled the Maverick, kicked the goddamn missile into gear.

By now the air around him was percolating with exploding flak shells. Doberman jinked hard, blood and gravity rushing to his head as he reached to key his mike and ask Shotgun what the hell he was waiting for. The ground rippled brilliant red as it filled the top and side of his cockpit's bubble glass. Doberman let the Hog fall into a swoop as he realized the triple-A had stopped; Shotgun had just taken out the gun.

Okay, he thought to himself, points for timing.

Without the Maverick Gs, Doberman could make out only shadows and fires on the ground. Swinging behind the Iraqi position, away from the Americans, he called Shotgun off, then fired one of the illumination flares his ground crew had packed under his wings. As the flare ignited beneath its slow-falling chute, Doberman spun back. The battlefield splayed out in his windscreen, Iraqi metal fat and juicy beneath him. He nosed down to get a good bombing angle, slanting onto the thickest part of the Iraqi position between the road and the side of a shallow plateau. A fat truck with a machine gun or something similarly impotent spat at him in the middle of his windscreen, while the shadows of rats scurried away. He stayed cool, in control, got his mark. He pushed the bomb trigger.

After he let off he realized he'd skipped his bing-bang-bam ritual. He also realized he'd drifted off target as he pickled. His iron landed well behind the truck.

Recovering, he temporarily lost sight of the battlefield and its white and red glow. Shotgun's plane pulled out about half a mile ahead; shadows danced against the stars as his wing mate's bombs exploded. Doberman banked, getting the battlefield full in the right half of his cockpit glass. There were a lot of small fires but as near as he could tell, no more tracers.

"What do you think?" asked Shotgun.

"I missed," said Doberman.

"No way. Everything's dead."

"I want to take another turn to make sure," said Doberman.

"If that helo's going in, he's got to go in soon. Fuel's low."

"Yeah, okay. Hang back."

Doberman put the Hog on her wing, tightening his circle to

shoot over the battlefield. Something about the fading glow of the ground bothered him.

The helicopter was an easy shot for anyone on that plateau. The pilot wasn't in radio contact with the ground forces and would have to take his time looking for them.

An Iraqi soldier could make himself a hero real quick by playing dead, then pop up with a little ol' SA-16 and whack the helicopter to Kingdom Come.

Even nail him with a machine gun from that hill. A lucky shot would take him down.

Nothing fired at Doberman. Still, it didn't feel right.

But damn, what did he want?

What was "feeling right" except some superstitious BS?

"I'm dropping a flare at the far end," Doberman told Shotgun. "Then let's take a fresh pass and see if anybody shoots at us."

"Got your butt," said his wingman.

47

OVER IRAQ
26 JANUARY 1991
0414

Talk about crappy timing.

Shotgun was pitching the Hog onto her wing, Jethro Tull was wailing about Aqualung, and the damn batteries in his custom CD player ran out.

"Hey there, Ack—wuhhhhhhhhhh-lunnnnnnnnggg . . ."

Click. Dead stop.

There was nothing worse than losing the juice on a golden oldie. Shotgun hit the player several times as he swooped behind and to the east of Doberman, both Hogs waltzing slow and easy over the entire Iraqi position, easy targets at five hundred feet, the flare above them.

Son of a bitch. He'd changed the batteries before the last flight. And they were alkalines. No reason for them to give out, especially now. You needed a sound track this low.

And damn, he loved the classics.

Shotgun felt a little naked, hand on the throttle, ready to flood the gates if his RWR or instincts told him something was coming. His eyes darted in every direction, scanning the ground like sophisticated radar.

Worst thing was, he didn't have spare batteries aboard.

Inexcusable really. Kind of thing they drummed into you in basic, for christsakes, like always check your fuel before taking off and never go anywhere without extra underwear.

The Iraqis, obviously unaware that he was vulnerable, made no move to attack. Shotgun pushed the Hog around into a bank, playing follow the leader. As he did, his fingers flew into his suit, flicking the player on and off, hoping to squeeze a last volt from them.

Still nothing.

Maybe he could get one of Clyston's guys to rig up some sort of power draw off the Hog itself. Need a transformer or something, but how hard could that be to get?

Hog's only flaw—no built-in stereo.

"See anything?" asked Doberman.

"Nah."

"Let's take another pass. I'm going lower."

"You worried about something?"

"Just making sure."

Shotgun was just starting his turn when Doberman barked something over the radio. The front of the lead plane began spitting bullets, tracers dancing a tight line down to the edge of the hill. Shotgun swooped around and upwards, trying to quickly build altitude to get his own run in, but by the time he was reoriented it was over. The flare gave him a good view; nothing was moving. Doberman was already circling out.

"Shit, what happened?" he asked Doberman.

"Thought I saw something. Maybe not."

"Dead now, if anything, Dog Man," said Shotgun.

"Yeah, okay, I'm bringing the helo," said Doberman.

"I'm doing a pass and clearing west." The Hog gave Shotgun a throaty roar as she hunkered down into the fumes of the vanquished enemy. She loved being here, and snorted for more, as if the cannon's ammunition drum were overloaded and she could only get some relief by blowing a couple of hundred rounds.

Shotgun wanted to oblige her, and scanned the approaching

shadows and curling smoke for signs of the enemy. He realized now that he shouldn't have cashed his chips in for the buggy ride—what he really wanted, damn it, were those night-vision-binocular things he'd worn. That was what he was talking about. A pair of those suckers and he could see fleas moving down there.

Something was running in the corner of his screen, down on the flat plain where the commando helo had gone down. He gave rudder to line up better, trigger ready. Every part of his body was in the windscreen, inching into the target.

One shadow, two, three.

His guys? Or the enemy?

Damn music would have told him. Music gave him a sense of things. Flying without music was like flying blind.

Worse.

The helicopter was between him and his target. He slipped right, riding the Hog as slow as an old pickup truck in reverse. It wasn't easy to nail something as small as a man.

Wax 'em or let 'em go? He strained to get a good view in the darkness.

Should he shoot or let 'em go?

Clash song.

Which was another thing: He'd left his Clash CD back at King Fahd.

Shotgun swung low, pushing the Hog into the dirt. The three shadows loomed in the crosshairs. He had them easy, felt the trigger starting to give way under the pressure of his finger.

Something made him hold off. They kept running as he passed. He picked the Hog up by her tail, flopped around and back for another pass. He was barely twenty feet off the ground and going slow enough to land.

His guys or the enemy? The helicopter popped up from behind a small rise not far away. These guys could take her out with a popgun.

The Gat jumped up and down below his feet. He had all three shadows dead on, dead if he wanted, but now, only now.

Had to be his guys.

If they weren't, his guys were dead.

"It's always tease, tease, tease, tease," he sang, supplying his own version of the Clash song.

Definitely his guys. He gave them a barrel roll as he went overhead.

"We got something moving up there on the highway, ten miles," said Doberman. "Other side of Sugar Mountain. They're cranking."

"I got people moving here."

"Ours," said Doberman. "Helo's got 'em. Come on."

Shotgun leaned his head back as he accelerated to follow. What song should he try next?

48

The Cornfield
26 January 1991
0418

Hawkins gripped his grenade launcher as a second shadow erupted near the tank, this one bursting into a brilliant ball of fire.

"The Hogs!" Ziza shouted as the dark shadow of an A-10A crossed against the flickering flames. A stream of green tracers erupted from the Iraqi antiaircraft gun—and then it too erupted in an explosion. Hawkins and his two men stood and gaped as the warplanes ripped up the enemy. In less than ninety seconds, the entire Iraqi contingent had been vacuumed away. A flare exploded above; the commandos watched in awe as the ugly forks of death mopped up.

The A-10's were the last things the Iraqis had been expecting. They were about the last things Hawkins had been expecting as well.

But shit damn, they had great timing.

"Let's go," he shouted, jumping into gear as the airplanes took a breather. The three commandos began running toward the open plain where they expected the helicopter to appear.

He'd taken two steps when Hawkins felt something in his leg tear. He began to limp, then nearly fell over.

One of the Hogs came in low, thundering overhead. They were supposed to be quiet for jets, but damned if the plane's engines didn't sound like tigers spoiling for a fight. Pushing back to his feet, he decided he loved that sound.

The helicopter came over the far hill and blinked a searchlight, either to show them where it was or to tell them to get their butts in gear. His leg was fucked up bad, and he felt blood as he reached down to hold it, hobbling forward. Turk grabbed him by the arm, half supporting, half pushing.

The Hog took another turn overhead, like a sheepdog pushing her lost lambs toward the shepherd. The helo was less than fifty yards away, loud and beautiful in the fading flare light.

Hawkins would have sworn the A-10 pilot gave him a victory roll before pulling off.

49

OVER IRAQ
26 JANUARY 1991
0419

Heavy felt the F-111F move ever so slightly to his left, Klecko compensating for some turbulence.

In the next instant he found their target.

"Yes!" he shouted, and the plane popped upward, and in the next few instants a million things happened, but as far as he was concerned, nothing, absolutely nothing happened: He kept the thin needle of laser light trained on one infinitesimally small shadow of a pipe. The plane banked and rolled out, wings swinging and Pratt and Whitneys whining; the Paveways edged their fins and adjusted their glide slopes, striving toward the laser pinprick. Heavy just sat there, all 136 pounds of flesh, bone, and muscle thrown into a small dot in the middle of a thin shadow near the center of his target screen. His eyes, his brain, his fingers were all there, all locked, as much part of the bombs as part of him.

The shadow mushroomed into whiteness once, then again and again. The fourth bomb either missed or malfunctioned or he just totally lost it. They were gone now, cranking away, accelerating toward home; he let himself ease back, taking a break to celebrate.

"Good," said Klecko.

"Good," he said back.

And damn, his neck hurt like hell.

The Cornfield
26 January 1991
0419

Hawkins threw himself at the door of the helicopter. Turk grabbed him and pulled as the AH-6 began moving away, its pilot trying to get the hell out of there while the getting was good.

Hawkins rolled on the floor, got up, and then wedged himself between the two front seats. He was practically kissing the control panel.

"Go to Sugar Mountain." he told the pilot. "The rock quarry. We got two guys waiting for us there."

"With all due respect, sir, we're going to be lucky if we get back to the Fort. Real lucky," said the pilot. "Part of our tail's shot up and the gauges say the fuel's iffy. And that bomber's gonna hit it any second."

"Screw that," said Hawkins.

The pilot grimaced, but began an arc in the northward direction toward the quarry. Hawkins managed to squeeze into the forward seat, changing places with Quilly. He wasn't quite settled when the Hogs radioed the helicopter to tell the commandos they had spotted a new convoy heading east on the highway. The column had trucks and tanks and was about four, maybe five miles from Sugar Mountain.

"They're going to see us, maybe even beat us if they stay on the road," said the pilot.

"What about the Hogs?" Hawkins asked. "Can they take those bastards down?"

"One of them just called bingo," said the pilot. "They're low on fuel. They're engaging the vehicles on the highway but they're going to have to break off."

"Just get us the fuck there!" said Hawkins.

As the pilot picked up the tail and began scooting toward the mountain, the horizon flashed white. The Little Bird's FLIR went crazy for a second.

"Bomber just took out the bunker," said the pilot.

"Fuck," said Hawkins.

"Hogs are bingo. They're breaking off. What are we doing, sir?"

As much as he didn't want to leave his men, Hawkins realized going to Sugar Mountain now was beyond foolish.

In every battle, there was a time to regroup. It wasn't necessarily the time you wanted it to be, but if you didn't recognize it, you usually didn't get a chance to fight again.

"Back to the Fort," said Hawkins. "Son of a bitch. Son of a fucking bitch."

51

Over Iraq
26 January 1991
0419

Doberman squeezed his stick tight enough to wring water from it as he got the cannon into the second truck, hot uranium mixing with explosives as he erased the utility vehicle from the Iraqi order of battle. He tried pushing his rudder enough to get a shot on another vehicle, but ran out of space and time, pulling off and flashing to the right so Shotgun could come in on his own run.

He figured it was safer to smash them without using the flares; the shadows were thick enough, and while it wasn't necessarily easy to sort what was what, the Iraqis were totally confused and probably defenseless. The few thin tracers raking the air arced in the wrong direction.

Unfortunately, he was into his fuel reserves.

Time to go home.

Shotgun pulled up, his green and black camo a blur in the predawn light.

"How's your fuel?" Doberman asked.

"Yeah, I'm bingo."

Doberman got their position on the INS and called it in to the AWACS. Then he checked in with the commandos' helicopter.

"We ought to refuel at Apache," said Shotgun after they had set sail southwards.

"You figure out how to land in a thousand feet and take off again, let me know."

"They'll have fifteen hundred feet with the mesh they're talking about," said Shotgun. "That's more than enough."

"They got bullets and Twinkies?"

"Negative."

"Then I guess we're going back to Al Jouf."

"Man, you're a grouch in the morning. You ought to drink more coffee."

"Hold your thermos out and I'll grab a cup."

"You got it."

Doberman half suspected Shotgun might try it. He fought the twinge of fatigue tickling the corners of his eyes. Then he tapped into the commandos' frequency and hailed the helo pilot, who by now was almost at Fort Apache.

"I understand one of our guys was on your mission," he told the pilot. "Like to say hi if I can. Lieutenant Dixon?"

"Dixon's still on Sugar Mountain," said the pilot. "Squad leader got hurt and he stayed with him."

"What?"

Another voice, obviously angry, cut off the pilot's answer with a single word: "Out."

Even though he understood the need for silent com, ordinarily Doberman would have taken offense to the tone. But all he could think about was the hole in his stomach as his fingers reached to see if the throttle could cough up some extra horses.

PART THREE

OUT THERE SOMEWHERE

52

Sugar Mountain
26 January 1991
0420

One second, Dixon was cursing himself for not changing the rendezvous, for not finding a way to get the radio working, for sending the commandos to their deaths. The next second, he was throwing himself downwards, a shriek from far above vibrating at the back of his head, a jolt that didn't register consciously until after he hit the ground.

Dixon landed on Sergeant Winston as the first of the F-111's Paveways hit the hill beyond them. The ground shook and then seemed to slide away, the two-thousand-pound bombs acting like God's foot, smashing and grinding the Iraqi hilltop beneath its heel. Debris percolated through the air, small bits of rock and sand propelled like shrapnel. To Dixon it sounded as if the air were on fire.

Even though they were some distance from the target and had a hillside between them and the explosion, Dixon was covered with grit when the tremors finally stopped. His eyes burned when he tried to open them. He put his fingers into his mouth and tasted sandpaper. There was no moisture, nothing to help clear his eyes; he rubbed them, but the burning felt even worse. Blind, he fumbled for his canteen and managed to get some water on his hand. It was so cold it stung; he rubbed it onto his face, then splashed the canteen over his closed eyelids. Finally, the crap cleared out and he could see again.

He checked Winston. The sergeant was still breathing.

Dixon sat back against the rocks. He heard the whine of helicopters and Hogs in the distance, or thought he did. He waited for either the helicopters or the A-10's, but the sky remained empty. After a while, he couldn't even be sure he'd heard anything. The desert had a certain hum to it, a way of being quiet that was not quite silent. That was the only sound in his ears.

He decided to scout the other hillside, see what the bombs had done. He stood and stretched some of the cold from his muscles. Winston snuffled below him, alive but oblivious.

There had been days with his mother when he waited for hours, thinking she'd open her eyes—or more likely, die. This was different, he told himself; Winston was going to make it.

Assuming Dixon figured out how to get help. He leaned back down, making sure the blankets were wrapped tightly. Then he took a few steps away, looking carefully to make sure the position was completely hidden before tracking across the ledge and down to the road.

The door to the bunker was still intact. That surprised him a little; he thought the force of the explosion would have blown it open. As he walked up the roadway, giving the mines a wide berth, he saw a huge hunk had been taken out of the side of the hill. A pile of boulders lay on the ground. Dixon guessed that the damage had been caused by several laser-guided Paveways, probably two-thousand-pounders. He began climbing the debris pile, wondering what he would see.

He was nearly to the top when he realized that any containers holding chemicals or biological agents or even nukes might have been ruptured by the blast. Which meant that the dust he was climbing through could be poisonous.

There was no sense stopping—he was probably contaminated by now anyway. If that was the case, he might just as well see what was going to kill him.

Even so, Dixon went up the rest of the way more slowly, using the M-16 as a balancing rod so he didn't have to stoop down and actually touch the dirt with his bare hands. Two feet from the lip of the crater, the rocks began to slide; he nearly lost his balance sidestepping it, and then fell face-first against the hill.

He pulled himself up through the sand and small stones to peer over the edge. He held the night viewer close to his eyes, expecting to see a smoky hole and, the way his luck had run, ruptured barrels of green and purple crud oozing with instant death.

But he saw nothing. The crater was filled with dirt, sand, and stones.

Dixon nearly threw down the viewer in disbelief. He clambered over the side of the crater and slid down, half expecting to fall through the debris into the Iraqi shelter.

He didn't. The bombs had torn the hell out of the rocks. The pipe and its shaft were gone. But the crater surface was packed harder than a runway built to handle a wing of B-52Gs. The bunker lay below, bored into the rock at the base and protected by solid stone.

Dixon found a shorter way back to the sergeant, walking up the side of the crater and across a long, narrow ledge, through a crevice, and then up a steep hill that brought him just behind the position. He was not particularly careful as he walked, letting his gun hang down and kicking small rocks indiscriminately.

He could hear the sergeant's labored breaths as he climbed the hill. They were eerily like his mother's toward the end.

He checked him. Winston hadn't moved. It occurred to Dixon that he should have left him with the gun.

It would be a gesture of respect. Like the nurse who put the lipstick on his mom's lips the very last night. He'd always remember that.

Carefully, Dixon leaned down and took Winston's Beretta out. He started to put it in the sergeant's hand, but thought better of that—some sort of muscle contraction might make him pull the trigger. So instead he set it down within easy reach, as if the sergeant had just nodded off for the night. Then he packed the blankets back around him.

The question was, what should he do next? Wait here to be rescued?

Only choice. Most likely that meant waiting until nightfall.

That wouldn't be a big problem. Winston wasn't going anywhere. The only thing Dixon had to worry about was boredom.

The Iraqis might come to check out their bunker. That was fine, as long as he and the sergeant stayed put. There was no way to see their hiding place from the road in front of the door.

He took the binoculars as well as the NOD and climbed a few feet up the hill where he had watched the battle earlier. At full magnification, he could see a wrecked APC and maybe a truck; much of the battlefield was blocked off by the terrain. He found an easy way to the top of the rocks and used the binoculars, focusing first on the area to the east of the tiny plateau they'd watched the road from yesterday. He saw an Iraqi APC, blown half apart. The back end looked like a paper shopping bag that had been twisted into a small knot; he stared at the jumbled shape next to it, wondering if it was a rock or melted metal, before realizing it was a body. A tank, its turret cocked to one side, sat a few yards away. Its gun barrel had snapped in two, and the jagged end pointed like a stubby finger toward the rest of the battlefield.

A hundred yards away in the flats near the irrigation ditches sat an American helicopter. It looked untouched—in fact, it looked like it was about to take off. But it remained perfectly still.

Then he saw a body nearby, dressed in the brown camo the commandos all wore.

One of his friends, dead. He moved his viewer around, examining the area near the aircraft, expecting to see other bodies, but finding none. He swept back around to the body, his eyes drawn to it by some inexplicable force; Dixon found himself staring at the fallen soldier, wondering who it was, thinking that the shape of the body looked like Leteri, though he couldn't be sure. He stared, and wondered if he should go and bury the body. He stared, and wondered if the man had been in a lot of pain as he died.

He stared, and then the body moved, twisting and raising his head. The man looked directly at him, and for a brief moment his face was clear in the viewer.

It was Leteri.

In the next instant, Dixon found himself running down the hill toward the highway, determined to rescue his friend.

Al Jouf
26 January 1991
0500

The flaps on the A-10A snapped tight at twenty degrees as Doberman slowed to a figurative crawl above the tarmac at Al Jouf. The Hog nudged into her landing gently, rolling along the runway like a Mercedes out for a Sunday spin. Doberman trundled quickly toward the repitting area, determined to rearm and refuel in record time so he could return north. But even as the engines wound down he could see that wasn't going to happen; a Special Ops officer was waiting to take him and Shotgun directly to Colonel Klee for a personal debriefing.

Not to mention butt-chewing, since the Hog pilots had "forgetten" to clear their flight north with him.

"You pull a stunt like that again, Glenon, and I don't care what Knowlington thinks of you, your next post is Alaska. Yeah, you're right," continued the colonel as Doberman started to open his mouth, "you saved their butts. Damn straight. You were in the right place at the right time, and that's your job. You know what I say? You were fucking big-time lucky. You pull that crap again and you're in shit-ass trouble for the rest of your career. In fact you won't have a career except replacing toilet paper in johns across Antarctica. You got that?"

Doberman had expected some grief. Even so, it was a struggle to corral his anger. "Yeah," he spat.

"Tell me what you saw at the Cornfield."

The colonel didn't even nod as Doberman spoke. While Doberman's account was in the best Hog tradition—brief and to the point, without taking credit for anything he wasn't absolutely positive about—it should still have been obvious that they had saved the day. But Klee didn't so much as hint ataboy. He told them that Hawkins, the captain in charge of Fort Apache, felt the helo left at the ambush site was worth retrieving; the colonel began peppering them with skeptical questions. Doberman felt his anger stoking up again—he half expected to be asked why he hadn't tossed down a towrope and hauled the damn thing back home.

"Keep yourselves available," said the colonel.

"Excuse me, Colonel," said Doberman. "We'd like to get back in the air right away. The planes'll be rearmed and gassed by now."

"See, our buddy's still on the ground back there," added Shotgun. "We don't want him having all the fun."

"You're to stay here until I tell you to fly. That's an order."

Only Shotgun's tug kept Doberman from exploding.

"We saved their fucking butts," he complained to Shotgun outside. "His whole fucking operation would be smoke right now if it wasn't for us. Fuck him."

"You're misinterpreting him. It's a Special Ops thing," said Shotgun. "Like tough love. The way he looks at it, he was kissing our butts."

"Yeah, well, he can fuck himself. If it wasn't Dixon up there, I swear to God, I'd fucking punch him out. Let them throw me in jail or wherever the hell they want. Shit. I have a half a mind to tell Klee to screw off and just jump in the Hog. I'll bring the kid back if I have to land on the goddamn roadway and carry him on the wings. What the hell are you laughing at?"

"Man, your ears turn bright red when you get mad. You want to go find something to eat?" Shotgun asked.

"Screw yourself," said Doberman, storming toward the planes.

Doberman was still fairly ballistic when he reached the pitting area, where the Hogs were being presided over by Rosen and the rest of the Devil Squadron crew dogs. Doberman waved at the crew members, then sat sullenly on a small folding chair near the "dragon" used to reload the Warthog's cannon.

"Whose cat did you run over?" asked Rosen.

"Excuse me?"

"You in trouble for going north, sir?"

Doberman shook his head.

"You want some coffee, Captain?" she asked.

Rosen had a roundish face with a sprinkling of freckles. Her nose seemed to lean slightly, as if it had been broken long ago in a fight. Her impish grin revealed perfect teeth, and her eyes changed color in the light, sparking green from light brown.

"Yeah," he said.

Rosen disappeared, then came back with a thermos, two cups, and a small campaign chair.

"Mind if I join you?" she asked, unfolding the chair.

"Go ahead. I'm sorry if I barked."

"Oh, you didn't bark at all," she said, pouring him a coffee. She started to hand it to him and then stopped. "Oh."

"What's wrong?"

"Well, if you're going to fly again . . ."

"Of course I'm going to fly again. Don't worry about it." He reached and took the cup. "Hey, don't worry about it. My bladder's not that small."

"Colonel was mad, huh?"

"Fucking asshole prick."

Rosen nodded. "Colonel Knowlington'll back you up."

"Yeah. If I need it."

"Damn straight. He's very fair."

She sounded as if she meant to add "for an officer," but said nothing else. Doberman couldn't help but look at her breasts. They were well hidden beneath her shirt, but not so well hidden that he couldn't notice them.

She seemed inviting. Not in a sexual way, though. In a good-comrade, fellow-squadron-mate, crew-chief kind of way.

Damn.

"How's Lieutenant Dixon?" Rosen asked. "Did you talk to him?"

"He missed the pickup. He's still up there somewhere, probably on Sugar Mountain. That's the quarry where the F-111 hit."

"He missed it?"

"He decided to stay back with a wounded man."

"Wow."

"Just like Dixon, huh? We'll get him. I'm going to fucking get him. They're working up something now."

Rosen looked worried.

"We can handle it," Doberman told her. "You don't have to worry about us. I promise."

"Excuse me, Captain," she said, tossing her coffee onto the ground. "I have to go check on something."

Rosen had a strained expression on her face, as if someone had punched her in the gut. She got up from the seat and quickly began trotting in the direction of the crew tents, probably to a bathroom, Doberman thought. Damn food was screwing up everybody's stomach.

54

The Cornfield
26 January 1991
0515

From Sugar Mountain, it had seemed as if the entire Iraqi force had been wiped out, but even before he got within a mile of the battlefield Dixon realized that wasn't true. He heard an engine turn over several times, cough, and die out; then he heard voices, a strange cacophony he assumed must be Arabic, or whatever the Iraqis spoke. Dixon began tacking south, arranging the landscape in his head as he tried to remember not only what he had seen from the mountain but what he remembered from the day before. The sun was still just below the horizon, but there was more than enough light to see without using the NOD. He left the roadway and headed for the stream the team had followed the day before, stopping every so often to try to see where the Iraqis were. The helicopter—not yet visible—should lie about a mile northeast, beyond the empty irrigation ditches.

He had gone about a quarter of a mile along the stream when the truck engine kicked and caught in the distance, roaring steadily this time. Dixon dropped to one knee, scanning with the viewer in the direction of the noise. A broken tank lay near the western edge of the small plateau. He couldn't see anything else.

Dixon moved a few hundred yards further east. Stopping, he saw figures moving beyond the shell of another wrecked vehicle. A few yards further and he had several more wrecks in view. Finally, he saw what must be the truck, back near the road. He was three quarters of a mile from it, about ten degrees to the west of due south. Dixon turned carefully and scanned the area where he thought the helicopter should be; he finally found it further to his left than he had expected, but much closer, only a few hundred yards away. The rotor and the very top of the motor housing were the only parts visible because of the topography.

He scanned around in a complete circle. Nothing was moving. Stooping, he retreated further south before turning back in the direction of the helicopter and Leteri.

He began considering contingencies. If the Iraqis put up a flare, what would he do?

Throw himself face-first on the ground, push up his M-16, and kill them all.

Yeah, right. He would keep his head. Firing first would give his position away. More than likely they wouldn't even know he was there. Even if they did, the flare wouldn't necessarily give him away.

He would hit the ground and wait for them to make the first move. And the second. Firing his weapon would be a last resort.

Dixon walked and trotted toward the helicopter, going slightly uphill, for what seemed like an eternity, though by his watch it was barely ten minutes. He crossed a dry irrigation ditch, climbed back up, and finally had the helicopter in good view. But now he couldn't see the Iraqis or the truck, though he heard its motor still coughing away.

The Little Bird looked unharmed, sitting as if it were waiting for its pilot to hop in. Even if it were in perfect working condition, though, it wouldn't make any difference to him—the only thing he knew about flying a helicopter was that it was a lot different than flying a plane.

Maybe he ought to blow it up, to keep the Iraqis from getting it.

Right.

So where the hell was Leteri? Dixon scanned down from the helo's cockpit, in front and around the aircraft and then behind it, without seeing him. He took a few steps to his right and looked again. He was now less than twenty yards away, and could see fairly well without the NOD. He used the binoculars but still couldn't pick out Leteri.

Shit. Had he even been there at all?

Dixon took another step, still using the binoculars, hoping the whole thing hadn't been a hallucination. As he took a third step, he heard the truck motor cut off. He ducked instinctively, catching a shadow he hadn't noticed before on his left and to the north across another ditch. He brought the NOD to his eyes slowly and saw there were four Iraqis there, two pointing their weapons in his general direction.

They hadn't seen him, but if he stayed here they would. Dixon began moving slowly, as quietly as possible, hoping to get on the other side of the helicopter, which he figured was what they were interested in. He took three steps and tripped, found himself skidding face-first down into the ditch. He bounced against the stones and dust of the dry creek bed, lost his gun, and then found it again as he threw himself against the bottom.

The amazing thing was, the Iraqis didn't start shooting.

The NOD and the binoculars had fallen somewhere along the way. Dixon left them, crawling and then walking sideways along the ditch, which came halfway to his chest. When the tail end of the AH-6G hulked about twenty yards away, Dixon stopped and rested on his haunches, trying both to get his eyes to see more and his heart to stop pounding so he could hear where the Iraqis were.

The Iraqi truck started up again, revving in the distance, smoother now. It roared, then backed off, then started revving wildly. He thought from the sounds that it was stuck in the sand.

He hoped that the men he had seen had gone back to help get it free.

But where the hell was Leteri? Assuming he hadn't been hallucinating, the trooper must have heard the Iraqis playing with their truck earlier and taken cover. He couldn't have gone all that far; it was just a question of finding him.

The truck screeched and ran steady. It sounded as if it were coming toward him.

Dixon gripped the M-16 tightly and continued along the dried streambed. It got progressively deeper and wider, angling away from the helicopter and battlefield. Debris had been piled in several spots; finally he moved around one and saw a shadow ahead. It moved, and he realized it was a man.

"I figured you had to be around here somewhere, Joey," he said.

The man answered with an incomprehensible shout in a language that definitely wasn't English.

55

THE CORNFIELD
26 JANUARY 1991
0530

There was a moment when he saw him clearly, saw the confusion, the question, and the plea, the small comforts and desperate wishes welling in the man's eyes. The next second Dixon had pulled the M-16's trigger, holding it there long enough for the three rounds to smoke through the Iraqi soldier's stomach and chest.

The 5.56mm slugs streaked through his vital organs so quickly that it took a moment for the blood to flood into the holes they had made. The man stumbled back, dropping his Kalashnikov, aware he was going to die, aware of it long enough to begin to shake his head.

Dixon caught his breath somewhere down around his stomach. His legs began to buckle, and only the sound of Iraqis shouting behind him kept him from collapsing. He threw himself on the side of the ditch, waiting for something to shoot at. At the top edge of the dry creek a shadow appeared, a leg that looked like a thick cornstalk. He pushed the trigger of his M-16. The man went down, but Dixon realized he had actually missed, and now he had to move, and quickly—the creek side began boiling with lead. He threw himself back and ran to his right, nearly tripping over the Iraqi he had killed. As his foot kicked the man's rifle, he heard a fresh burst of automatic weapons behind him. Dixon fell against the ground. He crawled a few feet; realizing the shooting had stopped, he hauled himself up the embankment, rolling onto the nearly flat ground behind it.

As he tried to figure out where his enemies were, they did him a favor, firing off a flare from behind the truck. He froze as it ignited, willing his body to become part of the dirt he was splayed against.

The flare began dropping above and behind the closest Iraqis. It seemed designed to help Dixon instead of them, though of course the Iraqis couldn't have known where he was, nor that they were facing only one man and not an entire platoon. Eight or nine shadows moved forward across the open ground toward the creek bed where he'd killed the first soldier. They moved at glacier speed, obviously unsure of their enemy.

He edged backwards, but dared not move too quickly or much further. When they were at the lip of the dry creek, the Iraqi soldiers split into two groups. One held its ground; the other group moved off to his left, probably intending to roll up the flank of the creek bed. He guessed they thought he was hiding in one of the piles of debris.

The men on the other side of the creek bed were all fairly close together. He could nail them and then the ones in the creek itself with the M-16's grenade launcher.

Assuming he could figure out how to fire the damn thing.

He knew how to do it. It was easy, like a shotgun.

Dixon pumped and loaded, pushed his right knee down into the dirt to brace himself, and then pushed his finger against the launcher's thin metal trigger. As he squeezed, the gun rammed into his shoulder; he threw as much of his weight against it as he could, awkwardly dancing the weapon in a half pirouette that would have been comical under other circumstances. The whishing sound of the grenade zipping through the air was followed by a deep, authoritative bang; he had missed wildly, firing at least a hundred yards beyond and well to the east of his enemies. Fortunately, the Iraqis responded with equally misplaced shots, firing not in his direction but towards the explosion. He cocked again, pointing the barrel eastward into the creek this time.

As he was about to pull the trigger, something moved to his right. He swung around to nail it, catching his finger only at the last second.

"Lieutenant, shit. What the hell are you doing here?" said Leteri, hunkering toward him.

"I almost put a grenade right through you."

"Nah, I saw your first shot. You would have missed by a mile," he said. "You don't mind if I take a whack at that, do you?"

Dixon quickly traded for Leteri's gun, an H&K MP-5. A fresh flare arced into the air in the distance, this one igniting directly overhead just as Leteri launched the grenade into the soldiers on the other side of the ditch. The corporal pumped a fresh one into the chamber and let it fly into the far end of the creek itself.

Dixon leaped to his feet. The Iraqi truck was about a hundred yards away, heading in their direction with troops behind it and its lights on. He had a clear shot at its front end; he nailed the trigger on the submachine gun straight back, running half the clip through the front of the truck. He pushed the barrel upwards, working his aim with his body as if he were firing the cannon in the Hog, smashing the radiator and the hood and then the glass. He stopped firing, saw something move to the left of the truck, and emptied the rest of the clip at it.

He ducked down as he ejected, reaching to his pocket to reload, forgetting that he had only M-16 cartridges.

"They're out of ammo," said Leteri.

"What?"

"They just wasted their clips."

"They were firing?"

"The whole time," said the sergeant, passing him a pair of the

MP-5's long clips. "Now would be a good time for a strategic retreat, don't you think?"

"Okay," said Dixon. He jumped up.

"Whoa, Lieutenant. Afraid I can't go very fast," said Leteri, grabbing him. He pointed to his side, caked with a black substance that looked like tar. There was a second blotch on his leg. "My heard hurts too."

"Lean on my shoulder," Dixon told him, running back. "Wait—maybe we ought to blow up the helicopter first. You got more grenades in that thing?"

"Let's not fuck around."

Dixon hesitated for a second, unsure. Then something moved on the other side of the creek. That cinched it—he scooped down and backed into Leteri. "Get on. Let's go."

The soldier started to say something, but before he finished, Dixon had him on his back.

"Just hang on," Dixon said, starting to trot. "And try not to bleed on my uniform. I had it dry-cleaned yesterday."

"In that case I'll puke on you too," said Leteri as Dixon waddled away from the battlefield.

56

King Fahd
26 January 1991
0530

Colonel Knowlington wasn't terribly surprised to find Mongoose in Cineplex, even though it was relatively early. While there was no one else in the squadron room, he decided to talk to him down the hall in his office. Mongoose's grin practically lit the way.

"So?" asked the major as Skull closed the door.

"Sit down and relax."

"Colonel, look—"

"I want to ask you something first."

Mongoose's expression quickly changed. He was once more the solid-faced, on-guard DO who had done so much of Knowlington's work during the first weeks of the squadron's creation and deployment.

"What's your wife think of you staying over here?" Knowlington asked him.

"Does it matter?"

"It might."

"She thinks it's great," said Mongoose.

"You haven't told her, have you?"

"She'll go along with what I think is right."

Knowlington pushed his fingers along his left ear, then around to his neck. Truth was, he still hadn't made up his mind. It was going to take a lot to keep the major with the squadron, though he had no doubt he could pull the strings.

What he doubted was whether it was the right thing to do.

"Why don't you want to go back?" he asked. "Are you afraid?"

"I can't really explain it," said Mongoose.

"Don't you love your kid? I'm not trying to insult you, Goose. But what you're asking—it's unusual."

"I love my wife and my son. Shit, he was just born. Of course I love him. And I want to see him too. But not yet. Not until this is over."

There was pain on the major's face.

"I can't explain it," said Mongoose. "They're all I've thought about since I've been here. But to go to them now, it feels wrong. It feels like I'm running away when I have a hell of a lot more to do."

"It's not your fault you got shot down. I'm serious."

"Look, I ought to stay until this thing is over. Don't you think? How long can it last?"

Under other circumstances, Knowlington would have laughed for quite a while. Instead, he only said, "We thought that about Vietnam too."

"This isn't then."

"I know. Thank God."

It wasn't Vietnam, truly. Knowlington couldn't think of anything else to say, and Mongoose had obviously told him as much as he would—and maybe as much as he could.

"What about it?" the major asked.

"If you want to stay with the squadron, here, doing what you can, I don't see that I can really deny that request," said Knowlington slowly. "In a lot of ways, I owe it to you. But I'm going to have to get it cleared. You can expect half-a-million people to show up on your doorstep with questions."

"I can handle them."

Skull scratched his chin. "I have to be honest with you, Goose. I'm not exactly sure I'm making the right decision here."

"You are," said the major. And with that, he got up and practically ran from the office.

57

Fort Apache
26 January 1991
0605

The commandos owned the night, but the day belonged to the Iraqis. Any of a thousand things might give the commandos away, a passing Bedouin, a flyover by an Iraqi plane. They had lookouts covering the approaches and had the highway under surveillance for nearly twenty miles, but the general plan for dealing with the day was to lay low, hiding and sleeping as much as possible.

But Hawkins wasn't about to sleep. Nor did he think about the danger they were in, or his injuries. He was determined to get the helicopter and the men he'd left behind back. And he started working out a plan as soon as his AH-6G, now officially dubbed Apache One, touched down on the weathered concrete.

Apache One had been hit in several places, including its fuel tank; while they were lucky that the bullet or shrapnel hadn't ignited the fuel, the damage itself was minimal and easily repaired. More serious were the hits the electronics and rear rotor assembly had taken. His men could patch a fuel tank and bang out damaged metal under the direction of their injured mechanic, but they didn't know very much about electronics or propulsion systems.

The mechanic's splints made it tough for him to inspect, let alone repair, the damage. He was a gamer, but he didn't look in particularly good shape, and he was clearly exhausted after only a half hour's work.

It would be a bitch for him to get the downed chopper working if there was a serious problem with it. And if something went wrong with Apache One on the way, they would be truly fucked.

Colonel Klee had promised at least two more technicians; Hawkins decided to open the line to Al Jouf and find out if they were coming. He gave Klee the good news first—the Blue and Green teams had reported in; two Scud erectors and missiles had been smashed overnight.

"So how are we getting our helo back?" said the colonel in response.

"We'll get it," said Hawkins. "Am I getting those mechanics?"

"We're working on it," said Klee. "You have a runway yet?"

"In two hours, I'll have fifteen hundred feet."

"Too short."

"Can you send a Pave Low?"

"Not this morning, no way. Maybe tonight or tomorrow night, if then."

"Too long," said Hawkins. "If you have the mechanics, parachute them in."

"In daylight?"

"I'll take the risk," said Hawkins. "I'm not sure about getting the helo fixed without them."

"It's not yours to take. I'm also not crazy about breaking someone else's leg."

"Do a tandem if they're not jump-qualified."

"Easier said than done."

"But you do have the mechanics?"

"I said I'm working on it."

Hawkins frowned but said nothing. The colonel clearly didn't have anyone.

"We should have a BDA report on the mountain bunker in an hour," Klee told him. "I'll get back to you. Sit tight until I do."

58

NEAR SUGAR MOUNTAIN
26 JANUARY 1991
0643

Dixon carried Leteri a few hundred yards until they were sure they weren't being followed. Leteri managed to do fairly well the rest of the way on his own, though they had to stop a dozen times. The last time Dixon didn't think he'd be able to get going again; Leteri actually pulled him to his feet and gave him a push to help him along.

He told Leteri about the bombing raid and Leteri told him about the action at the Cornfield. An explosion, probably a mortar shell, had knocked the sergeant unconscious. He had a hazy memory of the Hogs attacking and the second chopper appearing, but he had blacked out again in there somewhere. When he finally regained his senses he was near the downed Little Bird; he had no idea how he'd managed to drag himself there, since it was quite some distance from where he'd been hit. When he heard the Iraqis fiddling with the truck, he went and hid in the creek. He had heard Dixon challenge the Iraqi soldier.

"I didn't challenge him," Dixon said. "Hell, I almost shook his hand, thinking he was you."

"Then you killed him."

"Yeah."

"First time?"

"Well, I got that helicopter when the air war started. Those guys probably died too. Except, you know, I didn't think about it. I was flying. I never really saw them. Not as people."

"First time for me today too. Except I didn't see them," said Leteri.

Dixon thought about the look in the man's face for only a second, then banished it, concentrating on keeping his momentum up. He felt as if a fire had started in the back of his head; it burned there to keep him going. His hunger was gone and he was beyond feeling numb or tired. His gut had grown raw with the will of survival.

"How are we going to take that bunker out if the bombs didn't?" Leteri asked as they got closer.

"I don't know that we are."

"We have to somehow."

"Yeah." Dixon walked silently. They were about a quarter of a mile from the road, on the opposite side from Sugar Mountain. He was more worried about traffic finding them than doing anything about the shelter. There was plenty of light and they had little cover on this side of the road.

"What do you think?" Leteri asked. "The grenade launcher?"

"Grenade's not going through that door. Turk said the C-4 wouldn't even take it out. Besides, we got other problems."

"Captain'll come for us, if that's what you're thinking. I know Hawkins. He won't give up. And neither will our colonel. He's a prick, but he's a good prick."

About a half mile from the quarry, they rested at a small group of rocks a few yards from the highway. Dixon paused for only a second, rocking his body back and forth. "I'm going to go scout the quarry," he told Leteri. "There's a back way up to the sergeant a few yards ahead. I'll make sure it's clear."

"I'm gonna come," said Leteri. "My side doesn't hurt as much as it did."

"Better to hang here," Dixon told him. "There's a hell of a lot of climbing this way, and if you go the other way, you'll be in full view of anything that comes down the road."

"I'll be all right."

Dixon examined the H&K. The fire in his head was burning steadily now; his eyes had narrowed their focus the way they did the last few seconds on a bomb run in a Hog. "You stay here," he said. "I'll be back. Take the morphine if the pain gets too much."

Without waiting for Leteri to answer, Dixon began trotting toward the highway, clutching the small submachine gun close to his side. The sun had started to warm the air; for a second, he felt as if he were running along the beach at his town lake, trotting for an ice cream or maybe back to the car for the stereo.

Then he heard the rattle of a truck. He dashed across the highway and headed for the back of the hill where he'd left Sergeant Winston. As he did, a small pickup truck crowded with soldiers appeared from the shadow of Sugar Mountain, kicking up dust and skidding to a stop across the middle of the road. Dixon threw himself behind the rocks, his heart lost somewhere in the dirt as the soldiers jumped out and took up positions all along the highway, less than ten yards away.

59

AL JOUF
26 JANUARY 1991
0650

Even though the tent was empty, it was hardly private; anyone could walk in at any time. And yet she couldn't control herself. For her entire military service, Rebecca Ann Rosen had steeled herself against exactly this open vulnerability and nakedness. But she was helpless now, sitting on the edge of the cot and shaking like a windup toy.

There were no tears at least, or hardly any. But the shaking was nearly as bad. It wasn't as if there was anything between her and Lieutenant Dixon, anything more than a single kiss stolen at one vulnerable moment. He might not even remember who she was.

That was nonsense. Of course he did. But he wouldn't think anything of it, or at least he would be surprised, maybe shocked, to see her like this.

And yet she couldn't stop.

I'm a useless blob, she told herself, pulling her arms across her chest. Stop. This isn't helping him. It isn't helping anyone.

But she kept shaking until she managed to think about the capo di capo.

That brought her back to center. Sergeant Clyston was the closest thing to a father she'd ever had. He was closer to her than her mother even.

Rosen saw Clyston's face now in the tent, the way he would cock his head at her and push his lower lip tight against the top. "F'ing hell," he'd say. "Rosen, there's a ton-load of work to be done yesterday. Get your butt in gear and see what needs to be done," he'd say.

"Yes, Sergeant. Right away, Sergeant," she'd say.

And so she did. She pushed her arms down to her side and took a huge breath, ending the shaking for good. Then she took out a small makeup mirror and checked her eyes and face.

She took another breath and got off the cot.

The two Devil Squadron Hogs—her Hogs—were ready to go. But there would be something else for her and her men to do, plenty. And in the meantime, she'd try to come up with something to wring more time on station for the Hogs. Tinman might have an idea; he was always good for some trick that had worked back in the Dark Ages before screwdrivers were invented. Actually, there was an even simpler solution: The A-10As had three hard-points plumbed for external fuel tanks. While the idea of using them to extend range had been rejected for several reasons at different points, it might be worth reconsidering, assuming they could get a few tanks out here. Rosen decided to check with Sergeant Clyston about it before going to Doberman; no use making a pitch for something she couldn't do. She headed for the command bunker, hoping that one of the colonel's men could set something up for her.

She found the colonel himself, frowning at an Army captain. Even though the two men were still talking, the colonel motioned her forward.

"Sergeant?" he said.

"Sir, begging your pardon, I was wondering if we could arrange a landline back to my chief. I, we, I didn't intend on bothering you with this, sir, but I was hoping to squeeze more time on station out of the Hogs and wanted to get his input, sir."

Rosen had thrown more than the mandatory number of "sirs"

in the air, and the colonel seemed at least partly amused. "You have to run down Major Mosely," he told her. "He'll set you up. Sergeant, let me ask you something—any of your crew know anything about helicopter electronics?"

"What electronics?"

The Army captain gave the colonel a look Rosen knew all too well—it meant, *See what happens when you ask a girl a serious question?*

She stifled her urge to forearm the bastard. "Sir, I've worked on the Pave Low systems, if that's what you have in mind," Rosen said, her eyes fixed on the idiot captain. "I've served as an instructor."

"What do you know about AH-6Gs?" asked the colonel.

"Based on the McDonnell Douglas 500M, they're powered by Alison gas turbines. The electronics suite is contemporary."

"Contemporary?" said the captain.

"It will do. It's Army." She shrugged. "You can't expect perfection. The power plant's a nice piece of machinery, though. Well done."

The captain started to say something that would undoubtedly have not been very pleasant, but the colonel stopped him. She could tell that Colonel Klee was the sort of officer who didn't smile much; nonetheless, he had the beginnings of a grin on his face.

"You know a lot about that aircraft?" the colonel asked.

"A fair amount, sir. It's not my specialty."

"You think you could help get one of those things in the air?" the colonel asked her.

"Sir, I'll bust my butt doing anything you want."

"That's not the question, Sergeant. Can you fix helicopters?"

"If there's a problem with the electronics I can take a shot at it. I don't know much about the weapons suite at all. That's Army, and I don't mean that disrespectfully. As far as the base-model mechanics, I helped overhaul Kawasaki license-built versions in Japan. I can fix the engine, that's nothing. Engines were where I started, and like I say, that's a nice piece of work, that one."

The colonel nodded.

"So where is it?" Rosen asked.

"Two hundred and fifty miles north of here," said the captain with a snide grin. "In Iraq."

"All right—Apache," she said, making a fist and swinging it in the air. "Let's go!"

The captain had undoubtedly expected her to faint if not burst into tears. But even the colonel was surprised by her reaction.

"Sergeant, did you understand what the captain just said?" he asked.

"Oh, he's just an asshole who thinks women don't belong in the service. Don't worry about him. He probably couldn't fix a flat tire. When am I leaving?"

60

Al Jouf
26 January 1991
0650

Doberman tried to work off his frustration by taking a walk around the base, but that was about as effective as using gasoline to douse a fire. When he realized he was starting to rant at an F-16 that was landing with battle damage for no other reason than the fact that it was a pointy-nose fast jet, he decided to take a different tack and went over to the Special Ops mess area.

Masters of the fine art of combat supply, the troopers had laid out an extensive breakfast spread that included fresh eggs and what at least smelled like fresh ham. Doberman helped himself to a bagel and pineapple jelly and sat at a small table. He had managed only a single bite when the gaunt figure of Tinman appeared before him, wagging a finger.

"A caul isk signk," said the crewman. His lips were bluish and his cheeks caved in; his white hair flared up as if an invisible wind blew through it. He looked like a portrait of the Ancient Mariner, tied to a lost ship's bowsprit.

Make that the Ancient Mechanic.

"A caul isk signk," he repeated.

"What the hell are you talking about?" said Doberman.

"He's telling you you were born with a caul," said a Special Forces sergeant, coming over with a tray. The man, not quite as tall as Tinman but nearly as lean, smiled and said something to the Air Force technician. Tinman's eyes widened, and the men began a conversation that Doberman swore was encrypted with a 64-byte key.

"So what the hell are you two talking about?" Doberman finally asked.

The sergeant gave him an apologetic smile. "Like I said, you were born with a caul."

"What the hell does that mean?"

"Well, for one thing, it means you fight demons. Well, you know."

Tinman nodded approvingly.

"No, I don't know," said Doberman. "What the hell language are you talking with him?"

"It's not really a language. Kind of a patois. Name's Joe Kidrey. I'm from Louisiana. Bayou country. Backwoods, though, even for there." The sergeant sat down across from Doberman. Tinman stood behind him, hovering like a shadow.

"Is that where you're from, Tinman? Louisiana?"

Doberman's question drew a short but indecipherable response.

"He says not exactly. Apparently it's a long story," Kidrey said. "I assume you don't want to hear it."

"No. But what's this caul all about?"

Kidrey scratched his eyebrow and gave Doberman an embarrassed smile. "It's this birth-membrane thing, comes out sometimes on a baby's face when he's born. My mom's a midwife. I guess you see it every so often."

"And I had one?"

The sergeant nodded. "Oh, yeah."

"How the hell would he know?"

"Oh, the old-timers know." Kidrey gave a half shrug. "Sometimes there's a birthmark."

"I don't have a birthmark."

The sergeant did the shrug again. "Anyway, the old-timers, I guess the thing is, it used to be rare to survive that, you know, at least without problems, so these myths built up."

"What are we talking about here, voodoo?"

Kidrey shook his head quickly, but not fast enough to keep the Tinman from launching into what even Doberman understood as an agitated denunciation.

"I'm sorry, relax, relax," Doberman told him. "You're going to have a heart attack. Shit."

Kidrey said something and Tinman calmed down. The Special Forces sergeant gave the pilot a wink, then turned back to the Ancient Mechanic and asked him a few more questions. Words flew back and forth, punctuated by nods and deep gestures. Doberman felt as if he had stepped into a carnival sideshow.

"Now I'm not saying I believe any of this, you understand," Kidrey told Doberman when the conversation ended. "But, did, uh, the sergeant here give you a cross or something?"

"He gave it to my wingmate. I don't believe in that superstitious crap."

"Oh."

Doberman didn't like his tone, but before he could say anything, Kidrey turned back to Tinman and resumed their coded talk. It was amazing to Doberman that someone as skilled as the Tinman—whose mechanical genius was obviously the only reason the off-the-wall fuel drop worked—could believe in witchcraft.

Or whatever the hell they were patoising about.

Kidrey finally turned back to Doberman with an apologetic smile. "Thing is, Captain, and like I say, I don't necessarily believe this, okay? But some of the old-timers, they see the world as kind of two parts. There's us, and then there's this whole other thing, spirits you'd call it. A few people can go back and forth."

"Back and forth what?"

Kidrey shrugged. "It's hard to explain, especially if, you know, you're not one of them."

"What's it got to do with me?"

"Well." Kidrey laughed. "I'm not saying it does."

"But Tinman does."

"See, the old-timers believe people with cauls are kind of special. They got the power. Like karma or something."

Doberman nearly choked. "You're talking about luck?"

"That's not it," said Kidrey, shaking his hand quickly. Tinman looked as if he was going to stoke up again, but the sergeant leaned back and put his hand on his arm, calming him. "They think it's power. Not luck. Definitely not luck."

"And I got it?"

"Oh, yeah, big-time. See, stuff like that cross he gave you is supposed to focus it. The whole thing comes from Europe or Africa or somewhere. I haven't a clue. The word my mom used means nightwalker in kind of pig-French. Don't use that word," he hissed quickly.

"What word?"

"The one you were going to use. With a W?"

Doberman had, in fact, been going to ask if Kidrey's mother was a witch. Instead, he glanced at Tinman, then leaned across the table and lowered his voice. "I don't want to get Tinman twisted up again, but you don't believe in this bullshit, do you?"

"Well," whispered the sergeant back, "I would say it's kind of in the category of stuff that couldn't hurt. You know, like throwing salt over your shoulder, lucky pennies, that kind of stuff. If you know what I mean."

Doberman leaned back. Tinman was nodding, a very satisfied look on his face.

The entire fucking world had gone nuts.

"Thing is, I *have* seen some stuff I can't explain," added Kidrey. "So you never know."

The Tinman pointed his crooked finger at Doberman. His eyes grew large and his cheeks began to inflate. Undoubtedly a huge pronouncement was on the way. That or the geezer was going to have a heart attack, which would screw them big-time.

"All right, all right, I'll take the goddamn cross," said Doberman. "Shit."

The Tinman's smile could have lit an airfield.

61

Al Jouf
26 January 1991
0705

As Wong had suspected, the bombs had not been sufficient to penetrate the bunker. He was annoyed, though not surprised, that his advice hadn't been directly solicited on targeting; it had been his experience at Black Hole that no one there appreciated his abilities.

Be that as it may, he had a relatively straightforward solution—take out the doors, which he calculated could be done with as little as 130 kg of high explosive.

It was beyond the doors that things got complicated. His experience with Russian sites featuring these door types told him that they led directly to a concrete-reinforced hallway precisely three meters long. At the end of the hallway—which had generally started as a mine shaft and been adapted—there would be a stairwell at an exact ninety-degree angle. It would contain twenty steps downward to the storage area in the direction of the passive ventilation pipe. From there any of three different configurations was typically employed. The result was the same, however—an isolated storage area. He now tentatively identified the materials being placed there as biological, thanks to an admittedly third-hand description of a truck and single courier that had appeared at the facility. He hesitated drawing conclusions from the absence of protective gear; the Iraqis had uniformly proven idiotic. Indeed, the incident could be viewed as a Rorschach.

"Which means what exactly?" asked Colonel Klee, who had sat through the briefing with uncharacteristic patience.

"Which means that it means whatever the interpreter wants it to mean," said Wong. "It's open to many possibilities."

"Like?"

Wong sighed. It was always such a chore briefing people outside their area of specialty.

"It could be that they assume we would notice a large force and they want to remain inconspicuous. It could mean that they were delivering lunch or paperwork or perhaps orders to someone inside, though I assure you this is an unmanned facility. It could and most likely means that they are simply stupid."

"There are definitely weapons there?"

"I didn't say that. I said there is a strong possibility. There are only indications and inferences. If they respond to the bombing, that would be another strong indication."

"You're talking like a goddamn intelligence officer again, Wong. I don't like it."

"With all due respect, you asked for my opinion. As far as being an intelligence officer, let me remind you that I am attached to Admiral—"

"All right, I don't want your goddamn Pentagon job classification again. How we going to blow this thing up?"

"If we merely block the stairway with enough rocks we will accomplish the same thing," said Wong. "And we can do so quite simply, though admittedly there will be a high coefficient of variables beyond skill involved."

"What the fuck are you talking about?"

"I think he's trying to say it'll take some luck," said Major Wilson.

It was the first time Wong had heard him say anything intelligent since they met, and he nodded before describing his plan.

Wong's preferred solutions called for an F-117A Nighthawk flying a pair of Paveways through the doors. The difficulty for the Paveways was in the first shot; if it was off target, it could trigger a landslide that would effectively protect the interior from the second explosion. Unlike a crushing blow inside, exterior damage could be removed easily and would present only a nuisance. The warhead of the Paveways was actually a bit bigger than optimum, and not perfectly shaped for this application. But the F-117's had a very limited choice of weapons if their stealth profile was to be maintained.

"What's your less preferred way?" asked the colonel.

"A Maverick model G could pierce the door, if it hit precisely three fourths of the way up," said Wong. "There is an advantage in that weapon since it is unlikely to trigger a shock wave of sufficient size to block the entrance, even if it's a little off-target. But the second missile has to follow no later than two seconds to take advantage of the initial shock and avoid the likely rockfall. While this could be theoretically accomplished—"

"Fine," said the colonel. "You check this with the A-10 pilots?"

"It was not my preferred option," said Wong. "Although the A-10As are equipped to fire the Mavericks, without the addition of a LANTIRN targeting system—"

"Can it be done?"

"Of course, but—"

"Well, make it happen," said the colonel. His tone suddenly changed, becoming almost charming.

Almost.

"But before you do, Wong, tell me something—you parachuted into North Korea with that Gregory Team, didn't you?"

Wong shuddered at the memory. He hadn't been able to find anything to eat but fish and MREs the whole two weeks in-country.

"Yes, sir."

"As a matter of fact, you have a class D skydiver's license and a jumpmaster's ticket, don't you?"

"I have done some skydiving, yes, sir."

"Oh, that's more than some," said the colonel. "That's more than most of my men. You're current?"

"I believe I am."

"You're too modest, Wong." The colonel shook his head, as if that were something he had never expected to hear himself say. "That Korean jump was a tandem jump, as a matter of fact, wasn't it?"

"As it happened."

"I like you, Wong. I really do. I want you to find Sergeant Hillup after you brief the pilots. I have another mission for you. Not quite as exciting as Afghanistan or Korea, I'll bet, let alone your Vietnam foray last year, but it ought to keep you awake."

"With all due respect—"

"This is right up your alley, Wong. Turns out you're the only person in my command qualified for a tandem jump that I can actually spare to make one. We lost our last mechanic on a static-line solo jump because he didn't know how to steer and hit the ground too hard. I can't take any more chances. We need someone who can do a tandem and set her down gently."

"Her who?" managed Wong.

"Sergeant Rosen." The colonel grinned. "You're going to deliver her to Fort Apache."

62

Sugar Mountain
26 January 1991
0712

Dixon rolled over, waiting for the Iraqis to appear. Instead, the truck screeched around in a circle and headed back in the direction it had come. He couldn't tell whether the soldiers had climbed back in or stayed, and for the moment didn't care. Scrambling to his feet, he proceeded as quickly and as quietly he could up the craggy slope.

The back of the hill could not be seen from the roadway or most of the quarry, but turning the corner to get back around to the spot where Winston was, Dixon was totally exposed. He hesitated, spotting the top of a vehicle or something near the entrance to the bunker; finally he felt he couldn't wait any longer and just went for it, crouching low and using the MP-5 for balance. He reached the rocks and slid in, just barely missing the prone body of the gravely wounded sergeant as he rolled onto his knees and craned his neck up to catch a glimpse of the enemy below. He saw the turret of a tank at the head of the path.

Then he felt the cold barrel of a gun at his neck.

"About time you got back," rasped Winston beneath him.

• • •

The sergeant could move his arms, but little else. He said he was cold. His legs ached as badly as the rest of his body; Dixon figured that was a good sign.

"I was worried you guys just left me," Winston told him. "I've been hearing these trucks for a half hour at least, but couldn't see what the fuck was going on."

"I wasn't leaving you," said Dixon. "I had to get Leteri."

"Where the hell is that weasel?"

Dixon explained what had happened. He then crawled back to survey the Iraqi forces from the rocks, exposed but just barely.

As Turk had suspected, the Iraqis had positioned the mines to enhance preplanned defensive positions. Dixon could see part of a tank—he guessed T-72—on Sugar Mountain's driveway. It was about fifty yards away on a diagonal, and to see more than just the gun and top of the turret he had to stand and expose himself fully, which he naturally didn't want to do. He had a better view of a second tank at the far end of the quarry near the highway, even though it was two hundred yards or so away. Four or five Iraqi soldiers milled around behind it; he assumed that the group included the commander, since men kept approaching and then leaving.

He hadn't seen any antiair defenses. Thirty seconds worth of Hog action and these bastards would be toast.

But he wasn't in an A-10. He might just as well fantasize about being on a beach with Christie Brinkley.

If the commandos came back for them, could they take out the tanks? If the Hogs flew cover for them, they could. It'd be a piece of cake.

Except for him and Wilson, who'd be right in the middle of the action.

Winston would be. Dixon could still get away. Once he was off the ledge, he could probably get back around the hill. If he trekked west a ways, he could find a spot to cross the road to Leteri without being seen.

But that meant leaving the sergeant, and that was unacceptable.

Dixon sized up the Iraqi defense. How much of it was blocked from his view? Half? A quarter? Was there another tank or three more? Mobile SAMs? Self-propelled triple-A?

His fingers were wrapped so tightly around the MP-5 that he had to pry them free with his other hand, then try to shake them back to flexibility. The fear of being spotted kept pumping adrenaline through his body, but he was tired as hell and ached everywhere. Dixon couldn't have eaten if he tried, but he was thirsty, and though he told himself it was better to ration sips of water, he found his eyes constantly wandering to the canteen at his belt. Finally he couldn't stand it, and slid back into the shelter next to Wilson to get a drink.

The sergeant's arm twitched, jerking the pistol to the side.

"Sergeant? You okay?"

The trooper didn't answer. His eyes had closed again. Dixon leaned down; for a moment he thought Wilson had died, but then he heard the sergeant's chest rattle with fluid as he breathed. He reached over to his forehead, gently placing the back of his hand against it to see if he had a fever. He didn't seem to, though as he pulled his hand back Dixon realized his fingers were so numb he might not be able to tell. He rubbed them together and then edged himself hard against the rocks, trying to find a semi-comfortable spot where he could remain hidden but see some of the Iraqi soldiers below.

A half hour later, the lieutenant heard the distant whine of an approaching jet. Several planes had passed far overhead during the last two hours, but he knew right away this one was different—it was low and it was coming right toward them. The sound increased exponentially, and even as the ground started to shake the jet was overhead and gone, fleeing so quickly that Dixon got no more than a glimpse of its shadow. He guessed that it was a recon plane, most likely a British Tornado tasked for BDA or bomb damage assessment.

The Iraqis behind the far tank threw themselves on the ground. They got up chattering, but they didn't seem to be congratulating themselves on their good fortune. The commander pointed and shouted, and Dixon saw two of the men run to the parked truck beyond the tank at the edge of the highway. They took something out and began climbing up the side of the mountain toward the bomb crater.

They were still in view when he heard something move on the hillside behind him. He swung around, pulling up the submachine gun, cursing himself for not keeping a better guard.

He just barely managed to keep himself from putting a half-dozen rounds through Leteri's face.

"Thought I'd see how you were making out," said Leteri, ducking down to cover.

"That's twice today I almost shot you," said Dixon.

"Put me out of my misery." He unclenched his teeth and smiled briefly. "I'm all right," he told Dixon. "Took me forever to realize there was only one guard watching the whole back end of the quarry. I got around him easy, but I kept worrying about running into someone else. Guess they don't know we're here, huh? How's Winston?"

"He goes in and out."

"That plane ours?"

"Yeah. He was checking for damage," Dixon told him. "They'll hit the bunker again. But before they do, we have to remove a slight impediment."

"What's that?" asked Leteri.

"Two of our friends over there just hauled something up the hill with them. I didn't get a good look, but my bet is that it was a shoulder-fired missile, probably an SA-16. Anything comes back, it's going down."

Al Jouf
26 January 1991
0730

"You're out of your gourd, Wong. No way anybody can guarantee those shots," said Shotgun. He shook his head and jerked his thumb back toward Doberman. "I don't even think the Dog Man could do it, and he's best Mav gunner in the stinking Air Force. Mr. AGM."

"I attempted to point out the difficulty involved," said Wong. "But the colonel—"

"I can do it," said Doberman. "I set up on the way in and hand off without firing, get both nailed down, dial back, and bing-bang-bam."

"Two seconds?"

"Precisely 1.8 would be optimum," said Wong.

"And you're going to get a solid aim point with the infrared?" said Shotgun. "Exactly three quarters of the way up?"

"Don't sweat it," said Doberman. Part of him knew that even physically hitting the buttons quickly enough to get the shot off fast enough was nearly impossible.

Another part of him knew he was going to do it. And fuck everybody else.

Including and especially Klee.

Shotgun, for maybe the first time he'd known him, was temporarily speechless. And Wong . . .

Wong was incapable of such a condition, unfortunately.

"There is a significant error coefficient," Wong said. He had a pained expression that made it clear he was about to barf up a dissertation.

"Tell me about it later," said Doberman. He turned toward the Hog pit area. "Let's go talk to Rosen and make sure the planes get a last-minute tweak."

"I'm afraid she won't be available," said Wong. "The sergeant and I are relocating."

"Where you going?" asked Shotgun.

"North," said Wong. "Very far north."

"I'm going to do you the biggest favor of your life, Captain, and forget every fucking word you just told me." Colonel Klee pushed his words out in a perfect imitation of the Big Bad Wolf blowing down one of the pigs' straw houses. "You get your fanny in gear and you do your job. I'll worry about who goes where, why, and how."

Doberman didn't bother biting his teeth together, or taking a breath, or counting to ten, or any of the one million things he'd done in his life to try and keep his temper under control.

They never worked anyway.

"Squadron personnel are my responsibility," he said. "And Rosen—"

"I expect that door down before 1100 hours. You got that?"

"Screw you."

"What?"

"Screw you."

Doberman stormed out of the command post so hot his head probably would have melted metal. Shotgun, who'd been waiting outside, had to run to keep up.

"Colonel didn't appreciate your pointing out to him that Rosen's female, huh?" said Shotgun.

Doberman didn't answer.

"Kind of funny if she becomes a war hero, don't you think?" Shotgun began trotting to keep up.

Doberman wasn't quite sure where he was going to go. He wanted to hop into the Hog and take it straight north to Baghdad and give Saddam a Maverick enema.

Then he'd come back and do the same for Klee, the shithead.

"You sure you want to take both shots? I mean, I know you can make them, that's not what I'm talking about," said Shotgun. "Hey, for a little guy, you sure walk fast."

Doberman stopped short. "Who the hell says I'm little?"

"I do."

"Screw yourself," said Doberman, walking again, this time even faster.

"You got to play cards with me tonight," said Shotgun behind him. "I figure we can win enough for a couple of nightscopes. These guys think Baseball's something you do with a bat."

Doberman had known Shotgun for a long time, and there was no one he would rather fly with. O'Rourke was the best wingman in the Air Force, period. But there were times when he was just too much to take. He was always making a joke about something, or finding some way to bend the rules in his favor, or just ignoring them. It wasn't just that he flouted convention; he thought the laws of physics were optional.

"Screw you, Shotgun," Doberman said. "We got to get in the air, right now, and I don't want any more of your bullshit."

"Hey, Dog Man, hold up," said Shotgun, trotting beside him. "Yo, man, you got to calm down a bit."

"I am calm."

"Listen, Dog." Shotgun's fat fingers grabbed his biceps like a vice. Doberman swung around, ready to slug his friend for joking around.

But the look on his face stopped him. Shotgun's words came flat and calm and cold, as direct as the arc of a bomb on a ninety-degree drop.

"Your job now is to stay level," said Captain O'Rourke. "You're going to be the squadron Director of Operations when we get back to the Home Drome. You and I both know it. Everybody's going to depend on you. You can't let your anger go like you used to. Shit, Dixon and those Special Ops guys are depending on you. Me too." He tightened his fingers on Doberman's arm. "I got your six. No matter what. That's for real. But you level off."

"Yeah, I know," said Doberman. He pulled his arm free. "Damn. I'm pissed."

"I couldn't tell."

"What?"

"Nothin'," said Shotgun.

"You're looking at me like you got a question."

"You sure you can make those shots?"

"In my sleep," said Doberman.

"That's what I'm talking about."

Doberman started walking again. Truth was, it was hard for him to stay pissed at Shotgun. It was hard for him to stay pissed at anyone. Except Saddam and Klee.

He could do the shots. It was physically impossible, but who the hell cared. Line 'em up and spin the bottle. One-two, bing-bang-bam.

He'd have to lose the thumb thing, though. Bad habit anyway. Just a tic. Where the hell had it come from, anyway? It was a superstition—bullshit.

"Here's what we're going to do," Doberman told Shotgun as they walked. "We get the Hogs gassed and we support the helos at their cow field or whatever the damn pickup is."

"Cornfield."

"Yeah, good. We load up for bear, help them get their helo, and make sure Dixon's okay, then we nail the motherfucker door."

"You sure we have the fuel to do all that?" Shotgun asked.

"No problem."

"We don't get Sugar Mountain the colonel's going to be mad, no?"

"You want to hit it while Dixon's still there?"

"No way."

"Then we better make sure he gets out, right?"

"That's what I'm talking about."

Walking made Doberman feel better. So did having a plan. So did knowing he was going to get Dixon the hell out of that shit.

"Hey, listen, I'm sorry," he told Shotgun.

"Yeah, my ass you're sorry."

"I got the shots," Doberman told him. "No offense, but you know I'm better than you."

"I ain't offended, Dog Man. You're Mr. AGM."

"You got that cross thing Tinman gave you?"

"Um, well, kinda."

"Kinda?"

"The little doohickey spring that connects to the batteries in my CD player snapped. I thought it was the batteries, but it was just the spring."

"You used the cross to make the connection?"

"Hey, it's silver. Best conductor in the world. But listen, I can probably find something else."

It was just a goddamn superstition.

"Don't worry about it," said Doberman. He took a step and stopped, then reached down and yanked off his boot.

"Yow, what a stench," yelped Shotgun. "Whoa—what the hell are you doing?"

Doberman held the small penny he'd found on the tarmac the first day of the airwar.

Luck? Power? Spirit world? Nightwalkers?

All bullshit.

He flung the coin into the desert.

64

Over Fort Apache
26 January 1991
0835

This wasn't going to be too bad. Sure, the ground looked like a splatch of her grandma's old blankets and her teeth were already chattering with the cold, but Rosen was sure she could make the jump. Captain Wong claimed to have done this hundreds of times, and Wong wasn't the type to exaggerate.

Which cast his comments about the location of the base in a certain light that was hard to ignore, though she was trying her best to.

A lone crewman waited with them in the rear of the MC-130E. The plane had dipped to ten thousand feet and started a banking turn, which Wong had warned her would signal they were approaching the drop zone. She cinched the strap on her helmet and put her hands up as the captain snugged their two-place harness tight; there was no backing out now.

He nudged her, and Rosen began waddling over to the rear ramp. A Herc crewman lugged her packed tool kit, which had its own parachute and static line, alongside them. Rosen had expected to be almost sucked out of the plane, but standing on the open ramp, she felt no more pressure than she might have on a diving board.

Nerves, though, that was something else. Wong folded his arms around her waist and pushed his legs into hers for the final three feet. She stiff-legged toward the edge, then closed her eyes.

He'd told her to relax and above all not push against him when they jumped; parachuting was more a surrender to the wind than a dive into the air. And besides, if she moved too sharply she would whack him in the balls.

Or testicular region, as he'd put it.

Rosen tried to make her body limp as she felt the plane disappear beneath her right foot; the next instant her lungs disappeared from her chest and her stomach mushroomed. Eyes closed, she started to flail with her elbow, then stopped, realizing she was falling.

Or flying.

She opened her eyes. Becky Rosen was truly flying, the brown earth spreading out all below her, clear blue sky surrounding her head. Her head floated in nirvana-land, and she felt her jumpsuit ripple against its cuffs as the wind gusted. Wong had told her about arching and how to spread her arms and legs in the basic free-fall position; she realized now that her body had naturally moved there, arms and legs bent perfectly, as if she had done this a million times. Wong's body surrounded her, holding her much more tenderly than she would have imagined.

It was like being in a dream, this falling.

Then she felt herself yanked backwards, from the waist and then the shoulders and then her legs. She stood up. She felt a different kind of tug and once more they were flying, though this time much slower and in an upright position. Rosen could see only the leading edge of the oversized chute above her head, but she could feel the captain maneuvering it, steering the chute through the air as if he were a glider.

The earth was no longer a blob. She saw a flat space before

her, long and narrow—the Apache runway. There was a large lump and several smaller ones at one end.

It took quite a while before she realized that the large lump was a helicopter under a camo netting. The objects nearby were shelters dug into the dirt.

Wong steered the chute around into a miniature landing pattern as they approached. He had told her something about landing, but she was damned if she could remember what the hell it was.

Run?

No.

Roll?

No.

That was what he didn't want her to do.

Step off like an escalator had been what he said.

Unfortunately, she remembered too late, after he had flared the chute and plopped onto the ground in what would have been a perfect one-mile-an-hour landing into the wind. Rosen lost her balance and fell over. Wong lost *his* balance and tumbled on top of her; the chute pushed them along the runway toward a group of Special Ops soldiers who were trying hard not to give themselves hernias from their laughter.

"You're a girl," said one of the soldiers, helping her up as Wong unsnapped the tandem harness.

"Wow, something weird must have happened on the way down," Rosen said, pulling the shoulder straps away.

"You're a fucking girl," repeated the trooper.

"I'm not fucking you, Sherlock," said Rosen. "Or anyone else up here. You gonna stand there gawking, or are you gonna get me to that helicopter you want fixed?"

SUGAR MOUNTAIN
26 JANUARY 1991
0855

William James "BJ" Dixon had spent a great deal of his life wishing to become a fighter pilot, and then working toward that goal. It had taken a lot of sacrifice on his part, hard work, and once or twice some decent luck to accomplish that goal. But he had always been willing to do whatever it took; the dream had defined him, and he would sooner have thought of slicing off his arm than giving it up.

He had never, in all his life, dreamed of being a ground soldier, much less a commando. A year ago—a week ago—the idea of running around with a gun deep in enemy territory would have seemed about as likely as starting at quarterback for the Green Bay Packers in the Super Bowl.

But he was here, and his life was now defined by two irrefutable facts:

The man with the SA-16 had to be eliminated.

The only one who could do it was Dixon.

He expected Leteri to protest when he told him what he was going to do; Leteri did, suggesting that he go instead. But it was obvious to Dixon that he'd never manage to get across the ledge and around the mountain to surprise the Iraqis.

Leteri also mentioned another alternative.

"We can just bug out."

"How the hell are we going to do that?" Dixon asked him.

"I'm not saying we should," said Leteri. "I'm just saying it may be better than committing suicide."

"You gonna leave Winston?"

"No."

"If Hawkins sends a helicopter for us, these bastards will nail it," Dixon said. "Those shoulder-launched missiles are tough to get away from. Even the Hogs are meat." He got up. "I'll leave you the M-16 and grenade launcher. I can't use it for shit anyway. You okay?"

"I'm okay."

"Take care of yourself."

"You too."

This time, Leteri didn't offer a salute, and Dixon somehow interpreted that as an even higher honor.

He had to crawl the first ten yards to get around the side of the hill, but beyond that it was safe to walk, protected both by the ridge and the Iraqis' own overconfidence. They weren't necessarily incompetent, Dixon reminded himself; they were just so far behind the lines that they couldn't imagine American soldiers were sitting right next to them. He guessed that he would act the same way hanging out at Cineplex in Hog Heaven.

The fire was burning again at the back of his head, stronger now. His eyes were hard little spotlights, searching the rocks. The MP-5 was part of his hands; he didn't have to think about it as he moved.

A lookout had been posted at the end of the ravine he needed to climb down to get around the ridge and up onto the cratered hilltop where the missile launcher was. Dixon had a clear, easy shot of no more than ten yards with his gun—but no way to take it without alerting the entire Iraqi contingent.

The soldier faced the road, alternately standing and sitting, a

Kalashnikov hanging loosely at his side. Dixon was only partly protected from his view by the corner of the rock face and some large boulders, but the man's attention was focused entirely on the road beyond him.

Somewhere in the foggy early days of his ROTC training, Dixon had learned how to smash the back of an enemy's skull with the butt end of a bayoneted rifle, then twisted the gun around and stab him in the throat.

Or the heart. He couldn't remember which. He did remember that he hadn't done very well in any of those exercises.

And anyway, how did you attach a knife to an MP-5?

If he could sneak up close enough to the man, he could smash him across the side of the face with the gun. Then he'd haul out his knife and finish him off.

Dixon judged that the soldier was twenty pounds lighter and maybe six inches shorter than he was; he ought to be able to take him in a fight, especially if he was able to surprise him.

Could he? The ground seemed fairly stable, no large rocks or boulders to trip over.

Ten yards. Two seconds?

More like three or four. If he got off cleanly.

The Iraqi started to turn in his direction. Dixon ducked back behind the rocks, barely in time.

Or so he thought. For as he held his breath, he heard the man starting to climb toward him.

Dixon pushed his knee against the rock and bit the corner of his lip, trying not to breath, not to exist. Retreating was impossible; there was no cover behind him for five or six yards.

His finger edged lightly on the trigger of his gun. He'd kill this bastard at least, and two or three of the next men who came for him. Dixon pushed his right shoulder up, steadied himself for a shot.

The man stopped right next to the crevice wall, not three feet away around the corner, and began fumbling with his clothes.

He was taking a leak.

Go!

Dixon caught him in the side of the head, smashed him with

the hard stock of the machine-gun butt. Stunned, the Iraqi fell backwards, his gun falling away. Dixon went after him, losing his balance and plunging his gun barrel-first into the soldier's chest. The man struggled to turn over, both of them sliding downwards. Dixon took two wild swings, then lost the gun somehow, tumbling against the Iraqi and feeling a hard knee in his ribs. The fire in his head flared; his right fist found the soldier's chin once, twice, three times in succession, pounding the man temporarily limp. Without thinking about exactly what he was doing, Dixon snatched his knife from his belt and stabbed it into the man's throat. He slid it around, slashing inside the wound as if he were taking out an apple core.

Finally, he realized the man was dead and jumped up mid-stab, took a step backward, and picked up his gun, conscious of the noise they had made and worried that someone might have heard the commotion. He held both the submachine gun and the knife in his hand; ducking down, he scanned the area, kept his breath still nearly sixty seconds, listening for the sound of men running to avenge their comrade's gruesome death.

All he heard was silence. He straightened, then stooped and wiped the bloody knife blade on his pants leg. He slid the knife back into its sheath, and saw that his uniform was black with the dead man's blood.

Pants still undone, the Iraqi sprawled obscenely on the hillside, blood oozing from his neck and chest. Dixon saw him and felt a twinge of compassion; he went over and pulled the man's pants closed.

That was the old Dixon, the good, overachieving kid next door whose impulses sometimes led him to do foolish things but whose conscience never let him forget them, the kid who wanted not to fail and struggled to do his duty. That was the kid who had screwed up his Air Force career, nearly given up his dream, to stand by his mom at the end. It was the pilot who had aced every test but always worried he was a step behind where he ought to be.

A new self hauled the dead Iraqi up into the crevice out of sight, dropping him quickly and unceremoniously against the side of the rocks. He let the dead man and his old self go without wasting a moment thinking about the frenetic impulse to kill that flamed like kerosene in his hands and eyes. He felt the fire in his head and let it push him up the ravine toward his goal.

66

Over Iraq
26 January 1991
1005

Colonel Klee made one slight concession to the Hog drivers, Doberman specifically. He sent one of his flunkies to tell Doberman that if he wanted to go north early in case they were needed with the helo pickup, that was all right.

Doberman wasn't sure how the colonel figured out that he intended on doing so anyway, but it didn't alter his opinion of him. He hadn't thought Klee was a fool, just a douche bag.

They tanked after taking off to gain a little more time for the mission. Done, Doberman pushed his plane out over the desert toward central Iraq. Truth was, both planes and men were being stretched beyond reason, but he couldn't give a shit about that. Numbers, formulas, all that crap—that was engineering, and right now he didn't care for any of it. He was driving a Hog.

Still, it was a long haul north with little to do except sweat. He kept turning his eyes back to the Maverick's small television monitor, thinking about the double whammy he had to make.

What if the lock drifted or got lost or he couldn't get the little pipper precisely right as he rode in? What if somebody started firing at him, broke his concentration?

If anybody could make it, Doberman could. No bullshit. Mr. AGM.

Just like he could hit an inside card to make a royal flush.

If there was such a thing as luck, his was for shit. He had the luck of Job. Period.

Maybe he should've gotten the cross from Shotgun after all. Or at least not thrown the penny away.

Fucking goddamn crazy people were polluting his mind.

"Devil Flight, this is Apache Air One. Are you reading me?"

Doberman acknowledged the helicopter's call and took his coordinates, then gave a quick glance to the map on his knee pad. They were right on schedule, right where they were supposed to be.

"We are one-zero minutes from the Cornfield," said the commando captain in the helicopter.

"Acknowledged," said Doberman. "Wait for the green light."

"That's cross at the green, not in between," joked Shotgun over the squadron frequency as Doberman found his way point and made a slight course adjustment. He didn't bother acknowledging, listened only to the Hog and his breath as he slammed onward.

Five minutes later, cued not only by the INS but by the highway below, Doberman pitched his wing over and fell toward the ground. The Hog grunted appreciatively, readying her cannon as she accelerated, steadying herself under her pilot's hand into a stable downward plunge that gave Doberman a perfect view of the countryside. The disabled AH-6G sat directly in the middle of his HUD. The remains of the Iraqi column sat on the lower ground a few hundred yards away, the broken tank at the top left of his screen, and now the other vehicles behind it as Doberman began pulling the stick back, easing out of the dive at a still somewhat safe four thousand feet. He was pulling over four hundred knots, cranking by on his first run to see if there was anything below still moving. He was past the highway and large stream, then pulling around; trailing in Devil Two, Shotgun told him nothing had moved.

"This one's low and slow," Doberman told him, already stepping the Hog down into a more leisurely glide. He could see some tracks leading off the highway, but couldn't tell if they belonged to the wrecked vehicles or someone else.

If it was someone else, they'd come and gone. The tank and APCs the Hogs had splashed sat like twisted wrecks, forlorn and waiting to be claimed by the junkman. Nothing moved.

He wasn't letting Apache One take a chance, though, not with Rosen aboard and Dixon depending on them. He slipped back around and stepped down to Hog country—five hundred feet, speed dropping now to just under three hundred knots, tiptoeing over the enemy's dead bodies. The downed helicopter sat in front of the shallow plateau, looking as if she'd just set down. Doberman put the A-10 on her wing, waltzing through yet another pass, this one as close to a walk as he could manage, though he was still moving so fast he couldn't be positive there wasn't someone hiding in the wreckage.

But no one had fired at him, and the arriving helo was now under two minutes away.

"See anything, Dog?" asked Shotgun.

"Looks clean," he told him. "You?"

"Negative," said Shotgun.

Doberman saw a small bee zipping in from the southwest. It was Apache One.

"Green light," he told the commandos. "Kick ass."

"Kick it yourself," was the reply.

67

Over Iraq
26 January 1991
1015

Rosen jumped out of the arriving helicopter right behind Captain Hawkins, tool case in one hand and an MP-5 submachine gun in the other.

She would have traded both for a manual. She was a damn expert in avionics and com gear, a whiz at everything electronic, and had worked on gas turbines enough to smell like them—but her mind went blank as she ran toward the other helicopter.

Just fuzzed. She knew it would come back, but until then? She glanced quickly at the top of the other helicopter and its tail, saw that they were intact, then lugged her tools into the cockpit.

"Hey!" she yelled behind her. "Where's my pilot?"

"Here," said the man, a tall, chain-smoking Floridian whose name was either Slim, Bim, or Flim; she couldn't remember.

"Start it up," she told him.

"You don't want to check it first?"

"Maybe nothing's wrong. Start it up. If it works we'll worry about it later."

"What about the rotor blades?"

Rosen gave the pilot a look that made him climb inside. She took the copilot's seat and examined the interior; nothing was obviously out of place, except for the bullet holes in the windshield. That and the dead pilot's blood.

"I'm trying to turn her over but I get nothing," said the pilot. "Instruments are dead. Engine should be coughing and the rotors cranking, see? You gonna check it now?"

"Good, we're looking good. Kill the power. Don't smoke until I'm sure there's no gas leak," she said, zipping open her tool kit and then clambering out the door and climbing between the rotor and the roof. Her mind was still a TV caught between stations, showing nothing but fuzz.

Then it cleared, and she saw a motor laid out perfectly in her head.

Trouble was, it didn't belong to the AH-6G, or any other member of the MD530 family. In fact, it didn't belong to an aircraft at all.

It was a good ol' Chevy 350, V-8, stock, untuned, rusted even, lying in the center of the vast engine compartment belonging to her grandfather's Impala.

Heck of a motor, just not what she wanted to be thinking about right now.

The stream of bullets that had taken out the pilot had made an arc up to the top of the glass across the roof and rotor mechanism. The slugs seemed to either have all missed or grazed off. There were dents in the faring but nothing serious.

"Don't fucking smoke!" she shouted to the pilot as she slid off the front of the helicopter.

"It ain't lit!"

She climbed over the rocket launcher and hung beneath the body of the aircraft. A spray of bullets had nearly shot one of the bottom right-side access panels off. The metal was so loose that a touch of her screwdriver kicked it away.

And damned if the problem, one of them anyway, wasn't right in front of her—the bullets had chewed up one of the wire harnesses.

Hey, ignition system, no shit. That was exactly what was wrong with Grandpa's Impala. Except it had been squirrels, not 30mm bullets.

There was a warren of wires here, enough to keep a squadron of mechanics busy for hours testing and tying them together.

Best punt, as Sergeant Clyston would say.

"Okay, Slim Jim, hey, come here," she shouted. "And for christsake, don't fucking smoke!"

The pilot slipped out of the chopper. Rosen was used to Air Force pilots, most of whom ran instead of walked. The Army Special Ops pilot had a much slower approach to life, ambling around to her.

Or maybe she had just been thrown into overdrive and the rest of the world was at normal speed.

"You see colors?" she asked.

"What do you mean, colors?"

"You color-blind?"

"No."

"Good. This is gonna be kind of like a game, except it's not."

Rosen took a roll of spare wire and electrical tape from her toolbox and threw it to him. Then she explained how to strip the ends off the wires and reattach them. She emphasized the importance of getting the color coding absolutely correct—they could easily short out something important if they didn't.

"We going to reattach every one?"

"Only if we have to," said Rosen. "Every five wires, you go see what works. When we got enough attached we call it quits. Just shout before you turn the key."

"What are you going to do?"

"Number one, I want to make sure the gas tanks aren't leaking before you blow us all to bits."

"It ain't lit," he protested, taking the cigarette from his mouth.

Hawkins saw that the survivors from the firefight, or maybe reinforcements, must have taken away the dead, including the Americans. Relief mixed with anger as he surveyed the scene;

taking the bodies back would have been difficult if they couldn't get the second bird going. The captain called his two men back and made sure they had carefully gone through the site. He knew, of course, that they had, but asking was part of his job and they accepted it without complaint, assuring him the Cornfield was "clean."

"Wait for me at the helo," he told them, trotting over to Rosen. She was working on something at the tail end of the aircraft.

"How long?" he asked.

"If this rotor control and the wires are the only problem, I'm thinking another ten minutes, fifteen tops. I found a couple of shorts back on the engine and instruments and got around them. The rest of this isn't serious at all."

"What if they're not the only problems?"

"Well, I think they are. The blades are all good, the engine itself wasn't hit, and there's gas. The infrared radar's out and I won't vouch for anything electrical until the engine's humming, but Slim Jim ought to be able to fly it back."

"Gary's his name."

"Yeah, whatever. You want to help get some wires patched?"

"Thanks, but we're going to leave you here and get our guys," said Hawkins. "You run into trouble, call us. We'll come back and get you out."

"What if the radio doesn't work?"

"If we don't hear from you, we'll come back," he told her, already trotting toward his helicopter.

68

SUGAR MOUNTAIN
26 JANUARY 1991
1015

There was no way he was sneaking up on this guard, and no way he was getting lucky enough to dump him easily either.

Twenty feet of rubble and a seventy-degree slope separated Dixon and the soldier posted near the summit of the cliff. The man had his side to Dixon, and his back to the lip of the bomb crater where the Iraqi with the missile was. And he was paying attention to his job—Dixon had to duck back around the cliff wall as the man walked his short line back and forth across the ledge.

Rush the man now and everyone would hear. Dixon might be able to kill him, then get up over the lip of the crater and take out the man with the missile, but only if the second man wasn't armed. And only if this guard was the other soldier he'd seen climbing the hill with him.

Too many ifs.

He could wait until he heard a plane. The Iraqis might find him by then, though.

Dixon could walk back around to the other side and try to get a firing position. That would take at least forty-five minutes, and he'd be in the open much of the way.

If he went back and put on the uniform of the man he'd killed, he might be able to get close enough to take them out before they realized he was an American.

Covered with blood and too small.

Dixon stuck his head around the corner of the rocks. The guard had walked further along his lookout ledge and was out of view, though Dixon could hear his footsteps scrunching in the dirt.

The ledge the man was walking on blocked most of the cliff face directly below from his sight. If Dixon could go down about twenty feet and then tack out across the rock face, he'd get by him without being seen. He'd be only a few yards from the side of the crater, with a good view of the soldier with the missile.

From there, though, he'd be in clear view of the guard.

Have to take him and the missile handler out very quickly.

Doable. Then fire the missile into the dirt.

Better yet, into one of the tanks. If he could figure out how it worked.

Dixon studied the cracks on the quarried rock face below the guard. It wouldn't be easy.

Doable, though. Best way.

The guard turned and Dixon ducked back into cover. He'd have to wait until the guard was about halfway before starting.

He was going across. It would take fifteen minutes and some luck.

Make it ten, he decided. And screw luck.

69

THE CORNFIELD
26 JANUARY 1991
1027

"Try it!" Rosen shouted.

Nothing.

But damn, all the wires were together, she had current, there was definitely fuel. What the hell?

Her fingers were just touching the body of the engine when she felt a vibration. At first she thought it was an electrical shock; she yanked her hand back as the turbine coughed.

It started, coughed again, and stopped.

Progress.

"Shit," said the pilot.

"Give it another shot."

"These things are supposed to start right up."

Rosen rolled her eyes. Pilots.

Sergeant Clyston wouldn't have this problem. When he told a pilot to do something, they damn sure did it.

It had to do with the way he used his voice.

"Give it another shot," she said, trying to sound exactly as the sergeant would.

The engine cranked to life.

"Let it run!" she shouted. "I have to make some adjustments and see what I can do about the panel. Then I'll get the radio to work."

"Radar's out. No radio," said the pilot. "How the hell am I going to fly without a radio?"

She turned back to the engine shaking her head. Pilots.

70

SUGAR MOUNTAIN
26 JANUARY 1991
1028

Dixon slid his hand into the crack, pushing it sideways to get as secure a grip as he could manage before swinging his right leg toward the foothold. His boot slipped and he had to strain to hold himself up; he pushed off with his left foot and caught a foothold just as the ache in his arms became unbearable. Dixon took a breath, then inched his left hand to the same crack as his right, pulling his body across the face of the rock as he found a new place for his right hand. He had maybe five feet to go, five easy feet; all he had to do was get there and he'd be beyond the guard and have a line on missile-boy in the crater. His head felt as if it were sagging backwards and he was tired as hell, but he wasn't stopping now. He flexed his shoulder muscles slightly, heard the guard's footsteps approaching above him to the left, and froze, waiting for the man to walk past, turn, and go back the other way. While he waited, Dixon plotted his next two handholds—large, square notches on the rock. He had a good ledge for his feet, though it was a bit of a stretch to get to the holds. As the guard turned and began walking back, Dixon moved his right leg, found solid footing, then pulled for the new spot. He was there, he had it, only two feet to go and he'd be on the rocks scrambling toward the top.

Something gave way behind him.

Rocks tumbled. There were curses and people running. Dixon threw his body into a ball and plunged to the right, landing hard on the rocks at the side of the hill where he'd been aiming. He pulled the submachine gun up, ready to take a long blast, make something out of nothing before they killed him.

But the shouts weren't for him. A helicopter was approaching, a dark bee in the distance.

And something else, something that exploded nearly straight down from the sky, something that came faster than an archangel and with considerably more prejudice, not to mention a lot more firepower.

The Hogs had arrived.

71

OVER IRAQ
26 JANUARY 1991
1031

Shotgun had both tanks at about eight thousand feet and three miles off, a turkey shoot for the Mavericks, which were salivating on his wings and who could blame them? But he had to hold them in reserve, in case Doberman missed. As unlikely as he knew that was, it was the plan, and so Shotgun merely sighed and soldiered on, squaring up the iron bombs instead. He fixed the Hog's nose at nearly a ninety-degree angle toward the ground, about as close to a sure thing as you could get.

Finger itching on the pickle button as he framed the first tank in his HUD, Shotgun decided that *The Price Is Right* was what he was looking to play here.

Or rather, *The Bomb Is Right.*

"Who's today's lucky winner, Johnny?" he asked as the target grew fatter and juicier. "Why, it's Tank Number One, a lovely little T-72 model fresh from the factory at Minsk. I know it's not really Minsk, Bob, but I just love saying that. Minsk. Minsk.

"And what have they won?

"Why, two lovely five-hundred-pound bombs, right down

the poop chute," said the pilot, releasing his bombs and pushing the stick for a quick drop on the second tank. It was close to physically impossible to nail them both on the same swoop given their separation and his angle, but Shotgun went for it anyway, swinging the Hog's wings and seeing the tank flutter toward the aim point but then fritter away. The Iraqis actually had the gall to try to shoot at him as he began to pull back on his stick; a fair-sized knot of soldiers appeared in the center of his windscreen and he had to exercise an extreme amount of willpower not to toss his bombs at them, saving the heavy iron for the tank.

Which really he should have gotten on that first run, tough angle or not. Problem was, he hadn't gone with the flow, Shotgun decided. He'd gone with a game show, when he should have just gone with *The Boss.*

No problem. He clicked the play button on his personal stereo and dished up "Thunder Road." At the same time he slammed the Hog into a butt-crunching, face-slamming negative-G turn and climb, looping out at the top and nailing down into a dive toward the tank. The Hog snapped her tail and began picking up speed, revving with pleasure as her pilot decided to use the cannon instead of the bombs. This was what she was designed to do, unzip Soviet tanks, and even if this wasn't Europe and the big hunk of metal in front of her was technically bigger and thicker than her designers had envisioned her frying, the Hog had fury and momentum on her side.

The tank commander's 7.62mm winked at the plane as she came, and it seemed to Shotgun that a bullet or two actually grazed off the lower titanium hull.

"Don't do that," Shotgun warned. "You're only going to piss her off."

The tank commander obviously heard him, for the stream of bullets veered away.

"You know what I'm here for," sang Shotgun, echoing Bruce as he pressed the kill button. His first bullets greased harmlessly across one of the Dolly Parton plates at the front of the T-72. The stream moved upwards, sloshing left and right until

Shotgun found the relatively soft top of the turret. Then he nailed it down, riding the rudder pedals as his uranium slugs erased the bastard's top and back end.

Shotgun let off on the gun, pulling up and sailing over the rock quarry, considering whether to find something else or get some more altitude. He was just beginning to bank when Doberman started shouting in his head. A frantic warning cut through the chaos, drowning out the Big Man's saxophone.

"Missile on the hill! Missile on the hill!"

72

SUGAR MOUNTAIN
26 JANUARY 1991
1031

Dixon scrambled to his feet as the bombs separated from Shotgun's Hog, aimed squarely at the top of the tank stationed to the east of the mountain. By the time they exploded, he was throwing himself forward over the edge of the crater, and in the same motion spraying the figure standing below him with bullets. Wounded, the man staggered backwards, away from the SAM pack. Dixon pushed himself to his feet, felt the ground exploding, and remembered the guard from the ledge. He lost his footing and fell, tumbling in the dirt against the jagged rocks, bullets flying around him. He tried to aim his gun, but lost his grip. He saw the guard, fumbled to get his finger back on the trigger. Someone yanked at his leg as he fired.

He missed the guard but made him duck for cover.

The man he'd shot was clinging to his leg, clawing at him and trying to grab Dixon's pistol. Dixon smashed him with the side of the submachine gun, crushing his own finger against the man's skull. He pushed back as the man managed to grab his pistol, then sent three slugs into the Iraqi's skull. Dixon threw himself in the direction of the missile pack on the ground, letting off a long burst from the MP-5 back in the direction of the ridge. The guard there ignored the bullets, firing at him. Dixon pumped his gun until the clip emptied. Finally the Iraqi soldier disappeared, whether hit or simply reloading Dixon didn't know and didn't care.

A heavy machine gun began peppering the ridge as he grabbed the SA-16 missile launcher from the dirt. He ducked, fumbling with the controls. When the machine gun stopped, he rose, propped the launcher on his shoulder and aimed it toward the Iraqis.

Nothing happened when he pressed the trigger. He had to duck down as the machine gun once again chewed up the rocks in front of him. Examining the launcher, Dixon saw there were two triggers, one a primer and one the actual trigger. As soon as the machine gun stopped, he jumped up and fired the heat-seeking missile downward in the direction of his enemies.

73

OVER SUGAR MOUNTAIN
26 JANUARY 1991
1034

Shotgun cursed as the SAM launched behind him. He kicked out flares and wagged his butt around and jinked crazier than a topless dancer working for tips before realizing the rocket had been aimed downwards. It flew straight into the hillside, bouncing off a rock before exploding. A sixth sense told him Dixon had grabbed the SAM, the kid deciding to play wingman without a plane.

Just then, the CD skipped four tracks. "Born to Run" slammed into his ears.

Talk about *karma.* At exactly the same moment, the helo pilot hit the radio and said he was coming in and could somebody do something about the machine guns? Shotgun lit the Gatling, aiming to ice the nests near the roadway.

He hoped Dixon, if that really had been Dixon, saw the helicopter and got his butt into the damn whirly sardine can. Playing Rambo in the rocks was all well and good, but it was time for him to call it a day.

74

SUGAR MOUNTAIN
26 JANUARY 1991
1034

Metal and pulverized stone hung thick in the air as Apache One raced toward the position Turk had given them. Hawkins started to warn the pilot about an APC with machine guns in their path, but he was already greasing his rockets and veering right. They flew directly over another gun position before spotting the hideout, well hidden on the hill next to Sugar Mountain.

Hawkins caught himself against the frame and thought they'd been hit, cordite and God knows what else blowing around his head. But the pilot was only trying to get down onto the hill as quickly as possible. The Iraqis were firing everything they had as the helicopter's skids neared the rocks. A grenade or something equally obnoxious exploded close enough to send dirt ripping through the rotors. The pilot shouted something, but Hawkins was out by then.

Hawkins saw Dixon squatting and shooting a few yards from the position; a grenade shot off in the direction of the Iraqis.

Sergeant Winston was lying behind rocks in a shallow trench right in front of Hawkins. As slowly and calmly as he could, the captain bent to him, waiting as Stone brought the backboard and stretcher.

"Take your time, take your time," he said, as much to himself as to Stone, and despite a fresh hail of bullets and screaming explosions all around, the captain made sure Winston's neck was secure as they lifted him out. He started to slip on the rocks, caught his knee against something hard, and felt his gut wrench. His head suddenly felt light, and he knew he'd been hit for the second time in two days—and this time it hurt like a sonuvabitch. He bent forward and managed somehow to get to his feet, pulled by the stretcher, and now they were strapping Winston stiff to the skids and the pilot was screaming in his face. They were aboard, Dixon scrambling and jumping in, and the helicopter got up into the air, the cabin shaking as it was laced with gunfire. One of the Hogs streaked in front of them, inches away it looked like, smoke and fury pouring from its mouth as it nailed the Iraqis who were trying to kill them.

"Tell them to do it. Take out the bunker," Hawkins heard himself say twice, three times, and he turned around to congratulate Dixon, make him an honorary member of the Death Riders because goddamn he deserved it.

Except it wasn't Dixon. It was Leteri, back from the dead.

And goddamn, though Hawkins was sure as shit pleased to see his man alive, what the hell had happened to the Air Force lieutenant?

OVER SUGAR MOUNTAIN
26 JANUARY 1991
1034

There was so much goddamn smoke it was screwing up the IR targeting head in the Maverick. Doberman cursed as the helicopter stayed on the ground, taking fire as the Special Ops people ran to retrieve their men. If they didn't move quickly, he was going to have to bank away and reposition himself to get a lock.

Shit, he was so low he could hop out and run alongside the damn airplane. These bastards were going to figure out where he was eventually and start firing at him.

And son of a bitch. He was bingo fuel.

"I'm going to cover for that helo," said Shotgun, slashing overhead.

"You check your fuel?"

"Can't see the gauge from here."

"Don't get in my fucking way," said Doberman. He kicked the Hog into a turn to reposition himself, not really mad but stoking his emotions anyway, building the adrenaline as he spurred himself into the fight. He got a strong whiff of kerosene or something in his nose, imagined that his fuel tanks had sprung a leak, and started to laugh because that was just ridiculous. The oxygen was as pure as heaven and he had a good view in the screen as he came back into his attack pattern, lined up and loose, feeling like he did the first time he ever fired a Maverick on a practice run—nailed that sucker, and nailed every one dead-on since.

The helo skittered away. Shotgun cleared.

His turn.

The Iraqis seemed to have a thousand guys down there, everyone of them armed with a machine gun, everyone of them blasting away at him.

Good fucking luck hitting me. And I mean that sincerely.

Doberman put his head nearly onto the Mav screen, leaning as close to it as his restraints would allow, big fat cursor nailed two thirds of the way up the door. Next and nailed. He let it go, squeezed, and kept going, up and on go, go, go, he pickled again—no thumb thing, no luck, no ritual, no bullshit, just squeezed the son of a bitch faster than anybody ever said possible, faster than any engineer would calculate.

He kept going, watching the first missile slam in, the second missile flying right behind it.

Doberman banked through the hail of nasty but small machine-gun bullets. It was all up to the missiles now, all luck if it happened the way Wong said it should.

Luck.

What the fuck.

76

SUGAR MOUNTAIN
26 JANUARY 1991
1034

Dixon threw the missile launcher away, rolling and scooping up the MP-5. He slammed a fresh clip into the gun and aimed it back toward the top of the crater, but there was no one there. He slid out to the side of the ledge, leaned his gun over and fired, then pushed his head down.

Nothing.

He scrambled ahead, the end of the submachine gun trained on the rocks. He reached the corner of the rock face without seeing anyone and ran across the ledge. Still no one appeared. He began picking his way down the boulders that had forced him onto the rock face earlier.

The helicopter's loud whine reverberated through the quarry. Dixon lost his balance, slamming his chin into the rocks but scrambling up immediately. He took two steps, then felt himself going down again, only half conscious that he was doing it on purpose. Someone was shooting at him from the edge of the crevice leading back to Winston's hiding place.

He pushed himself into the smallest space possible, waiting for the gunfire to let up. When it did, he reached up and let off a quick burst from his MP-5. When he raised his head to see where his enemy was, he spotted the barrel of the AK-47 coming out from behind two large boulders. Dixon ducked as a fresh round salvoed behind him.

It was only a single shot, poorly aimed. Dixon ripped a quick burst from his own gun. It was answered by another single round.

The Iraqi must be preserving ammo. Didn't matter now. Dixon decided he would fire again, wait for the round, then leap up and run forward. The two shots had flailed well to the left; he would hug the opposite wall.

The helicopter engine revved on the other side of the hill.

Dixon squeezed the trigger, waited for the Iraqi to shoot. He began running. He saw the gun barrel and a figure; he fired, squeezing the trigger as hard as he could, the gun's smooth burp pushing the metal stock against his ribs.

But only for a second, then nothing.

The H&K had jammed. Dixon squeezed twice as the Iraqi rose. He threw the gun and himself forward to the ground as his enemy fired a single shot. The bullet wailed harmlessly overhead, and as Dixon hit the dirt he saw the man trying to take better aim.

Dixon rolled over and grabbed for his pistol. He fired, saw the bullet hit.

Then he heard the sound of a steam locomotive whooshing from a tunnel. In the next moment there was a loud bang; then there was a rattling, muffled explosion and a second loud whoosh.

The mountain across from him shoved herself in every direction with a tremendous rumble. Something hit his head and he slid into a warm bed, every muscle relaxing, every ache and pain evaporating as a down-filled comforter slid over his body and his head nestled softly into a deep, deep pillow.

77

Over Sugar Mountain
26 January 1991
1042

The first missile nailed the door precisely two thirds of the way up, its warhead bursting a hole through the thick steel as easily as a screwdriver piercing a can of tuna.

The second missile wavered momentarily, just far enough behind the first to survive the initial explosion, but now confused, unsure where to go.

Electrons danced in its control module, feinting left, right, trying to compute whether the dust was a mere diversionary tactic, or if the world really had turned upside down.

Unsure, they took the course that seemed most logical to them, directing the Thikol rocket motor to keep on trucking, riding the straight and narrow.

Precisely 1.8 seconds later, the missile flew through the hole the first Maverick had created and entered a long, natural rock hallway. As it did, it ran into a shower of light debris.

Close enough, decided the electrons, and the warhead exploded, precisely on target.

• • •

Shotgun had managed to get his plane stable and ready to take the backup shot when the first Maverick hit. Staring at his small TVM screen, he saw the shadow of the second missile enter the cloud where the door of the bunker had been.

The explosion that followed rippled through a massive fissure in the rocks, a fault line planted a million years before by the churning of tectonic plates, aggravated by years of quarrying and amplified by the F-111 strike a few hours before. Sugar Mountain collapsed downward, hundreds of thousands of tons of rock and dirt burying the deadly toxins Saddam had counted on as his ultimate vengeance weapon.

"Lookin' ugly!" screamed Shotgun as he whacked the stick and jostled the Maverick, hoping to unleash it on one of the few remaining targets.

78

THE CORNFIELD
26 JANUARY 1991
1045

They were in the air, without radar but with the radio, at least enough of it to monitor the chaos at Sugar Mountain. Rosen hooked her arm around the restraints, her attention divided between the radio and the readings on the displays in front of her. The situation over at Sugar Mountain was chaotic as hell, but she recognized Captain Shotgun O'Rourke's voice screaming through the chaos:

"I just shacked the APC with my last Maverick. That was kick-ass, Dog Man. You double-banged the fucker."

The helicopter pilot turned to her, as if asking for an explanation. "I think that's good," she told him.

The pilot of the other helicopter made a transmission to the Hogs, reporting some battle damage and wounded.

"Is Lieutenant Dixon okay?" Rosen blurted out.

There was no answer. She knew she had keyed her mike because Slim Jim gave her a dirty look. That wasn't enough to prevent her from asking again, though this time she dressed the communication up with a slightly more professional tone, and added an "over" at the end of the transmission.

"Apache Two, this is Apache One. Lieutenant Dixon is not on board."

Cursing, Rosen grabbed the sleeve of her helicopter pilot. "Go over to Sugar Mountain."

"What?"

"One of our men is still on the ground down there."

The pilot said nothing, but gave her two answers nonetheless. One was with his eyes, which summarized the helicopter's precarious mechanical state, their low fuel reserves, and lack of ammunition in a look that clearly asked, *Do you think I'm out of my friggin' mind?*

The other was with his hands, which yanked the helo's control column nearly out of its bolts and put the AH-6G on a direct intercept for the foaming clouds of smoke that marked the Iraqi stronghold.

79

SUGAR MOUNTAIN
26 JANUARY 1991
1052

"Apache Two, this is Devil One. I copied that transmission. We will cover you to Sugar Mountain." Doberman let go of the mike key and ran his eyes quickly over the Hog's indicators—with the notable exception of the panel detailing his dwindling fuel supply.

"Got your six," said Shotgun.

He was as short of fuel as Doberman was, but it was senseless ordering him home. The two Hogs cut tight angles in the air as they whacked back toward Sugar Mountain.

"I'm thinking that must have been Dixon who nailed the missile launcher on the crater," said Shotgun. "That's just the sort of thing a Hog driver's gonna do, you know what I'm talking about?"

"We'll buzz the crater and have the helo follow us in," said Doberman, straining to see the quarry through the dust and smoke ahead. "Check for machine guns first, if you can find the damn things. I can't see shit."

He took the Hog into a shallow but quick dive, moving down through four thousand feet as he accelerated. The smoke, rocks, and wreckage divided into distinct clumps, several of which began to fire furiously at him from the periphery of the quarry. Doberman didn't have a particularly good shot on any of them and decided to truck on past, concentrating on looking for Dixon. He figured Shotgun would be more than happy to clean up for him.

Picking out something as small as a man from an airplane under any circumstances was extremely difficult. Picking out someone in the rocks from two thousand feet while people were shooting at him was nearly impossible. Doberman nonetheless pushed the Hog in, practically crawling as he scanned out the right side of his cockpit. Pulling off to the west, he took a slow orbit and watched as Shotgun mopped up one of the machine guns, letting the A-10As cannon eat up the dirt. The cannon's kick was so fierce that it slowed the plane down, nearly holding the Hog still as the bullets stuttered right and left. Shotgun worked the rudders like pedals on a piano, playing the Death March for the unlucky slobs who had dared aim at him. And then he was beyond them, spinning off to put his Hog onto another of the heavy machine guns, pelting it with the Gatling's big shells. Doberman winged through the haze and got a good view of the landslide that had deflated the storage bunker for good.

He couldn't see Dixon. Nor could Shotgun when he took his second run through. The machine-gun fire had stopped, at least. Doberman cleared the helicopter pilot in for a closer look.

As they watched the helo approach, their AWACS controller asked, semi-politely, if they had left the allied air force and established one of their own.

He had some pointed questions about fuel consumption as well.

"Somebody's feeding him information," squawked Shotgun over the short-range radio.

Doberman told the AWACS that they had the situation under control, then asked for the nearest tanker track, knowing before the coordinates came back that it was going to be tight.

One of the Iraqi machine guns started firing again as the helicopter pushed in. Doberman cursed, nearly pulling the wing off the plane as he spun the Hog to take the bastard out. The helo pilot yelled something he couldn't understand.

There was a dead man at the lip of the crater.

Helo was taking fire.

Doberman leveled off briefly and flailed back in time to see the helicopter work its way toward the back of the mountain of rumble. His Hog was sucking dirt now, down under five hundred feet, slipping to three hundred. Doberman spotted something brown moving in the crevice formed by the rocks just southeast of the hill he'd hit.

"Two bodies," said the helo pilot, except it wasn't the helo pilot, it was Rosen.

Something flashed in the corner of his eye.

"Watch the hilltop!" he shouted as he passed. He started to bank and transmitted the warning again, unsure if he had even keyed the mike to send it.

There was a gunner flailing at the helicopter. Shotgun saw him and was diving at the hill. The helicopter yanked away, bullets erupting from its side.

Shotgun yelled and the helicopter pilot yelled and Rosen screamed and in the middle of it all the AWACS controller, calm and ice cold, dished out a snap vector. Two MiGs were taking off from a nearby Iraqi airstrip.

"We're hit but we're okay," announced the helicopter pilot.

"Was that Dixon?" Doberman asked.

"Those bodies aren't moving," said Shotgun. "Dog, we got two pickups on the road in warp drive heading for Sugar Mountain. Got guns in the back, looks like."

"Okay, everybody get the hell out of here," said Doberman. "Take the AWACS vector, Shotgun."

"What about you?"

Doberman hesitated for a second. The kid was down there somewhere. Dead probably, but he couldn't leave him.

Dixon wasn't dead. No way. No.

Doberman's Hog was almost out of fuel, two MiGs were

heading this way, and more Iraqis were playing Rat Patrol. Dixon or no Dixon, he had to go.

There wasn't anything he could do for the kid now. No amount of skill—or luck or superstition—would help him. Neither would pounding the Hog onto the dirt.

"Yeah, I'm on it," he told Shotgun, slamming the Hog onto the getaway course.

80

Over Iraq
26 January 1991
1058

Technical Sergeant Rebecca Ann Rosen slid back in the hard seat of the McDonnell Douglas AH-6G, letting her submachine gun fall between her legs. She had nailed the son of a bitch on the ridge who'd fired at them; she saw the bastard fall backwards, saw his chest ripple red even as the helicopter jerked away.

But she'd seen something else, something more gruesome and bitter. She'd seen Dixon's body face-down in the rocks, dead.

She had no way of knowing that it was truly Dixon, except that she did. He was wearing the brown Special Ops camo, unlike the Iraqis. And besides, she just knew it.

Rosen picked up the submachine gun and folded it against her arms, resisting the temptation to smash out the front windshield of the helicopter in frustration, resisting the urge to scream.

"I think I can get us back to Fort Apache," said the pilot next to her.

"I know you can," she said softly, clutching the gun to her chest.

81

Over Iraq
26 January 1991
1112

"We got one chance," Shotgun told him. "And that's Apache. We're never ever making the border, let alone Al Jouf. We'll be walking fifty miles, at least."

Doberman didn't argue. He'd already plotted the course himself.

"Got your six," said Shotgun when he told him he was changing their heading.

From a purely technical, specs-on-paper point of view, landing on the short strip at Fort Apache wasn't an impossible proposition. The A-10As had been designed to operate from scratch bases close to the front lines. Apache was only slightly beyond what the plane's designers had in mind when they started processing the blueprints, and within what a majority of them would have considered an acceptable margin of error, given the circumstances. The planes were essentially empty. The light load meant they had less momentum to slow down, which in turn meant they'd need less runway than normal. They had a good head wind, not the stiffest, but definitely another positive factor. And these two pilots were without question two of the finest Hog drivers in the world, able to wring things from the plane that challenged if not defied the laws of aeronautics.

But there was always a gap between theory and reality, a huge space inhabited by human beings and metal, a place where things went wrong as well as right, where the fact that you had been flying for tons more time than you were ever supposed to became more important than any wing-loading equation. It was a place where even the bullets that had missed the plane mattered, where the torque of the last screw in the final slot might be life or death.

And it was a place of luck, whether Doberman wanted to admit it or not, finally spotting the tiny squint of dirt in his windshield.

"Damn short," said Shotgun.

"What did you expect?" Doberman told him.

"Hey, I got it, no problem," replied Shotgun. "I'm just saying it's short, you know what I'm talking about?"

The Special Ops troops were standing by at the far end of the field, off to the side in a small area that from here looked tinier than the main ring of a flea circus. They weren't there to applaud. Because the landing strip was so short and narrow, the Hogs would have to land one at a time, the first plane hustling out of the way to let the second plane in.

Since their maneuvers over Sugar Mountain had left Doberman with marginally more fuel than Shotgun, he told him to land first.

"See you on the ground," said Shotgun, working into the first leg of the landing approach. "Boy, this is short."

Doberman lifted his left hand and shook it, relieving some of the muscle stress.

At least that was what he'd intended. It didn't seem to do anything.

Shotgun's wheels hit at the very edge of the runway, the Hog nosing into a textbook-perfect short-field landing with a good hundred feet to spare at the end. Doberman practically whistled, trucking into position for his own landing.

If the Gun could do it, so could he.

He was tired as hell but the day was far from over. Taking off was going to be another test, assuming the Special Ops people found some jet fuel for them.

Hogs could probably run on moonshine.

Doberman put his head back on the job, slotting into a final approach as he set his flaps and prepared to duplicate Shotgun's perfect touchdown.

Except that the outer decelerons didn't deploy.

He knew instantly he had a problem, tried quickly to reset, felt his heartbeat go from overwrought to ballistic. The plane fluttered and threatened to turn into a spinning football. He had hydraulics, had everything, but for some reason the decelerons stayed flat on the wing. His altitude bled off and speed dropped, though not nearly enough as he fought to control the approach.

No way he was landing without either smashing in a heap or rolling off into the immense ditch at the not-so-far end of the cement. Doberman pulled off, his mind and hands whipping through the emergency-procedures checklist.

Nothing worked. The Hog's decelerons—actually split ailerons located at the far end of each wing outside the two-segment flaps—were critical for short-field landings. The bottom part slid down to supplement the flaps while the upper portion popped up like air brakes. Besides increasing the wing area and helping the plane slow down, the decelerons helped control a certain innate tendency of the plane to roll. Basically, they allowed the pilot to land on a dime without becoming a piece of lawn sculpture. Without them set right, Doberman needed a lot more runway than he had, and even then it might not be pretty.

Caul my ass, he thought as he tried everything he could think of without result. I got the stinking goddamn crappiest luck of fucking Job in the whole damn Air Force.

Of course, maybe this wouldn't have happened if he'd had the damn cross. Or the penny.

Doberman worked into a new approach and pressured the stick and pumped his rudders, trying to jink the damn things loose. But nada. He glanced at his fuel gauges. He was beyond dry.

How the hell was he going to land? Come in hot and roll off the end? That'd be fun.

Have to climb and bail. God, he'd break every bone in his body, not to mention the plane.

Shit.

So what would Tinman's cross have done? Made the decelerons work? Put a tiger in his gas tank? It'd be as useless as his gun.

The gun.

As he began to pull up out of his approach, an idea occurred to him that was so wild he knew not only that he had to try it, but that it would absolutely, positively work.

Or it wouldn't. He put his nose back toward the runway and cleared his head, moving around the Hog cockpit as calmly as an insurance executive cleaning up his desk for the weekend. He was in perfect position to land, damn decelerons still not deceleroning, speed still high, but otherwise right on the money. The plane nudged a bit, but he had her tight in his grip and she wasn't going anywhere he didn't want her to.

Doberman stared out the windshield. He could have been the insurance man, waiting at the twentieth floor of his high-rise, killing time at the window as he waited for the elevator to arrive. The edge of the runway came up big. His thumb danced over the elevator button.

Or rather, over the trigger of his gun.

Bing-bang-bam.

The Gatling's heavy burst shook the plane violently, and three things happened:

The Hog slowed down, as Doberman had hoped.

The Hog nearly dropped straight down onto the desert, which he hadn't.

The Hog's decelerons suddenly popped into action, helping him regain enough control and pull to a slightly cockeyed, burn-out-the-brakes, blow-the-tires, screech-to-smoky-halt stop a good fifty feet before the end of the strip.

As he popped the cockpit and threw off his helmet, Doberman looked up at the sky.

"I am one damn lucky son of a bitch!" he shouted.

"That's what I'm talking about!" shouted Shotgun, clambering up onto the wing. "You're also a goddamn show-off." Shotgun slapped the Hog in admiration. "Wish I'd thought of that."

EPILOGUE

GOING HOME

82

King Fahd
26 January 1991
1200

The general gave him the news about Dixon personally. Colonel Knowlington listened quietly, nodding ever so slightly when the Special Ops commander finished.

"Officially, he's MIA," said the general. "But someone saw the body."

"Okay."

"I'm sorry."

"It's war," Knowlington said. "I'm sorry to cut you short, but there's something I have to do right away."

"Sure."

The colonel left his office and walked directly to Tent City. He found Mongoose in his quarters.

"Hey, Colonel," said Mongoose. He'd removed the cast from his arm, though it was still in a light sling. "I've just been going over the frag."

"Don't bother. Get your bags packed. You're out of here."

Mongoose nearly dropped the sheets of computer paper containing the squadron's assignments. "What?"

"There's a C-5A going to Newburgh, New York, at three p.m. You're on it or you're court-martialed for desertion."

"You bastard." Mongoose jumped to his feet. "What are you doing to me?"

Knowlington said nothing, turning and leaving the tent.

"I won't forget this," shouted Mongoose, running after him. "I'll get you back, you drunk bastard. You bastard. You bastard."

Tightening the fingers in his right fist, Colonel Knowlington walked away.

83

SUGAR MOUNTAIN
26 JANUARY 1991
1200

His mouth was full. Warm lamb, scented with mint and a little bit of thyme, his all-time-favorite dish.

It was a celebration, in honor of his finally becoming a real, bona-fide officer. Mom blew out all the stops.

His cousins and aunt were there. His mother sat at the end of the table, smiling.

When he saw her, he knew it was a dream. For a moment, he didn't want it to end. Then he decided it had to. He pushed his arm under his chest, raised his head for a moment, collapsed back.

It was dirt in his mouth, not lamb.

He pushed up and heard the voices nearby, Iraqi voices.

His gun was lying a few feet away.

Useless. It had jammed.

A Kalashnikov was a few yards beyond it.

So was its owner. Dead. He'd shot him.

The pistol was on the ground. He bent and scooped it up.

He thought the AK-47 was empty, but he picked it up anyway. He grabbed the H&K as well.

The voices were louder now, no more than ten yards away, around the corner of the crevice. No way anyone was taking him alive. Air Force Lieutenant William James "BJ" Dixon put down the rifles and knelt on one knee, bracing himself in firing position, both hands wrapped firmly around the pistol.

A Note to Readers

While inspired by actual A-10A missions conducted during the Gulf War, this book is fiction. All characters, commands, and locations are to be interpreted as such, and in no case are meant to reflect on anyone living or dead, actual military procedures, practices, or whims.

Readers familiar with the A-10A facilities at King Fahd and Al Jouf will realize I've moved a few things around in the interest of the yarn. We haven't gotten the Jacuzzi yet, but Sergeant Clyston is working on it.

While Special Ops—Delta Force in particular—infiltrated a number of teams into various parts of Iraq prior to the ground portion of the campaign, Fort Apache is entirely a figment of my imagination. A discrepancy in declassified records has tended to reinforce certain rumors about classified A-10A Forward Operating Areas or bases, but none of the official documents I've seen specifically prove that Hogs operated from enemy territory. In any event, all activities north of the border in this book are fictitious.

As for the Special Ops missions, we'll probably have to wait years for the official reports to be declassified—and for the guys who were there to say what *really* happened. But readers can find some details of the missions in several readily available books. Among my favorites, because they cast the operations in their historical framework, are *Commandos,* by Douglas C. Waller, and *From a Dark Sky,* by Orr Kelly. Kelly's book focuses on the Air Force's contribution to Special Ops, a perspective often missed. Terry Griswold and D. M. Giangreco also include some stories in *Delta, America's Elite Counterterrorist Force;* if you've never seen how small an AH-6G is, you can get an idea from the photos included in their book. Some of the behind-the-scenes political maneuvering is hinted at in Rick Atkinson's larger history of the war, *Crusade,* a much different book than the others. And a personal look at the British SAS contribution to Special Operations in Iraq is told by Andy McNab in his first-person *Bravo Two Zero.* McNab managed to survive capture; his true story is more harrowing than any fiction.

A final note: Don't try Doberman's approach to short-field landings on your local shopping-mall parking lot. It beats the hell out of the landing gear and besides, results in a lot of broken glass.